"I know you."

While Virginia knotted the final bandage, Zack squinted up at her and attempted a smile, but it was weak and misplaced. Realizing how awful he must look, he took a hand and swept it through his black hair. He rubbed a hand along one thigh, trying to straighten his pants. With tenderness she noticed his denims were riddled with gunpowder holes, though, and his boots charred.

He reached out with a shaking hand and cupped his blackened hands beneath her chin.

Her skin tingled where he stroked it. She'd imagined his intimate touch for weeks, never guessing his first touch would come as a patient to a doctor.

"Virginia," he murmured, slipping back into darkness, into unconsciousness, and sending a shudder quivering up her spine. "We weren't supposed to meet like this."

* * *

The Engagement
Harlequin Historical #704—May 2004

Praise for the books of
KATE BRIDGES

The Doctor's Homecoming

"Dual romances, disarming characters and a
lush landscape make first-time author Bridges's
late 19th-century romance a delightful read."
—*Publishers Weekly*

"The great Montana setting and high Western action
combine for a top-notch romantic ending."
—*Romantic Times*

Luke's Runaway Bride

"Bridges is comfortable in her western setting, and her
characters' humorous sparring make this boisterous mix
of romance and skullduggery an engrossing read."
—*Publishers Weekly*

The Midwife's Secret

"This is truly a story which will touch your heart
and stir your soul. Don't miss this delectable read."
—*Rendezvous*

"This is a lovely story and delightfully romantic.
Ms. Bridges is in a class all her own."
—*Old Book Barn Gazette*

KATE BRIDGES

THE ENGAGEMENT

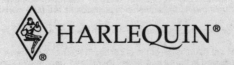

HARLEQUIN®

TORONTO • NEW YORK • LONDON
AMSTERDAM • PARIS • SYDNEY • HAMBURG
STOCKHOLM • ATHENS • TOKYO • MILAN • MADRID
PRAGUE • WARSAW • BUDAPEST • AUCKLAND

ISBN 0-373-29304-6

THE ENGAGEMENT

Copyright © 2004 by Katherine Haupt

This edition published by arrangement with Harlequin Books S.A.

® and TM are trademarks of the publisher. Trademarks indicated with ® are registered in the United States Patent and Trademark Office, the Canadian Trade Marks Office and in other countries.

www.eHarlequin.com

Printed in U.S.A.

Please address questions and book requests to:
Harlequin Reader Service
U.S.: 3010 Walden Ave., P.O. Box 1325, Buffalo, NY 14269
Canadian: P.O. Box 609, Fort Erie, Ont. L2A 5X3

This book is dedicated to my husband, Greg.

Chapter One

Alberta, May 1891

She was marrying the wrong brother.

Dr. Virginia Waters flattened her palm against the nervous tremble in her stomach. Dressed in her wedding gown for the final fitting, she stood before the pine mirror in her bedroom and tried to silence the runaway thoughts.

She was *not* marrying the wrong man. Wedding jitters were common, she told herself. Zack Bullock *was* the right brother.

"You look splendid in your gown. Bonnie indeed."

"Thank you, Millicent." Feeling guilty for her thoughts, Virginia smiled at the reflection of her uncle's housekeeper. In her late fifties, the pleasant Scottish woman pinned the hem as the satin train rustled around Virginia's long legs. A lacy V neckline swooped to Virginia's bosom; her velvet black hair, still damp and fragrant from her evening bath, cascaded below her waist. Crackling wood in the fireplace melted the chilly spring air while a kerosene lamp glowed in the other corner.

"I like the shiny fabric," said Emilou, Millicent Gray's

eight-year-old granddaughter and Virginia's flower girl, standing beside them holding the calico pincushion.

Virginia ran a gentle hand along Emilou's butter-colored braids. Everything was set for the wedding, three days away. A large wedding was expected; Zack was well-known in the community and Virginia was the niece of a prominent citizen. While friends and distant relatives fussed over details, she was grateful for their help but knew from painful experience that none of it mattered without her groom. None of it.

"Ask me another question from your book," said Emilou.

"All right," said Virginia, eager to oblige. She was less than four weeks away from writing her licensing exams, squeezing her studies into every stolen moment she could spare between her final practicum in this house with her Uncle Paddy—*Dr. Patrick Waters*—and her wedding preparations. "How many bones does a person have in their body?"

"Two hundred and six. We're all born with three hundred, but as we get older some of 'em grow together."

"That's right," said Virginia. "What's the longest one?"

"The femur in your leg." Emilou then reversed the questioning, in the game they'd been practicing. "What's the shortest?"

"The stirrup bone in your ear, one-tenth of an inch long."

The girl plopped down at Virginia's feet and slid a picture book of tropical animals onto her lap.

Virginia pointed to a painted giraffe. "Do you know that people and giraffes have the same number of bones in their necks, except giraffe bones are much longer?"

Emilou giggled. Virginia bent lower, kissed the girl's

chubby hand, then straightened in front of the mirror. She stroked the delicate fabric of her gown and wondered what Zack would think of it. Her stomach rolled again.

"What is it, Virginia? What's troublin' you?"

Mindful of the pins, Virginia turned so Millicent could unfasten the yard of pearl buttons down her spine. "I haven't seen Zack for five years. I thought we'd have the chance to reacquaint ourselves before our wedding day. I thought he'd be here to meet me a month ago when I arrived."

"You know the Mounties don't schedule when the crimes occur. When a policeman's called to duty, he has to go."

"What does Zack look like now?" Virginia asked between tugs.

"He's tall and big. Dark haired."

From her childhood, Virginia remembered him as a thin and wiry boy. He was almost ten years older and had rarely spoken to her. "Does he smile much?"

"What sort of question is that?"

"One a bride likes to know about her groom."

"I don't know how much he smiles. You know I don't know the man. Why don't you ask your uncle these questions?"

"Uncle Paddy thinks I'm being frivolous."

"From what I hear, Zack is a quiet man. He's legendary in his work. People say he's tough but fair."

Was it fairness Zack felt for her? Duty was likely driving him to repair the devastation his brother had caused.

Zack had first written her father, and then Virginia, that he was ready for a wife and for them to begin a family of their own. He'd written that it would be a marriage of mutual benefit and comfort, that he'd do his best to make her happy. But… "I thought I'd get to know Zack. Meet his friends. I wish we had more time before the wedding."

"Didn't he wire you he'd be here as soon as possible? Maybe he'll arrive on this evenin's train. Or tomorrow's."

Virginia nodded as her gown dropped, revealing a tight new wedding corset and crisp silk petticoat. She steadied her shaky breathing and made a crucial decision.

She'd give Zack all of her attention. She'd never let him know how deeply her love had run for his brother, Andrew. Although her heartache and anger at Andrew were still raw, she'd never make Zack feel as if he were second-best.

He had no time to think about his upcoming wedding.

"Take off your noisy spurs," Zack commanded in a whisper. Eleven men did as he asked without question.

Gripping two Enfield revolvers, Inspector Zack Bullock, known as "Bull's-Eye" to his men because he was their best marksman, inched forward through the moonlit cedars to the cabin nestled in the mountains. Although dressed as travelers and drovers, they were North-West Mounted Police, highly skilled federal agents commissioned to bring law and order to the West, and he was leading the troop.

Zack stopped to analyze the sounds. He *felt* his men stop behind him. Bullfrogs croaked in the icy spring air. The easy wind whispered across his unshaven face. A hawk fluttered through the sky; its wings sliced the golden moon, then touched down to the cabin rooftop, beside the smoking chimney.

They watched and waited as two night guards, criminals of the Stiller gang, lit a smoke. Four more killers were inside, either sleeping or securing the two hostages, or counting the money they'd robbed from the train two days earlier. The bastards had forced an elderly couple off the train with them—a jeweler and his wife, the O'Connolleys.

When the hawk cried into the night, Zack whispered, "Now."

They rampaged the cabin. The guards were overtaken. Zack kicked in the door, his leather duster flying at his ankles.

"Mounted Police! Drop your weapons!"

Four men hit the floor, guns drawn and firing. Zack threw himself onto the terrified couple in the corner. Rage filled him at the fear that had been instilled in two innocent people.

To protect them, he wasn't able to shoot till the criminals fled outdoors. Three were grazed by the Mounties; the vicious one, jumping on his mare, fired back at the unarmed jeweler. Zack cursed. Shooting at an unarmed man was despicable. Zack took careful aim with both hands—ambidextrous in his talents—and, as a cloud uncovered the moon, shot back.

"He's dead," said Sergeant Major Travis Reid two minutes later. "Right on target, Bull's-Eye."

Without pride or arrogance, Zack came to look at the man he'd shot. "Does anyone recognize him?"

"He's James Stiller's brother, Ned."

"What a waste." Zack lowered his head. It was always pitiful when a man died before his time. "We'll bury him here."

Ten hours later the O'Connolleys were safely back in their home in the mining town, and the prisoners delivered to the local jailhouse.

It was early evening when the Mounties loaded their muscled horses into the boxcars at the train depot. Zack smiled. He was going home to get married. Five Mounties would return with him to Fort Calgary for a week's leave. Six would remain here to continue the eleven-month hunt for the Stiller gang.

The fresh scent of lemons and raisins caught Zack's attention. Everyone was gearing up for spring. European tourists were arriving for the Rocky Mountain trails, farmers were picking up sacks of seed and homesteaders were streaming in for quarter sections of land.

Virginia would be waiting. The last time Zack had seen her pretty face was five years ago on New Year's Eve, when she was hired help at his family's hotel in Niagara Falls. She'd been clearing dishes when Zack had caught her by surprise beneath the mistletoe, stealing a midnight kiss. The kiss had been short and mellow but had left him with a fever of curiosity.

Thinking of how his brother, Andrew, had treated her, Zack shook his head in disgust. Marrying Zack was the last thing Virginia had expected, he believed, even fully wanted. But as the eldest brother he had the responsibility to fix things for her and her folks. Besides, he was ready for a wife. They'd be compatible; as a new doctor finishing her training, she'd spend much of her time on her work, leaving him alone to do his.

Zack boarded the third-class passenger car. The Mounties would have it to themselves for their three-hour trip across the prairies. Passing three constables, Zack slid in beside the sergeant major. Travis was an expert horseman, but Zack was taking a personal interest in training him how to track outlaws.

Two hours and fifty-four minutes later, a stone flickered beneath his wooden seat. Zack leaned over to scoop it up. It was an emerald-cut red jewel. Someone came up from behind him and started to say something as a light flashed outside the window. With a dawning of horror, still bent over but trying to struggle to his feet, he shouted, "Abandon the train!"

But an incredible, massive pain seared his chest. He heard the explosion, then felt twisting wreckage beneath his feet.

"Dr. Waters! Dr. Waters!" The night messenger raced to the house fifteen minutes after Virginia heard the thunderous explosion. Her heart thumped beneath her apron as she dashed with her uncle into the dark, chaotic street.

"What's happened, boy?" Uncle Paddy propped his huge forearms on looming hips.

"The train's been derailed! Someone threw dynamite! Ma'am, Zack Bullock has been shot!"

Heat drained from her pores. "Is he alive?"

"Yeah, but the Mounties' car was hit the hardest. They're callin' for you there!"

Virginia and her uncle were the only medical personnel in town. The fort's surgeon, Dr. John Calloway, was making his yearly rounds to the other forts, delayed by an outbreak of Rocky Mountain fever to the north. Whatever she could do for these injured men, she would.

She bolted to the station with her uncle. Dozens of people swarmed the platform. Many of the wounded, scratched and bruised had already been plucked from the train. Injured Mounties were propped against the station-house wall. She knew by their size and youth that they were police. She knelt beside two of the seriously injured. There was nothing she could do. They were gone.

"You help Zack," her uncle shouted, kneeling beside the Mountie with the broken leg. Horses whinnied along the tracks.

"Which one is he?" she cried.

"The one at the end with the injured shoulder."

Her mouth trembled as she peered down the line and spotted him. With a prayer to heaven, her thin skirts billowing, she ran toward him and fell to her knees beside him. "Zack…"

Someone had already placed a towel over the wound to try and stop the bleeding. Illuminated by the station-house lanterns, his looks came as a shock to her. The last time she'd seen him, he'd been dressed in a gentleman's suit, clean shaven with short hair, standing beneath a sprig of mistletoe.

Here he was a big, wild-looking man. Unkempt and unshaven. He struggled to rise. He mumbled something incoherent. Dozing in and out of consciousness, he wobbled forward. His long, dark hair glistened with moist blood, and the solid jaw she'd always remembered as being untouchable was lightly bearded.

"Save your strength," she told him, swallowing her terror, uncertain if he understood. His eyes closed. "Let me take a look."

Virginia pulled the towel off his left shoulder and winced. The bullet had penetrated from his back and exited out the front. Both wounds were clean and small but the front one was slightly ragged. From his asymmetrical movement, she guessed the bullet must have shattered through the clavicle bone.

With trembling hands, she pressed both wounds with bandages to stop the bleeding. He whimpered. Pain etched lines around his full lips. Virginia moaned in sympathy. She'd give him something to ease his agony as soon as she controlled the bleeding. She tried to fathom what had happened and tried to control her disgust. What sort of criminal beast could do this?

"A bloody ambush," said her uncle, tending to the man behind her. When she turned, she vaguely detected wine on her uncle's breath, but her concern was for the wounded. Injuries she'd never seen before and broken limbs she'd never dealt with as a student.

Virginia glanced at Zack's dark face. *We're to be married in two days.* She whispered, "I'm Virginia. It's good to see you after all these years, Zack. Open your eyes."

He didn't respond. He wasn't aware of her.

She fought her utter disappointment, but the pulse pounding in her ears thrilled to the joy that Zack had made it.

While she continued pressing his shoulder, tortured by the devastation of his injury and the loss of life around her, she recalled that, as a child, Zack's awful temper had made him the biggest scrapper in the neighborhood. In one of her first memories—when she'd been five and he fourteen—Zack had fought off five boys who'd started a game of throwing pebbles at a newly arrived immigrant boy from England. Even then, Zack had fought for those who couldn't help themselves.

"*Don't tell my ma,*" Zack had asked her as she'd brought him a hotel pillowcase he could use to tie his bleeding fist. "*She hates it when she sees blood.*"

His father had found out about the incident, though, and had given Zack such a walloping behind the hotel for jumping on the dentist's son that Virginia could still hear the thwack of the branch on the back of Zack's legs.

She'd stayed away from Zack and he'd never spoken to her much from that time forward. She'd preferred the company of his brother, who was nearer to her own age, who never raised a fist to anyone. But her friendship with Andrew had turned her world upside down and left her with a painful cavity in her heart. She'd trusted the wrong brother. She wouldn't make that mistake again. Zack was to be her husband, and she'd put her faith in him.

A train engine whistled. As if in a foggy dream, she realized the platform was covered with spilled fruit. They were sitting in a sea of lemons. Some of the yellow balls were scorched, some still ripe and golden, many rolling down the platform. In the foreground, young boys shoveled mounds of raisins back into barrels. The scent was strange, as burned juices mingled with sweet grapes.

With Zack's bleeding under control for a few precious seconds, Virginia drew up the morphine syringe. Trying to level her shaking fingers, she injected it into his good arm.

Zack murmured with his eyes still closed; Virginia faltered at the sound of his voice.

"I was bending over to get something off the floor… *something*…don't remember…someone startled me from behind and threatened me…" His body tensed. He jolted forward. His bloodshot eyes opened. His grip on her arm was ironclad. "What about the rest of my men? How did they fare?"

"Two didn't make it."

He leaned his head against the wall, closed his eyes and swallowed hard. His Adam's apple bobbed along his unshaven throat. "Which two?"

A feeling of inadequacy rippled along her spine. She didn't know the names of his men. She called behind her. "Which two, Uncle Paddy?"

"Peters and Littlefield."

Zack slumped. A sob burst from his lips.

Virginia felt the sting of tears behind her eyes but had no time to stop. She needed her strength to help him. Unbuttoning what was left of his shirt, she realized she couldn't remove it by herself. She took the pocketknife from her bag and sliced it off him.

Some of the hairs on his broad chest were lightly

singed, but most of his chest glistened with fresh blood. After cleaning it with antiseptic, she began her final bandaging.

One of the men helping her uncle set the broken leg was finally free to help her. Grimacing, she pressed Zack's left arm against his chest, and together they wrapped the linen gauze around his body as one unit. Zack's arm, held tightly against his chest, would support the injured clavicle.

Zack grumbled. "Stiller's going to pay for what he's done."

She didn't know who Stiller was, but wondered how Zack could be certain Stiller was to blame.

While she knotted the final bandage, Zack squinted up at her, as if noticing her for the first time. "You're a doctor."

Her hands fumbled. "Yes," she said, hopeful of the dawning glint in his warm brown eyes. She longed to know how she would speed up Zack's recovery from the pain she knew would follow this event. Physical pain would be the least of his problems, for he was sturdy. The mind-numbing inner pain of losing his friends wouldn't be so easily overcome.

"I know you," he whispered.

He attempted a smile, but it was weak and misplaced. Realizing how awful he must look, he took a hand and swept it through his black hair. He rubbed a hand along one thigh, a leg as thick and solid as a tree trunk, trying to straighten his pants. With tenderness, she noticed his denims were riddled with gunpowder holes, though, and his pointed boots charred.

He reached out with a shaking hand and cupped his blackened fingers beneath her chin.

Her skin tingled where he stroked her. She'd imagined

his intimate touch for weeks, never guessing his first touch would come as patient to doctor. Her long dark hair, knotted in one casual twist, glided along the back of her blouse.

"Virginia," he murmured, slipping back into darkness, into unconsciousness, and sending a shudder quivering up her spine. "We weren't supposed to meet like this."

Chapter Two

"Is the wedding on or off? You've got to make the decision within the hour, Virginia." Uncle Paddy removed his wooden stethoscope after thankfully confirming, as she had, that Zack's breathing was clear and regular. Physically, he was out of serious danger.

Her mind reeled with the thought of more decisions. How many had she had to make in the past two months?

Dawn light streamed through her uncle's spare bedroom, casting a brilliant streak across Zack's powerful set of bandaged shoulders. He and his iron bed were framed by rich blue wallpaper and glossy oak wainscoting. His black brows tightened in a mask of pain. They'd kept him sedated for eight hours, but hadn't wanted to give him too much medication while he was still unconscious.

Wake up and smile.

Filled with the looming fear that he might never awaken from unconsciousness, Virginia blinked her lids against dry eyes. They stung from the bright light and being awake all night.

Apprehension threatened to topple her out of control. She'd been unsure whether to marry Zack Bullock. She'd wanted more time before the wedding.

Well, she'd got it.

Guilt weighed upon her every time she looked at his troubled face. She hadn't wanted more time at Zack's expense. "It's possible Zack may awaken soon."

Uncle Paddy rested a giant hand on her shoulder. The touch of someone strong comforted her. Echoing from the street below, the sound of a team of oxen plodding through the dirt rattled the room's single panes of glass. "He's been delirious all night. Your wedding is only thirty-six hours away, tomorrow evenin' at six. What shape will he be in even if he wakes up?"

"The wedding details seem so trivial compared to what Zack is going through. Constable Johnson in the other room has a broken leg, and two of Zack's men need to be buried."

"Someone has to make the wedding decisions, darlin'. And they're not trivial. If they were, they'd be easy to make."

Teetering on the verge of exhausted collapse, she adjusted the kerchief around her head. She walked to the washstand and poured warm water into a basin, ready to wash Zack's face. It would make her feel better to do something for him rather than just sit and stare and hope for a miracle.

She mulled her options. For the wedding, her folks and Zack's had remained in Niagara Falls. Zack's were too elderly to make the seventeen-hundred-mile journey. Due to the busy tourist season, her parents couldn't leave their work at the Bullock hotel for the month it would take in traveling time, nor could they afford it. *It's best to plan your wedding this time without us,* her mother had said.

Virginia knew how terribly disappointed her parents had been over her breakup with Andrew. Although they meant well, it hadn't taken the sting out of their words.

"What should I do, Uncle Paddy? Should I postpone the wedding for a day or two, or cancel altogether?"

In a nervous habit, Uncle Paddy pressed down on the wire rims of his spectacles. She noticed that his glasses were a different pair than the first she'd seen him wearing a month ago—or perhaps he looked different because he'd shaved off his deep sideburns.

"How are you supposed to know when to postpone it till?" he asked. "It's not an easy thing to reschedule and then possibly have to reschedule again. You've got three hundred guests comin' from all over the countryside. Five wedding cakes to be baked—if they haven't been started already. Three sides of beef to be barbecued."

Uncle Paddy's upper lip caught against his brilliant gold tooth. "You need to decide this now. Telegrams need to be sent to the guests traveling from the next town, Red Deer. Including Andrew. He needs to be told about his brother's injuries."

At the mention of Andrew, at the thought of him coming here with his new wife, Virginia's fingers quivered on the pan. The water rippled. She set it down on the night dresser beside Zack and wiped her hands on her full apron.

The sound of the front door opening echoed up the stairs, muted somewhat by the plush rug in the upper hallway. "Good morning," they heard Millicent call.

"I'll go check on Johnson, then I'll ask Millicent to help you." Uncle Paddy walked through the open door, past the corn-husk broom and wooden bucket leaning against the frame. "I can head off to the telegraph office this morning. You've got ten more minutes to make your decision. Postpone or cancel."

Virginia sat on the edge of the bed. Beneath the colorful quilt, Zack's muscular body rocked on the mattress in response to her movement. His skin was tanned by prairie sunshine and chinook mountain winds. She'd never realized before how handsome he was. He'd come into his own as an adult.

God, she was still as intimidated by his bulk and strength as she'd been as a girl. He was obviously not as invincible as she'd once thought. She studied his sculpted face. What was he like as a fully grown man? He led a life wrought with danger to be sure, but after ten years, she imagined he'd become used to dealing with criminals. It was something she'd have to grow accustomed to as well if she were to be his wife.

In her mid-twenties, she was considered well beyond her prime to start looking for a husband. Many thought she should be grateful to Zack for offering marriage, only three months after Andrew had broken their engagement. She was grateful for several reasons. Zack had always been a decent man. She hated to admit there was more to her motivation…such as financial ties, with her beholden to his family.

She'd heard some people whispering how unlucky Zack was to get her for a bride. At her age, and with the day and night hours doctors usually devoted to their work, they'd speculated how little time she'd have remaining for a husband and children. Is that how Zack saw her? Was it possible to put him and family first, as she desperately hoped to do, while still tending to patients?

She wrung the washcloth, dabbed it against his cheeks, then outlined his straight nose. The heavy growth of stubble on his jaw accentuated the deep black of his eyelashes.

Andrew had sent his goodbye letter five months ago from Alberta. During the three-month interim before Zack had proposed, she'd been so hurt and sickened by Andrew that she vowed she'd never trust another man. She'd find comfort and meaning in her work and in her friendships, and not in a husband. Her friends from college had tried to convince her that not all men were like Andrew.

Six years of engagement, then a simple goodbye letter!

Then Zack had come along and she'd realized her desire to share her life with a man, and her overwhelming urge to have babies of her own were feelings from the heart she couldn't suppress. Zack was offering security and friendship. She hoped relying on him wouldn't weaken her dignity as relying on Andrew had. She could picture herself leading a quiet life with a quiet man, and so she'd said yes to Zack.

And she couldn't deny getting married would help her in her medical profession. How could she counsel people on personal matters of health and reproduction, sexuality and rearing children, if she remained a virgin forever?

Secretly she was hoping Zack would teach her how to enjoy the intimacies of lovemaking. To help her overcome her formality and awkwardness around men. As a growing girl, she'd often wondered about the repressed affection between her parents and had wished she'd known what went on behind closed doors. Sometimes she'd heard muffled groans at night coming from beneath their bedroom door, but she'd never so much as witnessed a kiss between her parents.

One time as they were leaving for church, she'd seen her father's hand stray to her mother's bottom for half a second, and the vision had scorched itself into Virginia's mind.

Intimacy was something she'd craved in her girlhood. Andrew's light pecks had implied more to come, yet her craving remained unfulfilled.

Sighing, she turned to rinse the washcloth. Zack's unexpected grip on her arm startled her. He mumbled softly.

She leaned close to his face, inhaling the musky scent of him, straining to decipher his speech.

His eyelids fluttered but didn't open. She had an uncontrollable urge to touch him, so she leaned over his chest, bosom pressing against his arm, and kissed his closed eyelid. She liked the feel of his muscled biceps pressed against her plump breast. His eyelid fluttered beneath her lips, like a bird's wing grazing soft blades of grass. It tickled.

"Don't tell my mother," he whispered. "She hates it when she sees blood."

Oh, Zack. Did he recognize it was her sitting next to him? Was that why he was repeating those words?

"Virginia?"

She gasped softly. He *was* regaining the lucidness of his mind. "Yes?"

"Is it raining?"

"No," she said with a skip of her heart. "The sky is clear."

A smile flitted across his face as he turned his head away. "I dreamed it was raining lemons."

She felt herself pale at the enormity of what had happened to him and his men, then got on with her task.

After they'd brought him here, all of Zack's clothing had to be cut off him. She'd done it without a moment's hesitation and had tended to the tiny burns on his legs. Twenty-one in all. Pulling back the sheet to reveal one muscled hairy thigh, she noticed the burns looked much better today.

When she was nearly finished, she heard footsteps in the hallway. Uncle Paddy stuck his shiny head through the door. "Well? What's your decision?"

She slumped beneath her uncle's compassionate stare

and prayed with all her heart she'd never regret this moment.

But her solemn hopes sank like a stone to the pit of her stomach as she said, ''Please cancel the wedding.''

''Watch out for your pretty new bride….'' The threatening words hammered through Zack's mind as he slept. It was a man speaking. The words had been unclear during the commotion of the train explosion, but crystal clear in Zack's subconsciousness now.

At the sound of a child's voice, Zack opened his eyes. ''You've got a giraffe's neck,'' said a little girl.

Bandages woven around his chest hampered his movement in bed. He squinted in the sunshine bursting through the lace curtain to find a young girl in blond braids staring at him.

He blinked several times, trying to orient himself, trying to remember his dream, but was unsuccessful. ''Please tell me I haven't awoken in *Gulliver's Travels* as a giraffe-man.''

Sitting in a rocking chair and clutching her leather-bound copy of *Gulliver's Travels,* she giggled, revealing a pretty row of crowded upper teeth. Had she been reading to him?

''What's your name?'' he asked.

''Emilou Gray.''

''Where am I, Emilou?''

She patted her frock. ''You're in Dr. Waters's house. Someone shot you in the shoulder bone. Dr. Virginia says it's called the clavicle.''

''Virginia?'' Panic tore through him. *Virginia.*

He was getting married.

But he didn't recall getting shot. He rolled over, his upper body quaking in a dull throbbing pain. It radiated from the tip of his left shoulder right through his chest and to his fingertips. He groaned, swinging his feet over the edge of the bed. Dizziness fogged his brain. ''I've got to get up.''

Emilou ran out of the room screaming as Zack hit the floor. ''He's fallin' over! Dr. Virginia! He's fallin' over!''

Damn!

Sprawled on the pine floor, with his shaven cheek squeezed against the cool glossy boards, he tried to force his arms to help him. Weakness won out. It felt better not to move.

When a slight breeze stirred the hairs at the back of his legs, he realized with a jolt that he didn't have a stitch on.

A woman raced into the room. He felt like an idiot. A long navy skirt grazed the muscles of his back although he could only see her boots.

''Good heavens, Zack. You must be feeling better.''

He had been, but not with Virginia staring down at him. He recognized the soft tenor of her voice and, Lord, she sounded good.

He was struck by the ridiculous nature of his posture.

''You must be little Virginia Waters,'' he mumbled to her polished black heel.

''And you must be my groom,'' she replied softly.

He smiled at her sense of humor, then winced from the pain of moving. ''Do you think I'll ever get out of this position?''

She paused. ''I'm looking to see where I can best grab you.''

''Don't look too hard. Grab me anywhere except my shoulder.''

''I gave you a dose of morphine thirty minutes ago so

hopefully the pain is subsiding, but it's probably made you woozy on your feet.''

''Is that why I'm down here?''

''That,'' she said, moving her warm fingers along his waist, ''and you've lost a lot of blood. And maybe…'' She didn't finish. Instead, she crouched beside him and placed another warm hand at his neck. ''Bend your knees. Can you try and stand?''

With a groan and lots of pulling and yanking, he tottered on his feet. She was right. The pain eased almost instantly. He wavered from light-headedness but she didn't let go.

''Who shot me?''

''We're not sure. Somebody at the train station.''

He tried to concentrate, tried to remember his dream, tried to remember if anyone had been there with him, but couldn't recall.

Having a woman's arm wrapped around his waist for stability wasn't helping to clarify his thoughts. He felt strange, especially being naked.

They shuffled toward the iron bed. He looked down into her speculative bluish-green eyes, but she didn't seem to know where to look. There was a pretty, tiny mole beside her left eye, which had always accentuated her femininity. But with her black hair astray beneath her kerchief, cheeks and lips reddened from bending over and the blood rushing to her face, she looked as if she'd been scrubbing floors.

''Thanks.'' The word seemed clumsy. He felt as if he'd known Virginia *once* a long time ago; the woman standing here felt like a polite stranger.

The awkwardness in the air irked him. Had they always been this awkward together?

Maybe they had.

He eased himself onto the bed and pulled the cotton sheet safely to his torso. The mattress springs squeaked beneath his heavy weight. He assessed the well-defined red lips and the splatter of freckles across her wide cheekbones. "You let your hair grow."

Her lips dimpled. "You haven't seen it for a while."

"What was the other reason?"

"For what?"

"You said I was on the floor because of the morphine and because I'd lost a lot of blood. And maybe...but you didn't finish the sentence."

Her black lashes caught the sunlight. "And maybe because, since I've known you, you've always wanted to be standing on your own two feet. Eager to run from anything vaguely resembling a bed."

"Ah." He nodded. "But I no longer run so eagerly from *all* beds."

She turned crimson. Up to this point, she'd looked like she'd been trying to ignore the fact that she was clothed and he wasn't.

It had been a long time since he'd been with a woman who was embarrassed about *his* nakedness. How would she react with him when *she* was naked? His eyes strayed to her worn cotton blouse as he imagined the full, soft breasts beneath it.

In the past, he'd always been attracted to very feminine women who wore fancy lace trim and frilly parasols, who were in need of rescue themselves. Virginia didn't seem to need rescuing...but maybe she did, from his brother and his brother's mistakes. She'd always been so much younger than Zack that he'd never thought of her in the heat of sexual attraction. The thought now brought him to the brink of self-awareness.

There was a lot of information to take in around him.

In a way he *did* feel like Gulliver awakening in a strange world. "I've been injured. Will I recover completely?"

"There's a good chance."

A chance? "Will I be able to shoot as well as I did before?" Dammit, he was a marksman. When he'd first begun practicing ten years ago, he'd sometimes practiced for five hours a day, putting everything he had into it.

"You're right-handed, yes?" she asked.

He nodded.

She smiled weakly. "Your right hand's unharmed."

What the hell kind of answer was that? "And my left? I could shoot just as good with my left."

She hesitated, and in that half a second, he felt disaster. "We'll see."

He leaned back against the headboard, supporting his bandaged side. "You haven't caught me in the best of circumstances, Doc."

Most of his pain had left, but he imagined from the size of his bandages that it would return soon. The bed felt tight and small. He rubbed his temple with his good hand, the right one, trying to remember anything that had happened to him. "You weren't supposed to see me like this until our wedding night."

Her eyes opened wide. She glanced down at his bare chest then trailed the length of his leg. "Right...oh..." She turned away to open the window, sucking in fresh air.

He'd meant the comment to be lighthearted, but it only intensified the silent charge between them. She was so shy.

They were going to be married...Was that *tonight? Tomorrow?*

"Turn around and say hello to me, Virginia."

She swung around. Her face was still stained with color.

She stumbled forward, holding out her hand and offering an uncertain smile. "I'm glad you're home, Zack."

Lying on the bed with sheets tumbling around his tanned skin, he frowned and clasped his large hand over hers. *A handshake?* That's what he got? He'd expected her to lean over and hug him, perhaps riddle his neck with soft kisses. Surely, he didn't look *that* bad.

He rubbed his prickly jaw. The bristles were longer beneath his chin than on his cheeks. "Who shaved me?"

"I did."

"You didn't do a very good job."

She smiled this time. "I didn't know there were so many little contours on your face."

He nodded and they stared at each other—Virginia, stiff and uncomfortable, crossing her arms against the intriguing rise of her chest, Zack fascinated by the shy woman he was about to wed.

With a nervous clearing of her throat, she helped him sit up, then placed his comb and dental brush with soda powder at his fingertips. With his thoughts still in a fog, he prodded his memory to return. A deep voice echoed in his mind, *"…your pretty new wife…"*

Fear pricked down his back. "What day is it? What happened at the train station?"

"I'm not sure it's good to tell you everything at once," she said, stepping back.

Finishing with his toothbrush, he gaped with astonishment, rankled by her reply. "Not good to tell me?" No one ever withheld information from *him*. When Zack Bullock asked, folks answered.

"Because of your health. I'm your doctor, and I think it's best—"

"*I* think it's best you tell me what I ask." He watched

her stiffen. A strand of long black hair fell across her shoulder, softly framing her face. "Right now."

She blinked, opened her mouth in hot defense, then sighed. "Do you remember anything from the train station?"

He squinted and tried to focus. "A lot of mass confusion. An explosion of some sort."

"Someone dynamited the passenger car you and your men were in."

"Me and my men?" An awful memory came crashing down on him. Nausea burned up his throat. "Oh, no. Peters and Littlefield."

He gave a choked, desperate cry. His friends were dead. Gone.

Zack had worked with men before who'd died in the line of duty. But never while working alongside him.

And never when he'd been in command.

He felt his throat tense up, but refused to succumb to the emotions threatening to spill—despair, hurt, rage, guilt, embarrassment that Virginia was witnessing his reaction.

He had to *do* something. He swung his legs over the iron bed. "Where are my clothes?" He scanned the room. "Where are my pants? I've got to go to their families. Peters has a wife and children. I've got to take care of their burials—"

She put a hand on his. Her skin was hot and her pulse beat rapidly above his own. "It's too late, Zack. They were buried yesterday."

His shoulders drooped against the headboard.

A moment of silence passed as fresh anguish darkened his pain.

"But I remember things from yesterday," he said, rubbing his jaw, determined to take control. "I remember talking and being on my feet. I remember Emilou reading to me. I could have made it—''

''You were in a daze. I told them to go ahead without you.''

''*You* did?'' He glared at her. She pulled away beneath his scrutiny, clamping her fingers roughly against her breast. He struggled to curtail his anger, but it coursed through his veins and exploded from his mouth. ''What gave you that right? They were *my* men under *my* command. They were *my* responsibility!''

Stumbling away, she fingered the hem of her apron but didn't respond.

Damn his anger. Damn the circumstances. *Damn James Stiller.*

He heard voices downstairs, then Dr. Patrick Waters stepped through the door, crowding the bedside with his presence. ''Zack, I can hear you down the stairs. I'm glad you're feelin' better, but you sound like a grizzly bear wakin' up after hibernation.'' The man looked from Zack to Virginia. ''What's the problem?''

Agony stole its way to Zack's heart. Cameron Peters and Timothy Littlefield were gone. Zack had been their commander for three years. He should have prevented their deaths. He should have been there for their families. What kind of friend was he? He looked away from Virginia to the window to hide his shame.

''What day is it?'' he asked.

''Monday,'' she replied.

''Monday?'' He squinted. ''Didn't I leave on the train on Thursday?'' He sprang upward. ''What about our wedding? *Saturday's* wedding?''

''It was called off.''

Anger flushed his skin, but he thought before he spoke this time. Of course the wedding had to be postponed.

He'd been unconscious lying in bed. But the question escaped from him nonetheless. "Who made that decision?"

She swallowed rapidly. "I did."

"You alone? Again?"

She fidgeted. Her faded white blouse spilled from her cinched waist, and the pleats of her navy skirt fell softly against the curve of the hidden thighs beneath. He knew it had to be tough on her while he was lying in bed, useless, but she seemed unapologetic for making vital decisions without him.

Paddy spoke up. "She discussed it with me. You couldn't have gone through with the wedding, Zack. It's ridiculous to think otherwise."

Zack nodded. "I *do* understand. The wedding had to be postponed. When did you postpone it till?"

"I wasn't sure what to do. Or when you'd wake up."

"You *canceled* it?" This time he cursed. She didn't understand the rules of their engagement. He was in charge. They were *his* rules. Why hadn't she simply postponed the wedding for a week?

"You're quick to jump to anger," she said, "because you're ill. You're not yourself."

Zack heard the footsteps of two people coming up the stairway—one heavy, one light—then saw his brother Andrew and new wife, Grace, standing at the door.

His fair-haired brother knocked lightly on the open door and smiled. "We heard the commotion. You're finally awake. Can we come in?"

Uncertainty pierced Zack's confidence. He thought he'd be ready for this moment when he and Virginia and Andrew would meet again, but he wasn't. And he had more important things to think about, such as the passing of his men. This was too much for him to deal with.

Chapter Three

"Please do come in, have a seat." Virginia took a deep breath and tried to stabilize her bouncing pulse, stepping back from the bed so Andrew and Grace could enter. She flushed with the humiliation of being stuck with both brothers in such intimate quarters.

Strings of dried fruit and herbs—always stored over the winter in these spare rooms—hung from the ceiling beams above their heads, adding a pleasant fragrance to the room. The two-story board-and-batten house was one of the largest in the frontier town; visitors were always welcomed. Andrew and Grace were no exception.

Andrew, as tall as his brother but blond with a neatly trimmed goatee, smiled at Virginia. She nodded blandly in response. Before these past few days, she hadn't seen him for two years; he'd grown more muscular since working on his ranch.

Their ranch. The one they had *together* agreed they'd live on after marriage, where she would open her practice.

"We're not intruding, are we?" Andrew asked her.

He was a capable, excellent rancher from what she'd heard.

Virginia's stomach tightened as she met his coaxing

gray eyes. "Not at all." For Zack's sake, she would not be rude to his brother, nor would she cause problems for Grace who, God forbid, seemed to be unaware that Virginia had once been engaged to her husband. For six years!

Virginia supposed that to this point, the secret had been easy to keep. Andrew had been living in Alberta for six years while Virginia had attended college in the East. And *their* big wedding had been planned for Niagara Falls.

"It's good to see you both," said Zack, but he was obviously still struggling with the grave news about his men. Virginia worried about telling him more and wondered if, now that he was conscious, she should up his dose of morphine. The amount she'd given him wouldn't hold him long.

Andrew and Grace entered with laughter, such a stone's difference between Zack and Virginia's awkwardness. On Friday evening, three hours after receiving Uncle Paddy's urgent telegram, the couple had rushed here to see Zack, then had gone home to tend to their ranch for two days. They'd returned early this morning on their wagon for more visiting.

Other than obligatory polite greetings, and although they were sleeping in the bedroom across from hers, Virginia had pretty much avoided them. She *had* been busy, tending to the wounded man in the next room and the local patients she and her uncle had received at his door.

Zack stretched his legs.

"How are you feeling, Zack?" Grace clutched her husband's elbow. She was beautiful and polite. Her copper hair, parted in the middle, braided and coiled around her ears, shone like healthy wool.

"I've been better," said Zack. "But thanks for coming to cheer me up."

"That's wonderful." Andrew lightly patted Virginia's back, offering condolences of happiness that Zack had finally awoken. Virginia felt her face heat. She lowered her eyes. Being touched by Andrew felt unnecessarily intimate; she fought her emotions. She no longer wanted to be pulled in his direction.

Zack was staring at her. She squirmed beneath his gaze. She didn't want Zack looking for signs of significance between her and Andrew. Her feelings and obligations were firmly planted elsewhere. They would all be growing old together as a family and needed to put this behind them.

But then to her horror, Grace kissed Virginia's cheek as she passed, followed by Andrew, who briefly did the same.

Virginia wanted to scream. There was no significance, she told herself. None. But sneaking a peek at Zack's cold expression, she sensed his disappointment. He'd received a handshake from her, but Andrew had taken a kiss.

Virginia wondered what went on in Zack's mind when he looked at his brother. It couldn't be easy for Zack, either, knowing how much in love she and Andrew had been—or had seemed to be—during all those years of chumming around together, attending parties and family dinners, always holding hands as soon as they were out of her parents' sight.

"Yes, I'm so pleased Zack has pulled through." Virginia slid to the side of Zack's bed and stroked his free hand, to make it clear where she stood.

Zack seemed surprised by the gesture. One dark eyebrow lifted in her direction. His lips quirked with humor. He gave her a yank at the back of her skirt, forcing her to sit down on the bed beside him, then placed his hot hand between her shoulder blades. Good grief, he was having fun with her. The heat of his touch seemed to burn the fabric itself, tattooing her skin with his imprint.

"You had us worried." Andrew sat down on a wooden chair beside his wife, beneath the sunlit window.

"I'll be fine. Right, Virginia?"

Virginia nodded.

"She was just telling me what happened at the station that night," Zack explained. "If you all don't mind, I'd like to hear the rest of it. What happened to the other three men who were with me?"

"Constable Hank Johnson is fine, but he's broken his leg. It's the tibia below his knee, thankfully not the femur. He's in the other room."

"When can I see him?"

"You've already seen him, briefly yesterday when we had you on your feet. You shared a cup of coffee."

Zack's face strained. "I don't remember." He ran a hand along his bandages.

"The pain is back, isn't it?"

"Yeah."

Virginia glanced at the pocket watch pinned to her blouse. "The dose only lasted forty-five minutes. I'll up it next time."

"I don't want to be groggy."

"But the pain—"

"I can handle it," he insisted.

At the boom of his voice, Virginia glanced at the other couple. Grace had lowered her eyes and Andrew frowned.

"Fine," said Virginia. She had no desire to push him. "We'll find a dose that's good for you."

"No more than what you've given me already. As you said, I'm woozy enough as it is, and I can't manage an investigation if my mind isn't working."

Virginia turned to look at him. He thought he could

head an investigation in his shape? It was the medication speaking.

If he wouldn't listen to her, then she'd get Uncle Paddy to reason with him. For now, she kept silent and gave him better news. "The other two men with you, Sergeant Major Travis Reid and his younger brother, Constable Mitchell Reid, are fine. They had a few scratches, but I gather from where they were seated in the car, they didn't fall far when it flipped."

Zack's mouth rose in relief. The smile transformed him. He no longer looked like a disgruntled bear. "Were any other passengers hurt?"

"No," she said. "Only minor cuts and bruises. The blast was centered on the Mounties' car."

Zack nodded, lost in thought. She wondered if he remembered the name Stiller, but decided not to tell him here in front of the others. Besides, if she did, he was liable to jump up this minute, put on his holster and run out the door without regard to his condition.

Virginia turned to her guests. "Would you like some tea or coffee?"

"No thanks," said Grace. "It's close to lunchtime and we—*I*—promised I'd help Millicent peel all the potatoes she'd need to feed these hungry men."

"How's the ranching coming?" Zack asked his brother.

"We're about to start planting as soon as the land drains from the spring melt. With this hot sun, it'll only be a few more days. And most of the cattle survived the winter."

Andrew went on about his irksome ranch, while Grace and Virginia nodded at each other. The image of having a friend, a close sister-in-law who lived within ninety miles of Virginia, would be blessedly welcome. If it weren't so painful for Virginia to glance in Andrew's direction, she'd willingly open her arms to Grace. A little more time was all she needed, she promised.

Grace patted Virginia's hand. "You two look good together."

Virginia mumbled her thanks as Zack's eyes flickered at the comment. He looked to his brother who was still talking, then gazed up at Virginia.

Yes, Virginia wanted to say to him. *Your blasted brother hasn't told his wife a thing.*

How much longer could Andrew hide it? It might be a secret in the town of Red Deer, but it wasn't a secret in this town. Uncle Paddy knew, as did Millicent. Didn't Andrew realize it would be better if he told his wife himself than for her to hear it through gossip?

But then for Andrew, silence was the easy way out.

Virginia tried to blink away her pain.

Why couldn't he have waited for her? Their years of friendship had turned into years of sensual longing. At the age of sixteen, Andrew had promised to marry her. He formally proposed two years later. At the time, she'd spent two summers with her Uncle Paddy in Saskatchewan— and her dearly departed aunt, before they'd moved to Alberta—watching Uncle Paddy in his practice as he tended to elderly folks and sick children. She'd wanted to study medicine, too, but her parents couldn't afford to give her an education. Andrew's folks had stepped in saying they'd be thrilled to have a doctor in the family. They had willingly and proudly put her through college, believing her to be their future daughter-in-law.

But those five years while she completed her education were a long time waiting to marry; Andrew had obviously thought it too long. As planned, he'd come west to buy his ranch and she'd thought she'd be joining him. He'd organized the wedding with her to the finest detail before he'd one day written, five months ago from Alberta, that he'd married someone else.

Could Virginia blame him for falling in love with another woman? Six years apart had been a lifetime.

My apologies, he'd written in his letter. *I hope this won't affect our friendship.*

Won't affect our friendship! So help her, she fought the urge to reach over and throttle the man. The humiliation of facing family and friends...the embarrassment of neighbors' gossip...

And to think what Andrew had put their families through. He'd left Virginia owing his folks a fortune for her education. No one had known what to do about it. It wasn't her fault that Andrew had walked away from her, but they expected repayment of some sort. Although embarrassed and humiliated, Virginia thought it only fair to repay their generosity.

She thought she could repay them over the course of ten years of working, if she didn't interrupt her practice to have children. Her folks were fraught with concern that they'd have to sell their modest home and work for the rest of their living days to repay tuition and boarding costs for medical college.

That's when Zack had stepped in. By marrying her himself, the Bullocks would still have a doctor in the family as they'd once proudly declared, and Virginia wouldn't need to repay a cent. Zack had never once mentioned the money in his letters, but the burden had been silently lifted off her shoulders.

"I hear a new wedding date needs to be set," said Grace.

"It does," said Zack.

"When will it be then?"

"We're discussing the possibilities."

"We'd like to make sure that Zack is feeling one hundred percent better," Virginia said cautiously.

Zack winced. "I'm fine."

Andrew stroked his goatee. "We'll be in town for another day and a half. Why don't you let us plan a get-together tomorrow evening and you can announce your new date then."

"No thanks," said Zack immediately. "We can do this on our own."

"But maybe it's a good idea," said Virginia. "If we could gather my bridesmaids and your groomsmen and a few of our friends, we could pick a new date that's good for everyone." Immediately after Zack's injury, she hadn't been thinking clearly about how soon they should reset a date. But considering the recent tragedy, she knew they should set the date a few weeks away, perhaps a month or even two.

Zack turned his attention to Virginia. "Maybe we'll get married quietly."

Virginia considered it. She wasn't against the idea. Maybe Zack preferred a smaller wedding, something modest, out of respect for the men who'd lost their lives. "That might be best."

He patted the back of her waist, and she felt him relax. He seemed to appreciate her answer. A quiet, quick wedding. That would suit her.

Virginia looked at her watch again. "Excuse me, but I'm due to help my uncle change a dressing in the next room."

She leaned over Zack and planted a gentle kiss on his cheek. The untouchable jaw wasn't made of granite; it was soft and bristly. With a private, amused smile, knowing it was the first kiss they'd shared since his proposal, she made to get away, but he tugged her back by her skirt.

"Not one on the lips?"

Virginia felt her color rise.

She leaned over and lightly brushed her lips against his. At the contact, he moaned beneath her and she felt a shiver run along her back. Mercy, how would she be able to handle a man like this one?

In bed and otherwise?

With a quick goodbye and an aggravating wink from him, she fled the room, thankful he didn't burst into laughter behind her.

Gathering her composure in the hallway, she called for Uncle Paddy, but he didn't answer. Constable Johnson was dozing in his room when she walked in. He was healing nicely and she was grateful. But like many of the single Mounties, his family resided back East, so he would be alone during recovery.

Medical instruments and trays were spread on the night dresser beside him, but his leg bandages remained intact. Uncle Paddy had been here. She wondered why he'd started, then left.

The constable opened his eyes. "Your uncle's gone."

"Where did he go?"

"I'm not sure. He started to mumble."

"I'll look for him and be right back."

"Virginia? I don't know if this has any bearing, and I know a lot of men who take to drink when they're under pressure, but your uncle's been hitting the rye."

Disappointment surged through her. She'd believed after his past problems with alcohol, Uncle Paddy was a teetotaler now. "Thank you for telling me. I'll make sure...I'll be the one to change the dressing. Perhaps he's had an early lunch and a glass of something with his meal."

She walked into the hall and leaned against the cool

wall for a moment to catch her breath. The oval staircase shone from fresh polish, and thick new candles sat in the crystal chandelier hanging above the stairs.

Uncle Paddy…*drinking again.* She'd heard rumors in town about his drinking binges of three years ago, how the surgeon from the fort, Dr. John Calloway, had helped him through it. She'd thought her uncle had no recent setbacks. Was it affecting his work again?

When she heard Andrew coming out of Zack's room, she darted down the hall to escape, but he caught her. "Virginia, hold on. We haven't been alone to talk since…for ages. You look wonderful. Utterly blossoming. I hope…I hope…"

Defiant, she glared up into his hesitant smile. "You hope what, Andrew?"

He reached out and stroked her cheek. "I hope that I haven't made a mistake."

She stepped away. Her mouth dropped in disbelief. How could he!

"Andrew?" Grace came around the corner. "There you are. I need help downstairs, please."

Grace pressed her shoulder against her husband's, and Virginia wondered if she was reading more into Andrew's statement than he'd intended.

What kind of mistake had he meant? A mistake that he hadn't married *her?* Or a mistake in the way he'd simply handled his rejection of her?

She didn't care to find out.

Grace retied her apron. "Virginia, there's a man downstairs who says he's a reporter. Mr. David Fitzgibbon with the *Calgary Herald.*"

"I don't know a Mr. Fitzgibbon. What does he want?"

"He says he heard that the inspector was awake for a

couple of hours yesterday and was wondering if he were alert enough today to be interviewed about the accident.''

"I don't think Zack would enjoy that. He feels awful enough as it is about the deaths of his men. Please tell Mr. Fitzgibbon that it's much too soon. Nudge him out the door.''

"What shall I tell your cousin?''

"Clarissa Ashford is here?''

"Yes. She's brought chicken soup for Constable Johnson. She'd like to deliver it to him herself.''

Virginia rubbed her cheek. Clarissa was friendly enough and eager to please, but a busybody. On the other hand, Hank Johnson was alone with no family to visit him. "Please tell her I have a dressing to change on the constable. Ask her to come back in an hour. I'm sure he'd enjoy her soup then.''

"And two more people arrived with that wretched stomach flu.''

"Oh, dear. Have you seen my uncle?''

"I'm afraid not.''

"Maybe he was called away for another emergency,'' Virginia rationalized.

"I daresay, otherwise he wouldn't leave you alone to handle all this.''

"Please ask the new patients to wait in the back room. It's more private than the sitting room, and there are buckets in case their vomiting persists. I'll get to them as soon as I can. Thank you for your help, Grace.''

Whatever Andrew had meant by his comment, Virginia had a sudden overwhelming sympathy for Grace.

Virginia left to finish her dressing change and called behind her shoulder. "Go with your wife, Andrew. She needs you.''

* * *

Virginia was in danger.

The next morning, Zack awoke from his nightmare with a start. Cotton sheets stuck to his sweaty arms. *"Watch out for your pretty new bride."*

Who had said that to him?

He watched shadows flutter on the ceiling rafters, weaving dark stripes around the hanging herb plants. He heard a rooster crowing in the neighbor's yard.

Beneath his command, two men had died. They might be after Virginia next. All because of Zack.

He'd shot and killed Ned Stiller.

Zack was sure James Stiller and his men had thrown the explosive charge. Someone in their gang had shot Zack at close range before the dynamite had blasted. Last night the superintendent and Travis had come calling on Zack and they'd pieced together some information. The other two men believed Zack had been shot through the open train window as they were pulling into the depot, but Zack kept his mind open. What if he'd been shot right in the car itself? His was a small wound made by a small pistol.

Who besides the other Mounties had been in the car with them that night? Or heaven forgive him for thinking it, but what if he'd been shot by another Mountie?

The only thing Zack could be certain of at this point was that Stiller wouldn't hesitate to blast Virginia dead.

Two Mounties were currently posted by the front and back doors of the house, protecting Zack and Hank in case of another ambush, but Zack's new insight from his dream meant he had to protect Virginia, too.

He rose and made sure she was sleeping soundly, then returned to bed. He dozed on and off till nine o'clock, when Virginia whispered a good morning and gave him an injection.

Through half-hooded eyes, he watched her. He'd never proposed to another woman before; he'd never come close. He'd always lived alone and been alone. He took *his* commitments seriously, unlike his brother, but nothing would come before Zack's duty to keep her safe.

How could he keep her safe unless he *disengaged* himself from her life?

He fought the idea all morning as she fluffed the pillows behind him, as she spread ointment on the burns of his legs, as she hummed while changing his pillowcase, explaining the arm exercises she wanted him to try.

He tried to sound casual. "Promise me you won't leave the house unless you tell me."

"Why?"

"I'm an overly cautious policeman, I guess."

She laughed gently. "I haven't been able to leave for days anyway because of the number of patients coming in and out of the house. Seems to be a stomach illness going around. All right, I'll let you know when I want to leave."

Zack wondered if his brother was targeted, too. He tried to think like Stiller did. A brother for a brother, why not? But whoever had been watching Zack knew he and Andrew weren't close. They barely visited. And no one had threatened Andrew like they had Virginia.

Nevertheless, Zack felt easier knowing Andrew was an excellent shot and always well armed. When Zack had first joined the Mounties, and then as he'd gained a reputation putting more than one vindictive criminal behind bars, he'd insisted his brother take precautions. Zack would again remind him.

Around noon in his room, Virginia brought him a tray of soup and biscuits. She watched him stumble around the bed.

"What is it that you're trying to do?" she asked.

"I'm putting on my holster—or at least trying to, with one hand."

"Let me help you—"

"No."

With rising impatience, she slapped the tray down on the dresser.

"I need to learn to do this myself. It'll be a couple of weeks before I can get my arm out of this sling, and you can't be here every time I need help."

"A couple of weeks? I recommend at least four in a sling. And surely you're not going to wear your guns while you're recuperating?"

"I'm a police officer."

"You're an injured man. You've been ordered off duty until you've healed."

His holster fell to the floor. He cursed in frustration. The shame and guilt of letting two men beneath his command die assailed him. Then his fury raged.

Virginia might be in danger, and there wasn't a damn thing he could do to protect her against the vicious animals if he couldn't even goddamn shoot.

Except tell her he no longer wanted to marry her.

The thought popped into his head. He groaned at what it implied. After how Andrew had humiliated her, how could Zack turn her away, too?

But that would be good, wouldn't it? She'd be furious and easily convinced to go home, seventeen-hundred miles away where she'd be safe, unattached to him.

She left the room to attend to the constable and Zack thought some more.

If he disengaged himself, she might never come back.

Why hadn't they tried to harm her already? Maybe the sick reason was Stiller wanted to torture Zack with the thought of harm, terrify him so much that he'd back away from the year-old investigation.

Never.

Why not go to Virginia and simply *tell* her she might be in danger?

Because that wouldn't help to keep her safe. Because it wouldn't stop the Stiller gang from coming after her. Stiller had to believe that Virginia Waters meant nothing to Zack.

Breaking their engagement would send her running from Calgary faster than any other reason. Zack had to quickly find a safe haven for her while he stayed behind to battle James Stiller.

When Virginia returned to his side, he studied the firm cut of her chin, the tilted, defiant face and the flashing dark eyes. Talking to Virginia was like talking to the commander. The dang woman voiced her opinion on everything Zack said.

He thought she'd be too preoccupied with her medical training to have time for much else, but unfortunately she was preoccupied with everything that concerned him. He could understand the worry of a new bride—but it didn't help him do his job. Knowing her, she'd object to his plan and demand they talk it through together.

There was no talking to these criminals. Virginia was an educated woman who'd never witnessed the dregs of society he had. The killings not just at arm's length down the barrel of a gun, but up close, with throats slit by hand-made knives.

"Zack, why don't we get a crowd together this evening, like Andrew suggested? It would do you good, as well as your friends. They've been asking and calling on you for five days straight. We can have the get-together in the parlor. I'm sure even Hank would enjoy it. We can get two men to carry him with his splints down the stairs.''

Zack leaned against the wall. If he announced the terrible news of his wedding cancellation to the crowd this evening, then word would get out faster to James Stiller.

Zack was beginning to hate himself already. ''How could we get the word out so quickly about a gathering this evening?''

Virginia smiled. ''We can tell my cousin, Clarissa. She knows everyone in town.''

With a glum expression, he stepped to the window and looked to the boardwalk and pedestrians below. Calgary was a haven for ranchers, businessmen, railroad tycoons and brewery owners. Farmers had recently developed a hardy wheat that could survive the cruel weather, and Canadian wheat was high in demand across North America. Hell, the town was also a cattle empire. Beef was packaged and shipped by rail all the way to the East Coast then shipped to England from there.

But along with all this money came the scum who lived off the labor of others. Thieves and killers.

Virginia came up from behind. When she wrapped her tender arms around him, he struggled to maintain his detachment.

''I should have said hello in the proper way to you before.'' She lightly brushed her lips across his good shoulder. The feel of her silken mouth on his bare skin made his muscles tighten. ''I'm sorry for what happened to you and for the loss of your men.''

He couldn't turn around. He couldn't hurt her.

''Zack, please, I know all this has been hard on you, but please talk to me.''

He swung around with such venom in his blood she backed away. With one arm in a sling, he took two hungry steps toward her, placed his right hand on the wall behind her head and looked down at the woman he'd proposed to. He tugged the kerchief from her head and roped her satiny hair between his fingers, inhaling the scent of Virginia.

She gasped. Her bluish-green eyes opened wide and her gaze dropped to his lips. Maybe she hadn't expected him to react so strongly, but his mouth came down hard on hers.

The heat of her lips penetrated his harshness, right down to his soul it seemed, but not before he took what he'd come so close to getting. Virginia. Little Virginia Waters.

The curves and contours of her body melted against his. The softer she felt, the harder he became. The simple strokes of her fingertips grazing his temples drove him wild. He ran his hand along the hollow of her spine, dipping lower and lower down her blouse, wondering what her skin would feel like naked, locked against his.

He felt her sigh and weaken to his touch. She tightened her breathing and embrace. Her warm hands came up along the muscles of his waist and he trembled at the erotic tracing of her fingers. Such a simple touch, but no woman had ever touched him along the recess of his waist. His thighs brushed the length of hers, and her breasts closed against him.

What he hungered to do was yank her blouse out of her skirt, lift the fabric and undo the stays of her corset. To touch her intimately, to stroke her breasts and kiss the rosy tips. He wanted to make love to this woman.

To kiss all the way down her rounded belly to her thighs until she cried his name and forgot about his brother's.

But what he did instead was pull away. He panted for air.

She studied his face, her eyes moistened with concern. He wondered if she'd ever come back to him after what he was about to do.

"Hmm." He shut his eyes against the regrets that would surely come.

"You're in pain. It's time for morphine."

"I don't care." He explored her lips again with a slow, deliberate kiss.

Breathless, she pulled her mouth away. "I care. I don't want to hurt you."

He winced at the irony and pressed his forehead against hers.

How could he turn her away?

Easily. If he cared anything about Virginia, he'd use the opportunity tonight to tell her he'd changed his mind.

Zack Bullock no longer wanted to marry Dr. Virginia Waters.

Chapter Four

Virginia wondered, as she changed into a fresh blouse, why she felt uneasy. It was likely due to the thought of her wedding. She'd barely reacquainted with Zack, and they were about to be married.

Three hours remained before her bridesmaids and Zack's groomsmen would arrive for the after-dinner gathering, but she'd have time enough to run her urgent errand.

"Where are you going?"

Zack's voice startled her as she dashed by his bedroom in the upper hallway. Skittish, she turned at the stair landing to look up at him. He towered over the handrail with his arm in a sling and white shirt buttoned askew—misbuttoned by one. He looked like a warrior, a wounded soldier who'd lost a battle but was up and ready for more. A sense of pride filled her; his work was important and she could understand why folks said he was so skilled at what he did.

"To the mercantile."

Zack's face knotted with disapproval.

Dampened by the overcast sky, the late-afternoon sun dimly lit the stair window, silhouetting the sleek lines of his jawbone and cheeks. His glossy black hair, overgrown to his collar, needed a good comb. He was, however, wearing his holster across his narrow hips, with two guns. It was strange to note his priorities. So he'd finally managed to get his holster on by himself.

His voice was firm. "I thought you were going to tell me when you needed to leave the house."

She felt chastised. "You were dozing."

"You should have woken me."

"Your rest is more important than tending to me."

"Virginia…you have to be careful in this town. It's not like Niagara Falls where everyone knows everyone and the tourists are unmistakable. Calgary's got a lot of drifters and gamblers and drinking men. Strangers blend in here."

She'd never thought of it like that, but she knew Zack was right. During the past month, it had already been her instinct to be more prudent than she had been back home.

"Considering what you've been through, it's natural for you to suspect everyone and everything," she said. "But living locked up in a house twenty-four hours a day is impossible. I can't last any longer. Your commander told me there's no sign of the Stiller gang in town. I've got calls to make and I need fresh air."

His brown eyes flickered over her blouse.

She was mesmerized at how handsome he was. She never would have described him like that when he was a boy. As a man, he was focused and confident. Everyone looked to him for leadership, and this quiet assurance was his most magnetic quality.

"You talk like a doctor."

The lines around his mouth deepened with anxiety—or perhaps a twinge of pain—and she tried to set him at ease. "I never go into dark alleys alone. If I go out in the evening farther than our neighborhood, I take someone with me. I never ride into the countryside without telling someone first.''

She took the three risers and stepped beside him, helping him straighten his shirt. ''Your shirt's not buttoned correctly. Let me undo this one for you.'' She pulled on the button. ''And I never accept peppermint sticks from strangers.''

The intimacy of her gesture didn't strike her until his dark head lowered over hers. Her fingertips brushed against his bare stomach. She felt his stomach muscles twitch.

He snatched and held her hand. ''It's a serious concern.''

She gulped at the heat of his touch, then pulled her arm back safely against her ruffled blouse. ''I know. I'm very careful.''

''I want you to take one of the two guards outside the door with you to the mercantile.''

''That's impossible.''

''Why?''

''Both men are with Hank Johnson at the moment. They carried him outside and are helping him practice with his crutches. He felt well enough to get up and walk to the privy for the first time.''

''Then wait until they're finished.''

''I don't have time to wait. It's four o'clock already. Besides, I've made this short walk many times before. The fresh air would do you good. Why don't you come with me?''

He stepped away and she noticed again the stiffness in his response. Since their kiss earlier, he'd been withdrawn. Hadn't he enjoyed the kiss? Had there been something more she should have done? She admitted, she hadn't had a lot of courting practice in her time, *none* in the area of the bedroom, but she would learn and come to please him as a wife.

In the secret conversations of women in her college, she knew that great pleasure was possible for them both. All Zack had to do was teach her. She hoped she could overcome her shyness to speak to him about it.

"Why don't you come with me?" she repeated.

When Zack didn't answer her, she struggled to understand him. He looked at her, then at the window with disdain, almost as if...as if he didn't care to be seen with her.

Voices rumbled from the parlor below. "Check."

Uncle Paddy and his good friend, Ian Killarney, were playing chess in the parlor as she'd often seen them do. It was still an amazing sight, considering Mr. Killarney's condition. He'd been blind for twenty years, but was still the town's best fiddler as well as undefeated chess champion.

Virginia tore away from Zack's glare and descended the stairs. She headed toward the front door to the hat rack and umbrella stand.

Zack followed, his muscled weight creaking down on every tread behind her. "All right, I'll come with you. I can see you're going whether I disapprove or not."

Exasperated but not willing to argue with her future husband, she peered through the archway, tying her bonnet's ribbon beneath her chin. "Uncle Paddy, would you like me to light a lamp? It's overcast outside and dark in here."

She struck a match and lit the hurricane candle lamp.

"It doesn't matter to me whether you light a lamp or not," bellowed Ian Killarney, running his hands over the top of several chess pieces. They were playing on the special chessboard he brought with him two evenings a week to play.

The chessboard and pieces were carved crudely from wood, smoothly polished by all their handling over the past twenty years. The white squares sat higher than the black ones by an eighth of an inch, due to the extra layer of oak that had been glued to each square. Mr. Killarney differentiated the white from black chessmen because a small triangle of wood had been notched at the top of all the white pieces.

"I can beat your uncle even if it's pitch-black in here."

"Very funny, Ian," said Uncle Paddy. "Rook to knight two."

Mr. Killarney ran his hands over the chess piece Uncle Paddy had just moved and chuckled. He moved another piece. "Queen to king bishop six. Checkmate."

Uncle Paddy sank back into his chair and sighed. He hadn't seemed himself for days. What was troubling him? She was a little tired of living with disgruntled men.

"You should have seen that one comin', Paddy. What's on your mind?" asked Mr. Killarney.

"Work," he grumbled, but Virginia wondered if that was all. She'd approached him earlier about his drinking. He confessed he'd had a drink with one of his friends just before noon. Since no harm had come to anyone because of it, Virginia hadn't pressed him further. Goodness' sake, her uncle was forty years older, and she had no right to reprimand him.

Virginia turned around in time to catch Zack watching in marvel as the two men cleared the board. She recalled a month ago when Mr. Killarney had dropped by for the first time and she, too, had been mesmerized by the blind chess player.

"That's incredible," Zack whispered. "I've heard of

Ian Killarney but never seen him play chess." Zack drew closer and introduced himself.

"Do you know how to play?" asked Mr. Killarney.

"Not as well as you, sir."

"Any time you need a lesson, I'd be happy to oblige."

Zack chuckled along with him as Millicent came through the swinging kitchen door with a tray of biscuits and tea. She set it down on the table beside the men.

Mr. Killarney cheerfully whispered, "Thank you" and turned his head toward Millicent in such a loving gesture, it caught Virginia by surprise. The cataracts made his eyes cloudy, but his clean-shaven face and long gray hair gave him an air of distinction. He was handsome. When Virginia studied Millicent's face to see if the slender housekeeper had noticed Mr. Killarney's affections, Millicent's tender gaze settled on Uncle Paddy.

Millicent had feelings for Uncle Paddy.

Oh dear, thought Virginia, turning her attention to her uncle, who was sliding chess pieces into a felt pouch, noticing neither Millicent nor Mr. Killarney. What a tangled web between three old friends.

Zack nudged her shoulder. She felt his warm breath at her throat. "Are you ready?"

She nodded, leading the way to the front door. When she popped out a comb from one of the compartments of the front hall's Hepplewhite dresser, she handed it to Zack.

"Right," he said, sliding it through his hair. She enjoyed standing here in the tight corner with him, taking care of him and helping him, basking in the warm delight of being needed.

He propped his oil slicker over his sling and shoulder, then picked up her umbrella as she pulled on a shawl.

On the boardwalk they were met with a warm spring

breeze; the musky scent of a coming rain met her nostrils and she inhaled deeply. It smelled good, like the sweet coming of summer. They would have a glorious summer together, she and Zack as a newly married couple.

Andrew and Grace had gone visiting for the afternoon, but would return in time for this evening's get-together. At the thought of this evening's social, Virginia smiled. Clarissa had said she would invite everyone, and Virginia was grateful that it had freed up her time so she could see patients.

Zack scanned the street like a gunfighter on patrol.

"Inspector Bullock!" called a male voice behind them.

Virginia turned to see a slim man with straw-colored hair, a portable camera slung over his back and a monkey sitting on his shoulder. She backed away from the animal, the likes of which she'd never seen except in the Niagara zoo.

"It's my aunt's pet monkey, ma'am," he said. "He won't hurt you. He's tame. She got him from a passing carnival."

She nodded. The man and beast made a distinctive impression and she supposed the man enjoyed the attention.

He turned and extended a hand to Zack. "I'm David Fitzgibbon, sir. I'm a reporter—"

"With the *Calgary Herald,*" Zack finished. "You and your monkey have been around for a while. I know who you are."

"I was wondering if you could answer a few questions about the train derailment."

Zack turned away, adjusted his Stetson, then pressed his palm against the small of Virginia's back, urging her to keep walking. "No thanks, David."

"How about a few questions about your upcoming wedding, then?"

"Why does a reporter want to know about my personal business?"

"I write a weekly society column as well as reporting on the news. I heard your wedding was postponed. Folks in town like to keep up on these things. The paper goes to several surrounding towns, too, and it'd be helpful to folks if we announced your new date."

Zack's expression mellowed and he slowed his stride. "I see." He glanced at Virginia. An almost imperceptible redness washed his neck, as if he were embarrassed. "Why don't you come by the house—Doc Waters's house—later this evening. We're deciding on a date then."

Virginia frowned, expecting Zack to clear the invitation with her, but he kept walking, leaving the reporter behind. Why hadn't Zack asked her for an opinion? Not that she would have argued, but it would be a polite gesture to have been asked. She also noticed he hadn't mentioned a wedding date yet. She hadn't more time to think about it before they reached Rossman's Mercantile, and Zack was holding open the door for her.

She'd come to give Mr. Rossman an important message. The town's health depended on it.

Four-thirty was a busy time for shoppers, some of whom were leaving their own jobs for the day and preparing for supper. More than a half-dozen people milled the crowded floor, squeezing between pickle barrels, stacks of old newspapers, hanging rope of every thickness and boxes of nails.

"Mrs. Rossman, is your husband here?" Virginia asked the thirty-year-old ruddy woman behind the counter. Two small children played tag around her legs while she weighed coffee beans for a customer.

"He's in the back room, trimming wood for a customer. Rossman!" she hollered.

A thin sixty-year-old man, double the age of his wife, with white bristles, short white hair and spectacles popped out with a piece of pine. He handed it to a waiting man, who took it to the cashier. "Howdy, Zack. What can I do you for, miss?"

"I'm Virginia Waters, Paddy's niece." She'd start off slow but she'd be firm.

Mr. Rossman squinted. "I've seen you here a couple of times before. My wife served you."

"That's right."

"Whaddya need? More lace ribbon for your weddin' dress?"

"No, sir, it's about the raisins."

"Right over here." He led Virginia and Zack to a quiet corner and lifted the lid of a barrel. "Will a pound do you? Two, maybe?"

Virginia took her gloved hand and scooped a mound of golden raisins into her palm. Sand grains trickled between the cracks of her fingers. "You can't sell these anymore."

"I beg your pardon? It's loud in here. I don't think I heard you right."

"You can't sell these raisins. They're making everyone ill." She strained to be heard above the other voices. "Is there a place where we can talk in private?"

Mr. Rossman scowled and glanced at Zack, who looked equally surprised. Without a word of alarm to his customers, Mr. Rossman led them to the back storage room. Boxes and barrels filled every free space.

Virginia stepped to the back of the room, squeezing her skirts past the boxes near the open door, and counted nine more barrels. "When were these raisins delivered?"

"A few days ago. Why?"

"They arrived on the same train Zack did, last Thursday evening."

"That's right. I had the order in three months ago to California."

"Have you eaten any of them yourself?" She suspected the answer was no, otherwise he would have been one of her recent patients.

"No, ma'am. My family's not partial to raisins. We like dried apricots but they're not comin' in for a while."

"I saw these raisins when the train was derailed by the blast, sir."

"So?"

"I don't know how many barrels were spilled, but I saw a group of children shoveling them back into the barrels while I was there."

He leered at her. "So?"

"So the barrels are full of dirt and who knows what else." She felt intimidated by his glare. "There are mice beneath that platform. Half-a-dozen patients have come to see me and my uncle because of vomiting. The only thing these people seem to have in common, which I've traced to…are these raisins."

Zack folded his good arm across his sling and came forward to stand beside her. It was a comforting gesture of support. This was what it felt like to be a couple. She'd been alone for so long but now Zack was here beside her, soon to be her protective husband.

"That's nonsense," said Mr. Rossman. "I'm not throwing out good money on someone's idea of a—"

"I can quarantine the whole place."

"What does that mean?"

"If you don't get rid of these barrels right now as I witness their destruction, I can shut down your business till you comply. My uncle will back me. And so will the Mounties, right, Zack?"

Zack muttered beneath his breath. "Why didn't you warn me?" Then louder, he said, "She's right, Rossman."

The man swore a streak. "Your uncle's never given me trouble like this."

Virginia tensed at the insult but didn't blink.

"But listen, some of the barrels didn't spill," said the older man. "You can tell by the seals. The wax isn't broken. Can I keep those?"

"Maybe." She brightened. "Let's take a look."

By five o'clock, with Mrs. Rossman's help, they had salvaged three of the ten barrels. The raisins in them were clean and pure.

"Can I sell these as pig feed at least?" Mr. Rossman filled his wheelbarrow with the contaminated raisins and wheeled them outdoors. His back strained beneath his damp, wrinkled shirt.

"Not even for pig feed," she said. "They'll make the pigs sick. You can bury the raisins or burn them. And you also have to personally retrieve all the leftover raisins from everyone who's bought them."

"But that'll cost me a fortune!"

Mrs. Rossman poked her head out the door in passing. "I'll make sure he does it, ma'am." She turned to one of her youngsters, who was still climbing around her knees. "Can you git off my leg for just one moment, honey? Please go play with your brother!"

Zack and Virginia finished their business. As they were heading toward home and out of earshot, Zack moaned. "Could you please warn me the next time before you come out blasting with both barrels?"

He laid a solid hand along her back to guide her around

a passing couple. She reached out and squeezed his hand affectionately, and he reacted with a definite jolt. So he felt the deep attraction, too, the anticipation of their wedding night. He pulled his hand away, although his breathing was rattled. Mercy, did all men get as physically affected by the same rousing thoughts as women?

"I'm sorry I had to use you as leverage," she said, trying to calm her feverish images of Zack in bed with her. "It happened so fast and I wasn't sure how Mr. Rossman would take it. I realize the folks in this town don't know me as well as they do my uncle."

She *knew* she was getting special treatment and acceptance because of her likable uncle. And she was sensitive to the townspeople's resistance to meeting their first female doctor. Lord knows, in the letters she was receiving from her two closest female friends who'd graduated medical college with her, people in Vancouver and Halifax weren't taking any more quickly to women doctors than they were here.

Zack whistled. She felt engulfed by his massive build. "You're full of surprises."

Unable to resist the pull between them, she slid her arm through the crux of his good elbow. He stiffened in response and pulled away *again,* rubbing his other arm nervously. What had she done wrong? Was she being too forward? For heaven's sake, he was jittery. Maybe he wasn't feeling quite himself yet, she rationalized. Vestiges of his injury.

He stopped just as she was about to turn the corner, and she nearly toppled over him.

"It's Cameron's wife," he whispered, peering across the dirt street to where the new widow and her three children were heading down the crowded boardwalk. "I was going to visit her after I dropped you off at the house."

Virginia's heart tugged in sorrow for the young woman and her lovely children. And then it tugged for the agony etched in Zack's face. It was the first time he'd be meeting Lucy since the death of her husband.

"I'd like to say hello," said Zack.

Virginia nodded and followed him to the other side of the street. Yesterday, at his request, she'd brought a blank piece of paper, envelope and quill pen to his bedroom. He'd written a letter of condolence to the family of the other man who'd died in the blast, to Timothy Littlefield's parents in England.

"Hello, Lucy," said Zack.

Dressed in black from toe to bonnet, Lucy turned to them and winced at the sight of Zack. She paled but quickly recovered. Virginia was surprised to see her in the streets, but then, where else would the poor woman be? She had to run her errands, and she had three children as well as herself to feed and clothe.

"Hello, Zack." Lucy glanced at his arm. "I heard you were badly injured. How are you?"

He shook his head. "This is nothing. I'm sorry…I'm so sorry…"

"Thank you." Lucy lowered her eyes. She looked at her children. The two older girls, twelve and thirteen, were pointing at a pair of boots in the clothing store window, while the eight-year-old boy threw a pebble through the planks of the boardwalk.

Zack fumbled with his words. "I don't know how to explain what happened to Cameron."

"It wasn't your fault."

"If there's anything I can do, please let me do it."

"There's nothing. The superintendent and his wife have been by and…and everyone's been supportive…and

Cameron's last paycheck has been transferred to my name.''

"I should have been there for Cameron. And I should have been there for his service.''

"It was a nice service, Zack. Cameron would have thought so. He—he would have understood that you couldn't make it.''

Zack nodded. Lucy nodded. Each looked as if they wanted to say more but didn't know how to comfort each other.

Lucy turned her delicate nose to Virginia's direction. "Didn't you think it was a nice service, Virginia?''

"It surely was. I've never seen that many people in a church before. Although I didn't know your husband, Cameron was obviously a well-loved man.''

Zack spun around to Virginia. "You were there?''

Virginia nodded.

Lucy fingered the brim of her black bonnet. "Your kind bride-to-be said she was coming to represent her groom, since you couldn't be there. She took care of the children and she forced me to eat something to keep up my strength.''

Zack looked away. "I didn't know.''

"I'd best be going,'' said Lucy. "I've got supper to make. Please drop by anytime, the both of you. We'd love to have your company. Please don't be strangers. When you see me on the street, don't shy away...*please.*''

Lucy gathered her girls and said goodbye. The boy, Kyle, whispered to Zack in passing. His eyes were round and dark. "Do you know who killed my pa?''

Zack flinched and shook his head.

The boy turned away and followed behind his sisters.

Virginia couldn't shake Zack's sullen mood for the remaining two hours. When they got to Uncle Paddy's house, Zack slipped up the stairs and firmly closed his bedroom door. He refused her offer of pain medication and her offer for company.

There was nothing she could do to help ease the pain of losing his friend.

While dressing for the evening ahead, she questioned whether they were making the right decision to go ahead with the formal gathering of their friends.

But it was too late to change their minds, she realized, when she heard the knocker banging on the front door and the sound of laughter filtering up the stairs.

The faster Zack made the terrible announcement, he figured, the easier it would be on Virginia. Prolonging it would only prolong her agony and embarrassment.

Looking into the hall mirror, Zack adjusted the collar of his scarlet jacket, the official Mountie uniform he—and his groomsmen—would be wearing for this evening's social.

Everything that'd happened this afternoon had strengthened his resolve in knowing he was doing the right thing by setting Virginia free—free of him and free of danger.

His arm sling was cumbersome, but he was getting used to working around it, as well as the throbbing shoulder pain that never totally dissipated. He slicked his hair back, then ran a hand along his tight black breeches. Dreading the task that loomed before him, he pounded down the stairs toward the jubilant voices.

Laughter combined with the sounds of storytelling, music squeaked from the hand-wound gramophone, all amplifying the contrast between the sick feeling in his chest and the joy of the people around him.

Meeting Lucy Peters and seeing her children had deeply disturbed him. Up to that point, he'd been thinking that he should extricate himself from Virginia's life so she herself wouldn't be in jeopardy. He'd never thought about the effects of his own life being in danger.

Dammit, it'd never occurred to him that he, too, might leave Virginia behind as a widow if the Stiller gang caught him and killed him, finishing the job they'd started. The image of Virginia staring down the boardwalk at a fellow Mountie as he gave condolences for Zack's death had tortured Zack all afternoon. He needed to resolve this investigation and see the bastards responsible behind bars before he could plow ahead with hopes of marriage. Or heaven forbid, hopes of *children*.

He fully recognized that he and Virginia weren't in love. Breaking the engagement would be a blow to her pride, nothing more. The impressive woman he'd seen fighting Rossman today was strong and capable. She'd survive. Weeks or months into the future—hell, it wouldn't be longer than that to find Stiller, Zack desperately hoped—if Virginia were still available for marriage, Zack would go to her, explain, and they'd sort out their feelings from there.

A dozen men looked up as he descended the stairs.

Hank Johnson was there in a wooden wheelchair, his broken leg propped up on a stool. He'd managed to get into his Mountie's red jacket but had passed on the breeches, obviously too tight to pull over his splinted leg. He wore baggy trousers and Zack was glad to see him here.

"Bull's-Eye!" hollered Travis, flagging Zack into the parlor.

Zack strode to the group of uniformed Mounties. They carried shoulder holsters as part of their ceremonial uniforms. The guns hopefully went somewhat unnoticed by the women, but it wasn't lost on Zack that all the men were armed and ready in this dangerous time. He shook hands with each of them, aching at the absence of Littlefield and Peters.

"I'm sorry I'm late to greet you. It took a while to change into my uniform."

"Ah," said one of the married men. "That's where you should get your lovely Virginia to help you." He winked and the men laughed.

Zack felt his neck heat. He stretched his jaw and wiggled inside his tight collar. "Have you seen her?"

Travis nodded toward the kitchen door. "She's been in and out of the kitchen, serving trays of food and talking with her bridesmaids."

Someone shoved a glass of Scotch and water into Zack's hand.

"I really shouldn't," he began, then reconsidered. He swigged a mouthful. It sent a wonderful burn down his throat. Hell, he could use a whole bottle tonight.

He noticed Andrew and Grace standing in another corner, speaking with the reporter from the *Calgary Herald*. The reporter would soon have something to write about.

Groaning with his burden of decision, realizing he was about to reject Virginia just as his brother had, Zack looked away. But Zack was about to do it in a more public, humiliating manner. It was necessary to get the word out to Stiller as fast as possible and Virginia back on that train home.

His eyes were on the swinging kitchen door at the end of the parlor when Virginia came through it.

She was whispering something to her cousin, Clarissa Ashford, and a couple of other women Zack recognized from town whom he knew Virginia had chosen as bridesmaids.

Virginia bent over to offer her Uncle Paddy a refreshment from her tray when her lashes swept up to meet Zack's gaze. She flushed and smiled and his breath escaped him.

Yards of blue fabric brought out the river-blue of her eyes. Dressed very starched and proper, every inch of her body was covered by her jacket and matching skirts. A frilly white lace collar encircled her throat and draped right up to her chin. The silk edges cascaded from her throat like flower petals. Billowing blue sleeves and numerous pleats and folds accentuated her slender waist and upper arms. The feminine swell of her breasts strained beneath the black velvet trim of her yoke. Her pool of black hair wove up to her crown, exposing wispy tendrils at the back of her neck.

A schoolmarm was the first thing he thought of, seeing Virginia beside her friends. They had much more of their necklines and arms exposed in fancy ballroom dresses.

A shy, prim schoolmarm. Virginia likely wore bulky flannel nightgowns and muslin caps to bed, summer or winter.

She was a virgin, he had no doubt. And he'd almost been lucky enough to be her tutor.

"Hello, Zack," she said, inching her way toward him.

He bowed, unsmiling. "Hello."

"Were you able to rest?"

"A little."

"Good. Have you…have you got the time to come into the kitchen? We've been looking at the calendar. That is, my friends and I…looking at the possible dates."

"Virginia." He hesitated. "I've been thinking all afternoon. Virginia, I have to say that…"

"Yes?" She pulled closer, bending beneath his chin and looking upward so her face was inches from his. The scent of her freshly scrubbed skin rippled over him, blocking his concentration. The pretty freckle at the side of her eye accentuated the depth of her gaze. How could he do this?

"Virginia, this is awful news to bring to you...but..."

Her smile waned and her lips parted. Her forehead creased with uncertainty. "What is it? You're not feeling well?"

"I'm not feeling well, but it's because, I'm afraid...I don't want this marriage."

Blood drained from her lips, and her eyes opened with dismay. He couldn't have shocked her more if he'd raised his fist and smacked her face.

The tray slipped from her grasp and clattered to the floor.

The room stood still. All eyes riveted to them. Shame filled him to the core.

"I don't want this marriage," he repeated.

"Oh." She looked to the floor, bewildered.

Cupping her cheeks with trembling gloved hands, she then bent to her knees to pick up the rolling biscuits and egg spreads and pickles off the floor. Her friends were already scooping to help.

Zack gripped her arm and lifted her to full height. "Virginia, I'm sorry."

The paleness left her face, replaced by a deep, pulsing red.

From the corner of his eye, he saw the reporter taking out his notepad. It made Zack sick. James Stiller would soon hear of it, though, and that's what kept Zack going.

Virginia yanked out of his grasp with an incredible force he never thought her capable of, then backed away, making him feel like the sludge he was. "Why have you changed your mind? *Why?*"

The hurt he witnessed in her eyes tore him into a thousand pieces. "You need to return home. I don't feel any-thing for you. I don't want to marry you. Not now, not ever."

Her hand raised in a flash. Due to his years of training, he watched and waited for it and knew it was coming; in fact, he saw it. But he didn't duck.

The slap resounded off the walls and stung his cheek as if it had caught fire. It made his eyes water.

He deserved it. He deserved every bit of hatred he saw in Virginia's eyes before she turned and fled the room.

Chapter Five

The silence in the parlor intensified until it threatened to explode. To Zack, the invisible pounding felt as if someone had a large hand around his throat, squeezing the air out of his windpipe. Thirty pairs of eyes followed Virginia's fleeing figure as she ran up the stairs. Then the mortified and accusatory gazes slowly turned to his direction. He cleared his throat with self-disgust. These people were Virginia's friends. Although she'd only been in town for a month, it struck Zack how many friends she'd already made.

Clarissa staggered to the arm of a sofa. Her mound of chestnut-brown hair, pinned on top of her head, bounced. "I think I need my smelling salts. Good Lord, it's the same thing Andrew did to her."

"What?" asked Grace, standing in her simple country gown beside her husband. She looked to Andrew with a skewed expression. "*You* were engaged to her as well?"

"For six years," scoffed Clarissa.

Zack groaned. Causing trouble for his brother was not his intention.

Andrew squirmed and glowered at Clarissa, then back to his wife. "I can explain," he said.

Grace set down her drink. "Six years, and then you left her? Why?" She looked about the room at the staring faces, self-consciously bringing her hand to her throat, twisting her string of pearls. "Why didn't you tell me?"

"I didn't know how."

Grace's face flooded with scarlet patches. "Well, any way would have been better than this way!" She let her hand fly across Andrew's cheek. Another slap for another brother.

The reporter kept scribbling. Zack took a deep breath to calm his nerves. He hadn't intended on Grace getting hurt. The truth was bound to come out, but Zack regretted that he was responsible for causing this.

"Grace, wait." Andrew raced after her as she stormed through the kitchen door.

A commotion ensued. Chatter exploded from the group. Zack rubbed his temple. He should go to his room and get his bag. It was already packed. He intended on staying in the officers' quarters of the fort to figure out who had shot him, to study the other Mounties and see for himself if one had betrayed him.

Paddy blocked his path to the stairway. "What's the meaning of this?"

Not many men were equal to Zack's height and breadth, but Paddy Waters was. Although Zack was more muscled from years of strenuous activity, Paddy was intimidating.

"I'm sorry, sir, I didn't mean for this to happen."

Paddy's face reddened. His gold tooth glowed. "She's a fine woman, one who'd make any man proud."

Zack nodded in sympathy, but he'd come this far in the charade and had to carry through. Although he was silent, his gut churned.

"What's more, you told her here in front of everyone. Get out of my house."

The guests gasped. The reporter looked up from his notepad, shook his blond head, then continued scrawling.

Zack nodded. This was good. It was really convincing. The separation between himself and Virginia was already a mile wide. "Yes, sir, I'll get my bag."

"*No.* Get out *now.*"

The tremor in the old man's voice caught Zack by surprise. Maybe Zack had gone too far in this game.

Travis stepped beside Zack protectively, patting his good shoulder and steering him away from the old man. "I'll come back tomorrow and get your things. You better return with me to the fort."

Zack stumbled out of the house into the darkness of the street. The rest of the houses on the block were quiet in comparison. Every twenty yards, a lamppost lit up a patch of grass. Instinct made him glance up at the front bedroom window he knew to be Virginia's. The gingham curtains stood as still as death—not a movement, not a flutter. What exactly had he been hoping for? That he'd look up and see Virginia watching him? That maybe she'd wave to him and signal that she understood why he'd broken her heart?

"Do you have Scotch at the barracks?" asked Zack.

"I've got two bottles."

"I'll take one."

Zack stole a final glance at the lone window and steeled himself against the confounding ache in his own heart. But despite the uproar he'd caused, he knew he'd never regret what he'd just done.

James Stiller could go to hell.

Virginia prepared for bed, her eyes still puffy from crying. Dressed in a lumpy flannel nightshirt passed down from her grandmother, she shoved her hair into her nightcap. She plunged her face into the basin of cool water that rested on her dresser. What a colossal disaster.

How could he?

With a snap of anger, she reached for a towel. Her lashes flicked away cold water; her face sizzled and tightened with the rush of heated blood.

How could Zack Bullock be even more despicable than his brother? How could she have been so stupid to allow herself to be *jilted* by both brothers?

Discarded. Abandoned. Dumped like a problematic mule.

She was no mule!

But he was definitely an ass.

If Zack dared to ever show his face to her again, she would spit in his eye. She rubbed her face with a coarse linen towel, wishing she could scrub Zack from her brain.

He didn't want her. He wasn't attracted. She'd thought their kiss had ignited something special between them. Apparently she was wrong.

With a lingering lump in her throat, she told herself it was his loss to have released her.

She'd heard the commotion after she'd fled up the stairs, heard her uncle berating Zack, then the turmoil between Andrew and Grace. They'd left two hours ago for their home. Despite the knocking at her door from her cousin and bridesmaids for those same two hours, she'd told them all she wished to be alone.

She'd been deserted by her fiancé. Again. When the news spread, she would be the laughingstock of Calgary.

Andrew had left her and she shouldn't have made herself vulnerable to Zack. She should have devoted herself to her work to gain time and perspective on her circumstances, and not rush headfirst into another engagement. Giving in to Zack *had* weakened her.

And what of the money Virginia owed Mr. and Mrs. Bullock for her education? Had Zack thought of it? She had half a mind to tell Zack and Andrew to sort it out between themselves and leave her out of it, but when she thought of her struggling parents and *his* elderly folks, it crippled her anger.

How would her parents feel to know her second engagement had fallen through? She'd have to write to inform them. Or perhaps she should pack her bags and leave for home this instant.

Wondering what to do, she lowered her towel. She had no burning desire to run back to her parents to brag about her bad luck. But she also had no burning desire to stay here and face her humiliation.

She didn't matter to Zack. She didn't matter to anyone.

"Virginia," Uncle Paddy called.

Still solemn, three mornings later, she was dressing in her room when a soft tap sounded on the door.

"I know what you said last night." Uncle Paddy tried to convince her. "But come with me anyway. Meet me at six o'clock. Quigley's Pub always puts a smile on your face."

She yanked on her stocking. "I've no wish to go out for dinner this evening." No wish to traipse through town with all the brewing gossip. The bleeding biweekly paper had arrived before dawn today. Her photo and Zack's— along with Grace and Andrew's—were displayed smack in the middle of the local society news!

The shame!

"Mr. Killarney will be playin' his fiddle. You know how much it'll mean to him. I told him you'd be there."

She groaned and wondered if Millicent had read Mr. Killarney the newspaper yet this morning, as she did every

Friday when he arrived to share breakfast with Uncle Paddy.

Virginia tugged her dress over her head.

Then she realized with a sigh that if she were going to remain in Alberta to write her licensing exams, she'd have to face the public soon. Picking up her brush, she looked into the mirror and pulled the bristles through her hair.

"All right, if I have time after my patients. But I've got a late-afternoon appointment with an instrument salesman, so I may be a little late."

"Great, darlin', great." When Uncle Paddy muttered with glee, she shook her head and wondered what he was concocting.

"They're the finest bullet extractors made in St. Louis."

"I understand, Mr. Vanderveer—"

"Call me Yule, please."

"Yule, I'm late for a dinner appointment with my uncle. It's already seven-thirty."

Seated in her uncle's parlor, the youthful salesman scratched his dark chin and flashed Virginia a charming smile. His well-tailored navy suit accentuated a muscular build. He whistled. "Two doctors beneath one roof? Would you mind if I joined you? I'd like to show your uncle these items as well."

"I don't think—"

"Please allow me to pay for your meal. For such a beautiful young woman, it would be my honor."

Virginia felt her skin tingle but knew the man was full of malarkey. And she was staying clear of all men.

However, he insisted and she relented. When they left the house, one of the Mounties tagged behind in the semi-darkness, half a block away. It wasn't necessary in her opinion, but she felt protected. He would be around, she supposed, to protect Hank Johnson until he was transferred to the fort tomorrow. The fort's commander had issued the transfer request earlier in the day and Virginia wondered why the hurry.

Yule insisted she take his arm. He cajoled her with delightful traveling stories, beginning with his hometown of Montreal and ending in St. Louis for the entire five blocks to Quigley's Irish Pub. When they entered, Virginia adjusted to the dim lantern lighting. She noticed her uncle flagging her from across the room.

With Zack seated across the table from him.

Her heart bounced a beat. So this was the trick!

And seated right beside Zack with her arm intertwined around his was Clarissa.

Zack was with Clarissa?

"Let's go," Virginia muttered to Yule. The pub was crowded and people's heads were turning from her to Zack. Her bonnet, tied beneath her chin but sliding off her head, tapped along her spine.

"Why? Isn't that your uncle?" Yule waved to the old man, who was rising in his chair to greet them.

Zack was already standing, arm in a sling. Dressed in a black leather vest and black denim pants, he cut an impressive figure of power and strength—and caught the eyes of several women in the room. The pained, sour twist to Zack's mouth, however, indicated he was as surprised to see her as she him. The wretched man.

Spurned. Renounced. Tossed aside like a crooked stick.

"I don't like the company my uncle keeps," Virginia replied. She rubbed her moistened palms along her skirt pocket.

"That young couple? They look like pleasant folks."

Yule shuffled his boxlike leather bag to his other hand, leaned into the weight, then removed his bowler hat.

Quigley's Pub was the only drinking establishment in town that a lady could frequent and not feel ill at ease or improper, mainly because a sympathetic woman ran it— Travis Reid's sister, Shawna, and her husband, Mr. Quigley.

One side held a bar and pub, the other side was filled with heavy oak tables made for elegant dining. But this was the first time in a month's attendance that Virginia felt disconcerted.

Because of Zack.

Uncle Paddy plodded his way through the tables to her side. "You and Zack need to talk to each other." Then he nodded at her companion, the salesman. "Howdy."

"Hello, sir. I'm Yule Vanderveer, and you're in luck today for a wonderful new opportunity that's just arrived from St. L—"

"How could you invite Zack?" Virginia blasted her uncle.

Uncle Paddy adjusted his spectacles. "I admit my first response that night had been to slug him, but after seein' how miserable you were—"

"—the finest supplies from the Yoo-nited States of America—"

"Howdy," Uncle Paddy nodded again to the salesman, then whispered to Virginia. "You've got to come and talk to him."

Virginia scowled. "Clarissa can have him."

"Clarissa bumped into us on the boardwalk. She said she hadn't eaten yet and sort of…invited herself."

"—I've got a dozen different kinds of bullet extractors, hair tonics, reflex hammers, lancets and leech containers."

Uncle Paddy skimmed his gaze over Yule's bag, which

the man unbuckled, but grabbed her elbow. "Something doesn't add up, Virginia. Talk it over with him."

Yule held up a laryngoscope. "This is the latest from Boston. Comes with two mirrors. Why, the inventor even photographed his own larynx. With Edison's invention of the lightbulb, I imagine we're only years away from adding a light to this model so you can see down someone's throat. Ree-markable—"

"Shame on you, Uncle Paddy." Virginia reeled to the door, her dark hair swinging about her shoulders. "For getting involved in ludicrous matchmaking."

Yule's voice strained. "—gauze bandages that come in different widths, so there's no longer any need to cut them yourself—"

With a muffle, Yule stopped talking. Virginia didn't turn around to see why; she kept walking. The unexpected torture of seeing Zack again tripped up her breathing.

"Virginia." Zack's cool, husky voice rang through the air behind her. Her heart strummed; she froze in place. She couldn't turn around to face him.

Not ever.

Deserted. Forsaken.

She clutched her reticule. Zack touched her shoulders. His grasp was firm and warm around her skin. Beneath her cotton collar, tiny hairs at the back of her neck raised in gooseflesh. How could a simple touch affect her like this?

Don't place your hands on me, she silently pleaded, trying to pull away. Humiliation swept over her.

Despite his injured clavicle, his strength overcame her resistance. He spun her around to face him, hands still on her body.

They were standing alone in the noisy crowd. Uncle Paddy had taken Yule back to the table.

She'd promised herself she'd spit in Zack's eye next time she saw him, but cranking her neck to gaze up at his soft, dark features made her tremble in confusion. He was so much taller and bigger. His nearness disturbed her, excited her. She inhaled the clean scent of his skin. There was an air of self-control about his probing brown eyes that fascinated her.

His full lips quirked upward in an awkward, apologetic manner. "How are you?"

She sniffed with disbelief and didn't answer, pulling her shoulders out of his fingertips. His hands slid slowly across the curve of her back, tempting her with…crazy images of seduction. How did he expect her to be after how he'd treated her?

"It wasn't my idea to come here," he whispered.

She blinked. "It wasn't mine, either." Did he wish to speak with her now that they were together again? He struggled with something on his mind. Did he wish to explain himself?

If he did, she wasn't sure she'd listen. She willed her heart to stop skipping beneath her breast.

His trained gaze darted around the room at the people staring at them. With a self-conscious nod, he slid the Stetson from his hand to his head. "Well, then, have a good evening."

He was leaving her!

Again!

With a jolt of disbelief, she nudged by him, grasping her shawl tighter over her arms and pivoting so quickly her skirts twirled in a circle about her high-heeled boots. "I believe I was leaving first."

Just as she stepped closer to the front door, the reporter came crashing through it. David panted, out of breath. "Is she in here? Someone told me Clarissa Ashford had come inside.''

Virginia turned her head to her uncle's table. Aghast at the sight of the reporter glaring at her, Clarissa darted from Uncle Paddy's side, where Yule was sliding out his entire showcase of instruments, to join Virginia, Zack and David at the front door. ''What is it?''

''I found another one of these.'' David slapped a piece of paper onto a table. It was a Wanted poster, but looking at it upside down, Virginia couldn't fathom its significance.

''The photograph looks like you,'' Zack said to David.

''Damn right it is. Clarissa had my likeness printed on this Wanted poster as an April Fools' joke last month, and I'm still finding them tacked all over town.''

''You printed that inaccurate article on my father's jewelry business,'' Clarissa explained, fingering the floppy lace collar of her jacket. ''Just because one little watch wasn't working properly when we sold it.''

With his black string tie swinging about his throat, David snorted. ''Look what she had printed beneath my photo!''

Zack leaned over the table to read.

Virginia read aloud. '''Reward for the safe capture of David Fitzgibbon and his monkey—one sack of dried peanuts.'''

''You tell her, Inspector, that she can't do this to me,'' David pleaded.

''Clarissa, the man's right. How many of these did you post?'' Zack continued his questioning, but Virginia spotted her opportunity to escape. Just in time, too, for she observed Ian Killarney seated on the stage, lifting his fiddle beneath his chin. The atmosphere here was too crazy for her.

She pushed open the pub's stained-glass door and took a deep breath of night air.

The streets swelled with people out for an entertaining Friday evening. The log saloon house across the street two blocks away rattled with piano music. The mercantile ahead had a lineup out the door filled with rail laborers and miners, who were cashing their Friday paychecks there because the banks were already closed.

Couples of all ages strolled the windy boardwalk, some headed to the steakhouse for dinner, others to the pub or the fragrant bakery around the corner or the bath and barber house to get a shave and cut.

Virginia trudged alone. It was over between her and Zack. She'd seen the finality in his face as he'd donned his Stetson and looked about the room as though he couldn't wait to escape.

Why had he changed his mind?

She weighed the whole structure of events but came up as bewildered and empty as before.

She pulled her shawl close around her throat and shrugged her shoulders defiantly into the wind, determined to forget about the man who'd briefly possessed her heart.

Her eyes stung from the wind. Although it would be June in another two days, when the sun retired for the evening, the air turned cold.

Two miners whistled at her as she passed the mercantile's lineup. "Need some company this evenin', miss?"

A momentary spark of fear caught her, but she ignored the men and walked around them.

"Don't bother her," said a better-dressed fellow. He took off his sombrero and bowed. "She's a doctor and she don't need your company."

"A doctor?" said the wiry miner. "Well, well. A wor-kin' woman. Don't reckon I need one of those."

She flinched. Would any man need her? What would it feel like to stroll the boardwalk with a man who truly wanted her? Perhaps they'd be going into the steakhouse for a late evening meal, or buying hot-cross buns at the bakery to run home and eat in the privacy of their cozy kitchen. Maybe they'd stay home for the evening and read to each other in front of a fireplace, massage one another's muscles while sharing a glass of wine.

For six years, she'd attended college in Toronto and had stayed in a boardinghouse filled with five other women struggling for their right to an education. Not once had she questioned her decision to marry Andrew. He had been the strength and the goal she had worked toward, sending letter after letter to him in Alberta, writing to him about her friends and her problems. Not once had he written back that he doubted his love for her, that his future wouldn't coincide with hers after all.

And then Zack...he'd written her from the mountains that they'd look for a little house together as soon as they got married. She'd spent four weeks getting to know the neighborhoods of Calgary, cheerfully looking at every street as a potential home and future playing ground for their children.

Although her engagement to Zack had been ridiculously shorter, their breakup was almost more painful. She wasn't sure why. Perhaps because he'd told her in public in front of her friends and family, or maybe because it was the second time she'd been rejected, adding to her raw wounds from Andrew and stinging doubly more.

She heard someone calling, but the passing horses and rickety wagons muffled the sounds into one.

The loud thud of boots echoed on the planks behind her. "Virginia!"

She wheeled around, frightened with the expectation it might be one of the two harassing miners.

Zack? His muscled shoulders loomed over her.

"My God, Zack, you scared me."

He cursed softly as he peered into the shadowy forms of the street. "Where the hell is the Mountie who's supposed to be walking with you?"

"How should I know?" Her temper finally snapped. "Why are you bothering me?" She spun on her boot heel and whirled down the boardwalk steps to cross the street. "We've got nothing to say to each other!"

"Where the hell is he?" Zack chased after her. "Ah, dammit, there he is."

Virginia glanced over her left shoulder and saw the constable helping a miner to his feet in the dirt street. The Mountie appeared to be breaking up a fight.

"Virginia, please wait for him."

"Leave me alone."

"Virginia!" He caught up to her in three easy strides.

She swung back to avoid a team of oxen, then a man pushing a wheelbarrow. "Go jump off a big rock!"

When she darted through the crowd by the saloon, Zack muttered, "Hell, I'll have to walk you home then!"

"Don't trouble yourself!"

The wind blew cold around her ears. She stopped for a second to slide her bonnet to her head. She clawed the ribbons beneath her chin and raced away from Zack. "I don't ever want to see you again, do you hear me?"

She heard the thunder of two galloping horses in the darkness but didn't pay them heed.

Zack ran toward her, lunging at her, screaming, "Get down!"

"Stay away from me!"

The sound of a bullet zinged through the air. She felt her bonnet explode. The top of her head scraped painfully at the same instant Zack flung himself on top of her. Together, they hurtled down the steps of the boardwalk.

Chapter Six

Every muscle in Zack's body tightened with the heat of rage. Virginia was wounded.

"Everyone stay down!" Zack shouted, but the horsemen had already passed. Ladies on the boardwalk screamed. Men hollered and ducked, drawing their guns to protect their women.

Zack's injured neck and shoulder throbbed due to the fresh fall, but he ignored his pain as he climbed off Virginia. Beneath the flickering light of the lamppost and the swaying tin sign of the tailor's shop, Virginia sagged against his good side. Her eyes traced the outline of his face.

"Virginia," he said softly, untying what remained of her bonnet. A yard's clump of her black hair came off in his hand. He grimaced at the sight of her bloodied scalp. The bullet had grazed her hairline two inches above her right ear.

"It's only a graze," he murmured to calm her, although he trembled as he spoke. He scanned their bodies to find something to clamp the bleeding. With a stroke of brilliance, he slid the linen sling off his neck. He bunched the fabric and pressed it against her bleeding head.

She drew her brows together. "You need your sling."

He studied her tender face, at the upturn of lashes and the sheen of perspiration on creamy cheeks. He was responsible for her. For this. "You talk like a doctor."

She winced in agony.

Gently dabbing her scalp, he lifted the cloth but the wound was still bleeding. "It must sting like hell."

She closed her eyes and rocked as he pressed.

Cursing, he clenched his gun in his right hand, glancing down the street through the frightened crowd. Folks scrambled for cover behind hitching posts and wagons and jittery oxen. A pebble dug into his freshly ripped pants and bleeding kneecap.

The two gunmen on horseback were well out of sight. They were hidden beyond a wall of darkness, the sound of their galloping horses clomping past the brewery. With the trained discipline of ten tough years on the force, Zack listened and focused on the riders.

Faintly he heard the riders turn west toward the mountains. One horse wasn't galloping precisely perfect, as though it were protecting an injured leg that wasn't quite healed. When they'd raced by him before with flying hooves, he'd noticed as he went down that both horses were shod. And judging from the look of their supple postures, the men were young, in their twenties. Their saddles were new. Their rifle slings held eight-round repeating Winchesters. Guessing by their trappings, they had lots of money.

He knew, by the force of God, it wouldn't protect them from him.

After a moment of petrified silence, assessing that the danger had passed, people shifted from their places and came to help. "Is she all right, Zack?"

Zack scrutinized Virginia's pale face for impending

signs of trouble, but she looked staunch. Although weakened and dazed, she had minimal blood loss. Nonetheless, a spasm of alarm crawled up his back. "She'll be okay. The bullet missed her head and grazed her scalp."

"Who were they? Why'd they shoot her?"

"I think they were aiming for me." He *wished* they had been. He *wished* his plan had worked—that his disengagement from Virginia had fooled James Stiller. "They're part of the Stiller gang."

Dozens of faces bobbed around them. "What can we do to help Virginia?"

The young constable, who'd been busy breaking up the miners' fight instead of following Virginia, knelt beside Zack. "I can help you lift her."

Zack nodded as they yanked Virginia to a sitting position in the dust. There was no sense blaming the constable; he'd been pulled in two different directions at the same time. But looking at his crestfallen face, Zack knew the next time he had to make a choice, he'd stay with his prime assignment.

To Zack's irritation, the reporter pushed his way through the crowd, pulling out his notepad. "What happened?"

"Don't write about it, please," moaned Virginia. "Don't put me in the paper again."

Virginia's blue eyes lifted to meet Zack's brown ones. He flinched with a stab of guilt at what he'd put her through for the past week.

Zack had had enough of the reporter. "Virginia's got a minor injury, David. I need you to run into the saloon. Have them fill two buckets with clear warm water—heat it up if you have to—and bring it back here with towels for her head."

*"Yes, sir," shouted David, running down the boardwalk.

Zack knew the false task would keep David busy and out of their business. They'd be gone by the time he returned with the water. For her safety, they didn't need a journalist knowing where they were headed.

Zack pulled her to her feet. "Are you dizzy?"

"A little." When she tipped backward, he pulled her tight against his side. She was tall for a woman, but still a good six inches shorter than himself. His right arm spanned her soft shoulders. Her weight slung to one hip, one hand tucked inside her shawl, the other around his waist.

"Lean on me. I'll take you home." But he knew he wasn't taking her anywhere near home tonight. He'd said it for the sake of listening ears.

"Break up the crowd," he ordered the constable as he and Virginia walked south. "Don't breathe a word of this to anyone, but tell Paddy Waters to bring his medical bag to Superintendent Ridgeway's house. Then go to the fort and tell the commanding officer on duty what's happened. Bring three guards back with you to the superintendent's house. Fly as fast as your legs can carry you."

"Yes, sir."

"Can we help you down the street, Zack?" someone called.

He needed them to leave him alone so they wouldn't notice where he was taking Virginia. "No, go back to your homes. Make sure your families and children are safe."

That did the trick. People hurried away as he and Virginia disappeared into the alley. Their families were fine. It was him and *his* family the bastards were after.

"This doesn't look like the way home, Zack."

Virginia stumbled. He shortened his long stride so she could keep up, but he wouldn't stop for any reason. "We're going somewhere safer."

"Why did those men shoot me?"

He clenched his teeth at the injustice of her injury.

In his ten years of being a Mountie, he'd always scoffed when someone called him brave or labeled him a hero. Now he knew. It was easy to be brave when he was alone in the world.

How much harder was it when he was responsible for a woman...for the safety of their potential sons and daughters?

His greatest vulnerability—his feelings and hopes for a future with this woman—were turned beneath a magnifying glass to face the light for all his enemies to behold. God, they were like lame, sitting targets.

His plan had failed.

He inhaled deeply, past the lump of useless pride in his throat. "Keep walking, Virginia. When we get to the superintendent's house...I've got a confession to make."

"Were they shooting at her or were they shooting at you?" Superintendent Ridgeway spoke to Zack but hovered at the door of the parlor with eyes on Virginia, who was lying on the sofa of the Ridgeways' home while Doc Waters cleansed her scalp wound.

Virginia grimaced beneath her uncle's poking.

Feeling helpless, Zack cringed at her pain. "I believe they were shooting at her, sir."

"Why?"

"Because it's a good way to repay me for what I did to Ned Stiller."

"Even though you and Miss Waters are no longer engaged?"

Uncomfortable beneath the direct question, Zack shifted his weight, nervously pressing a hand along his pocket.

From across the room, Virginia's gaze shot to his. He'd thought she was too immersed with her injury to be aware of their conversation. The candle flickering on the end table highlighted her moist, matted hair. His mind swirled with a kaleidoscope of impressions—she'd never recover the growth of hair in that spot; she seemed so defenseless, splattered with blood; it was his fault that she was wounded; her eyelids were puffy; *she'd* spent the past three nights sleepless, too.

"I'd like to explain about our breakup," Zack began.

He was interrupted by the commander's wife, Annabelle, a plump round woman who spewed commands as easily as her husband.

"Let me help you with that basin," Annabelle said to Doc Waters, taking it from his hands and leading him out of the room. "Take what you need and come with me to the spring room for fresh water."

"Don't get up yet," Doc Waters hollered to Virginia from the hallway. "I'll be back with a mixture of laudanum."

Virginia swung her legs to the floor and eased her bandaged head between her hands. "I don't think I should drink anything, due to my head injury. It would confuse the symptoms if I…"

Zack's stance softened in her direction. Sympathy spilled into his voice. "You mean you can't take anything for pain?"

"Not quite yet," she groaned. "Not for another two hours, till we insure my injury doesn't take a turn for the worse."

"What should I be watching for?"

"When you lift the candle to my eyes, my pupils should constrict and dilate equally. I should remain oriented to time and place...my arm and leg movements should remain balanced."

He hesitated to ask what to do if those problems arose. He knew damn well it might mean she was having a stroke.

Zack walked to the sofa and knelt on the plush rug below her. He wanted to caress the knee beneath the smoothly draped fabric, or squeeze the soft curve of her arm, or run his thumb along her trembling bottom lip, but couldn't bring himself to such intimacy. "I'm sorry this happened to you."

The anger that she'd flashed at him in the pub an hour ago was gone from her face, replaced by a grim resolve. "You're not responsible for every criminal who rides into town."

"This time I am," he admitted with misery. "This time it's my fault."

She ran her bloodied fingers along her skirt. "What's the confession you said you had to make?"

"I had to walk away from our marriage, not because of anything lacking between us, but—" Stumbling with the awful truth, he rocked up from the rug to his feet, then lowered himself onto the other side of the sofa. His wide shoulders brushed against her slender ones. "I walked away because I believed—*I knew*—James Stiller would harm you if you became my wife."

She recoiled from him—ever so slightly, but not slight enough for him to miss it.

"Someone threatened me on the train before I was shot. They came up close behind and told me to watch out for the safety of my new bride."

Her blue eyes flashed. "That's why you said you no longer wanted to marry me?"

He nodded.

"To protect me."

He nodded again, hoping she'd understand and forgive him.

"Oh, I see," said the commander from across the room.

Virginia stood up on shaky feet and walked to the massive fireplace mantel. She gripped the polished mantel, took a moment to gather her thoughts, then turned around. Her black hair, messed up but long and loose, dangled about her shoulders. "Why didn't you come to me and tell me?"

He rose and stepped closer. She raised her chin with a cool stare.

"I thought if I backed away, if I proved to everyone around you that you meant nothing..." He swallowed hard at how incredibly difficult it was to say the words aloud. This was the little Virginia Waters he'd grown up with, who had learned to skip a rope in the alleyway behind his backyard and had learned to wash pots in his parents' wooden sink. He'd always been so much older, and smarter, and more decisive. How had she caught up so quickly?

"If I proved to everyone that you meant *nothing* to me, it would be the quickest way. I thought I could control the problem. I thought you'd leave town immediately."

"You should have explained it to me. I would have understood."

"You would have wanted to talk it over, to discuss an alternative. You know you wouldn't have accepted my decision without a fight."

She wrinkled her forehead. "I was about to become your wife. Talking things through is a part of marriage.

Instead, you treated me like an adolescent who doesn't know how to help herself.''

"I treated you with the utmost respect of a man for his bride. A bride who doesn't have the experience to understand the dangers of the situation. The fact that you were shot is proof that I was right to take extreme measures."

He reached out to touch her hand, but she pulled away. Then she winced.

"We should discuss this when you're feeling better," he suggested.

"We'll discuss it now."

"I don't want to aggravate your condition."

Her volatile expression conveyed her anger. "I would have appreciated being told that my life was in danger. *Is* in danger."

"If I thought for a moment that our breakup wouldn't stop James Stiller—"

"You said those terrible things to me in front of everyone at the engagement social."

"It was the quickest way to spread the news."

"Our horrible news was written up in the papers. And you planned it that way. You invited David Fitzgibbon."

"He invited himself to the social on our walk to the mercantile, remember? I simply took him up on a wonderful opportunity to spread the news—"

"Wonderful opportunity? Your logic is twisted. *I'm* your friend in this. Not David Fitzgibbon, not your men and your secret code of honor."

"It's my duty to protect the town and the people in it. I've spent ten years hunting criminals in the backwoods, chasing them through the back holes of dirty saloons and grimy mountain dugouts. Without getting into specific, sickening examples of the things they do to people, Virginia, you don't understand how their convoluted minds work.''

''I'm supposed to understand how *your* mind works, though. You were supposed to become my husband. If I can't go to you and if you can't come to me with our deepest, gravest problems, then it's not a true union in matrimony.''

''A marriage of harm is no truer.''

She blinked. ''Then you're better off on your own.''

He rolled his jaw at her summation.

''I think I understand what's happened,'' said the commander.

Virginia made her way to an upholstered chair but didn't sit. She went around it and dug her fingers into the back for support. Velvet curtains hung to the floor behind her and richly colored oil paintings covered the wall.

''Is there anything more that either of you are withholding?'' she asked bluntly.

''No,'' said Zack.

''You're sure? The both of you?''

The superintendent stiffened with her insulting question. Zack had never heard anyone speak to the commander in such terms. If the commander didn't reprimand her, it would be because she was injured.

''I'm sure,'' the commander replied, chomping on the unlit cigar between his teeth. He motioned to Zack to answer.

''I'm sure,'' Zack repeated.

It didn't seem to calm her. ''Despite the cruel way you severed our engagement, just an hour ago I wasn't certain whether I wanted to stay in Alberta or return to Niagara Falls. As much as I fought Uncle Paddy in meeting you at the pub tonight, I wondered if there was something… something that we hadn't said, that remained unsettled between us." Her lips clamped tight. "I'm packing my things and leaving on the first train east. I believe there's one in the morning."

She brushed by Zack, wobbly on her feet, heading down the hallway toward the voices in the spring room.

Zack grabbed her arm, curling his fingers around her elbow. He reeled her short of the door: "You can't do that."

"What am I supposed to do?" She yanked back her arm, closing her eyes for a second to combat what Zack supposed was dizziness. He wished she'd quit arguing and sit down.

"Should I go back to my uncle's? Put us all in danger? Perhaps the next time, Stiller and his men will use explosives and blow up the entire house. Ah, you see," she said when he raised his brows in surprise, "I *can* think like them. Millicent's granddaughter spends every afternoon after school helping me with patients. You didn't even recognize that she was to be our flower girl." Virginia glared into his eyes. "Maybe the sight of blood doesn't frighten you, but it frightens me."

"You can't leave," he insisted. "Not now."

"He's right," said the superintendent. "You wouldn't make it past the first train stop. Now that we know they're after you, I suspect Stiller's men would get to you as soon as you boarded. We don't know who these men are. We don't recognize their faces."

"Then what do you suggest, superintendent? I stay under guard at my uncle's home?"

"No." The commander twirled his cigar between his lips. "No, I think it'd be nearly impossible to keep you protected there. What I suggest is that you move your things to the ranch on Side Road Three. It's the Mounties' ranch. We use it to grow vegetables and raise beef for our troops. What we could do is instill half a dozen Mounties among the workers there as ranch hands incognito to protect you. And of course, Zack will be your twenty-four-hour personal guard.''

Panic assailed Zack. ''Sir, just a minute—''

The commander narrowed his eyes. ''Is there something more pressing you need to do?''

''No, sir, but—''

''With your busted shoulder, you're not on active duty. You've got one hand that can still shoot and protect, though.''

''But I was hoping to work from the fort to head the investigation for the Stiller gang—''

''You can head it from the ranch. When this is over and Stiller is behind bars, you and Miss Waters will both be free to go.''

''Sir,'' said Virginia, a blush racing to her cheeks. ''Is there anyone else besides Zack who could stay with me?''

Zack agreed with her. The plan was sound and Virginia would be safest on the Mounties ranch, but the plan didn't have to include him. ''Sir—''

Superintendent Ridgeway raised his palm. ''Enough said. You'll both stay here tonight. Annabelle will get your bedding. That's an order, Miss Waters,'' he said with friendly but unmistakable firmness.

Virginia's complaints dwindled to a squeak.

''One more thing,'' the commander said as he swung around to leave. ''I've never had to do this and I understand the commander before me had done it only twice in eleven years. You both say your engagement's off, so maybe this won't matter to you anyway. But as commanding officer for the district, I'm revoking my permission for you two to marry.''

Chapter Seven

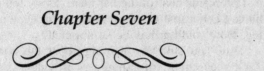

"How could he revoke his permission? We live in modern times and that's archaic!" The next morning Virginia tugged herself to full height in her mare's saddle, indignant that now two men controlled her life.

Zack reined in beside her on his stallion.

With laudanum playing in her system, she patted her bay's neck, struggling to appreciate the *good* things about the morning, but barely noticing the pleasant feel of the reddish coat and the black mane beneath her fingers. It was Zack's horse. He'd insisted she take the tamer one for their five-mile ride. He rode a striking, dappled-gray horse with white markings on its forehead, a beautiful specimen that flexed its gleaming muscles beneath Zack's capable hands.

She imagined they looked like a battered couple, Zack with his new sling thrust around his thick collar, she with her scalp bandaged. Earlier this morning she'd borrowed a small cowboy hat from one of the Mounties. It fit around the bandages better than her bonnet while still allowing the warm breeze to roll around her neck and through her hair. The leather ties tugged loosely at her throat.

The sound of horses' hooves on pounded grass bounced

off the grove of cottonwoods and aspens ahead. She wished Zack would ride farther away from her. She felt sandwiched between him, and the other six Mounties riding behind, and the wagonload full of her luggage that she'd packed half an hour earlier at her uncle's home. She had problems controlling her mare. Every ten minutes her booted calf came within inches of Zack's long muscular leg. How could a man be so muscled?

"Are you still complaining about the commander?" Zack's lean figure, his shoulders as wide as a stagecoach, profiled like a square against the breaking red sunrise. A green field of spring wheat rustled in the breeze behind his waving black hair. The wind filled the air with the heady scent of damp earth and a freshly shaven Zack.

"Why does it bother you this much?" he asked. "Half an hour ago you told me…let me see, you expressed it so tactfully…you said *I wouldn't marry a Bullock brother if I were the Queen of England and he were the last man on earth who could give me an heir for the empire.*"

Virginia scowled, as bothered as she was last night at bedtime in the commander's guest room, and as fuming as this morning upon rising to Zack's soft knock on her door. He'd slept on the horsehair sofa in the parlor. Quite well, he'd declared, which for some reason irritated her more.

"You wouldn't have my heir even for your empire?" Zack teased, giving her a slow smile that sent her pulse rushing. "Think of how disappointed your people would be."

"I think you and Andrew should marry each other and leave me and Grace alone!"

Zack didn't find that amusing, but the Mounties behind them laughed. When she smiled and nodded to the men, she noticed one of them staring at her ankles, which were covered by knee-high boots but displayed beneath her hemline. Zack shot the man such a maddening expression of possessiveness that all the Mounties reined in their horses and fell behind by ten feet.

She regarded Zack with disbelief. It disturbed her that she was disturbed. Everything about Zack Bullock disturbed her—his shameless confidence that he was doing the right thing; the arrogant smile he bore beneath his Stetson; the way his thighs dug into his saddle; the fact that *she* was counting how many calluses he had on his chiseled hands.

"The commander has every right to revoke his permission," Zack reminded her. "I had to go to him to *get* permission in the first place—every Mountie has to—and the commander doesn't want us getting married until you're out of harm's way."

"It's not that I want to marry you—*God knows I don't*—it's that I should have the right to make my own decisions. First I'm bossed around by you, then the commander."

Zack's cheeks curved upward, threatening another dimpled smile. "The next time you see him, why don't you voice your displeasure?"

"I have no problem voicing my displeasure." She pulled her reins to the left, trying to avoid a collision. The horse wouldn't listen to her, either. Every man, woman and beast seemed to flock to Zack.

Well, not her.

She yanked a little harder until the mare obeyed. "I'm sure the news of our false breakup and the commander's revoking his permission will be all over town this morning. Probably before the second shift of bread baking at the bakery."

"Our marriage plans are no longer a secret. I agree with

the superintendent. James Stiller might as well know you're under twenty-four-hour guard. He might not recognize the Mountie faces protecting you, but he knows we're here. You'll be safe.''

Fifteen minutes passed in misery. Why couldn't she keep her eyes on the horizon, on the prairies, on anything but Zack?

She blurted a question. ''Who were the other two women you mentioned earlier who had their weddings canceled by the previous commander?''

''Are you sure you want to hear it?''

She nodded.

''One woman was an old...*barmaid,* we'll call her. She serviced the upstairs saloon beds, as well, if you catch my meaning.''

Virginia felt her face grow hot. Of course she caught his meaning. She was a doctor and knew about the ways of the world.

Zack's mouth twitched. His square jaw and cheekbone stood out against the sun. ''She was a dozen years older than one of the young Mountie recruits and for some reason, he was smitten by her.''

''Were they...in love?''

''How should I know?''

''What happened to them?''

''When the commander refused him permission to marry, he quit the force and married her anyway.''

Virginia clasped her hands together over the saddle horn. ''How romantic.''

''Romantic? He left a well-paying steady job behind and two years of intense training.''

''They *were* in love. They were definitely in love.''

Zack turned his head and scrutinized her face, then lowered his dark lashes over her faded white blouse, dipping his gaze to her waistline and the spread of her skirts. Virginia squirmed with such an intense discomfort…feeling as if he were peeling off her clothing right beneath the sun!

"Their *love* didn't last long," said Zack, finally looking straight ahead so she could release her breath. "He took a job at the Wolf Saloon as a barkeep. The money wasn't that good, neither was the company. He started drinking and fighting and she left him."

"*She* left him?"

"I guess he learned his lesson about love, huh?"

"Is he that surly middle-aged man who stares out the front window of the saloon?" She'd never been inside the mysterious place, but she always walked faster when she passed by.

"The one with the handlebar mustache and scar beneath his left eye? That's him."

"Aw. The poor man is lonely now."

"Oh, would you quit?"

As they turned the final lap of trees, a cluster of log buildings sprang from a hillside. They were nearing the ranch. A bumpy road led them down the last quarter mile. It was a corduroy road. Constructed near the soggy banks of the Bow River, it was made of logs laid side by side. Age had sunk some logs deeper than others, but years of dirt, moss and grass had leveled the lower spots.

"What happened to the other couple who were refused by the commander?"

"She was the daughter of a con man. Claimed she had nothing to do with her father's crooked ways, but within a month of knowing her, the quartermaster at the fort had six months' worth of supplies stolen from under his nose. He couldn't see her flaws, I guess, because of all the love in his eyes."

Virginia clicked her tongue. "Are you always this pessimistic about love?"

"Realistic, not pessimistic. I've trained myself to see the character flaws in people. It makes me good at what I do. Is that so bad?"

"When you distrust everyone as a result, yes." She plunged into her next question without thinking. "What are my flaws?"

"Oh, no. I'm not getting into that."

"You're such a great judge of character, I thought you might like to share your expertise." She was crazy to ask the question. *Crazy.* She didn't care what Zack thought of her.

"You don't have any flaws."

"Don't be so condescending. You're speaking to me like an adult to a child if you think I believe that."

"Is that one of *my* flaws? What else is wrong with me?"

They passed beneath the cedar gates of the ranch. The horses slowed to an intimate pace and when Zack turned to her, awaiting an answer, Virginia felt a nervous tremble. A queer mixture of emotions passed through her—caution, yearning, disillusionment, the loss of a childhood friend. "I think this conversation is dangerous and we'd better stop."

"Dangerous? A conversation?" When the horses came to a stop at the hitching post outside the main house, Zack's focus lowered to her hands rubbing nervously on the saddle horn. "Maybe we'd better."

Three men popped out from the barn, another one from what appeared to be a meat smokehouse, and three more from the stables. "What are you doing here?" called one.

The Mounties around them explained as Zack slid off his horse and strode to her side to help her dismount. He ignored the others and concentrated on her. Two yellow mutts swirled about her mare's legs.

Feeling a bit woozy from being in the saddle and maybe from the dopey effects of the laudanum, Virginia accepted his offer. When she held out her hand, he crushed it with his.

She slipped out of the saddle and tried not to disturb his injured arm in the sling. The result was a clumsy dismount. She stuck out one hip for balance, then teetered so hard he pulled her closer within the circle of his arms. The wind licked at their perimeter. Her hat blew off her head to hit her between the shoulder blades. Her skirts draped across *his* thighs; her long hair mingled with *his* shirt collar. It felt insanely sensual.

"What else is wrong with me?" he repeated.

"Your biggest flaw as I see it," she said, peering up at him, marveling at the black flecks within the brown pools of his eyes, "is that you can't see the smaller vision for the bigger vision."

"It sounds like you've been giving this some thought."

"Four nights' worth."

His lips and the bridge of his nose were slightly sunburned. The redness blended with the overall tan of his skin. She pretended not to be affected by his ruggedness.

"What do you mean smaller vision versus bigger?" His silent expectation swelled as his gaze traveled from her eyes down to her lips.

He wouldn't *dare* kiss her....

"Take, for instance, our wedding," she said with a stumble. "You were so intent on canceling, you didn't care who you hurt along the way, only that it got you to your bigger scheme. Some might call you Machiavellian—the end justifies the means."

His eyes flickered with a sentiment she couldn't read.

Massive hands unlocked from her spine, loosening their embrace. ''Thank you for the judgment. I'll try to work on that.''

''You're welcome. Go ahead, tell me one of my flaws,'' she urged recklessly. ''Perhaps it'll do me good, as it's done you.''

''You sure you can handle it?''

''Of course.''

With an amused twinkle, he suddenly released her, then pulled down on his Stetson. ''You choose to tell people your opinion before they've even asked.''

While he whirled away to hitch his horse, her mouth dropped open with the unexpected sting of his barb.

She'd stumbled headlong into that insult. She bloody well had.

''Your uncle's here to see you.'' A constable knocked on Virginia's bedroom door.

''Thank you. He told me he'd be dropping by on his way to check on a patient.''

''He's waiting in the kitchen. Cook's makin' him coffee.''

Virginia left her bedroom and strode down the hallway of the log house. She'd been unpacking and resting for an hour, then had spent another hour reading her medical journals.

Zack's deep, low voice carried around the corner, then other men's voices mumbled in reply. She wondered what they were talking about.

Slivers of sunshine poked through the chinks between the log walls, painting gold stripes along her path. The solidness of the house and pine scent of the peeled timber appealed to her. The house was much bigger than she expected. It'd been built on high ground away from the flooding river and near half an acre of precious forest, which was difficult to find on the prairies. But then, the vegetation around Calgary was more foothill than prairie, a gentle transition between flat grassland and forested mountains.

The house walls rose to a steeply pitched roof with an overhanging interior loft. Floors were planked with mouseproof tamarack; windows were made of real glass and not oil-soaked paper; the kitchen was big, with a breathtaking view of the river below. And five bedrooms flanked the central room, which everyone referred to as the *great room*—a combined space of parlor and dining room.

Sparsely furnished, the ranch house was intended for men. There wasn't a doily or runner or quilt in sight that might appeal to a feminine eye, but the house was large and clean. Its proximity to town and to the river for fresh water no doubt made the property valuable and the reason the federal government had claimed it for their police force.

Six men plus Zack stood in the great room as she passed, hovering over a large map spread on the roughly hewn dining table. Zack pointed to different areas and spoke in low tones to his men. He never looked up at her until she passed by the table, and then he only nodded.

She responded with a stiff nod. So this was how it was going to be. He'd go about his business and she'd go about hers. That would suit her fine.

She was relieved to see Zack deep in his work already. The sooner he caught James Stiller, the sooner she could leave. In the meantime she'd work toward studying and writing her licensing exams, and finishing her practicum with her uncle. She was blessed to have someone with decades of experience to guide her. When this maddening confinement was over, she could easily transfer her license to another province.

Pushing open the swinging, double kitchen doors, she called out, "Uncle Paddy?"

Seated alone at the kitchen table, apparently surprised by her quick entry, he fumbled to clear the table of his books.

"I brought your mail. I'll bring it by every few days when I'm in the area."

It was a letter from the district government about her examinations, confirming dates and times. She placed it in her pocket, then came around to his right side and peered over his rolled-up sleeves.

He'd been reading from a book entitled *Herbal Remedies for Easy Use* but quickly slammed it shut. He stuffed a magnifying glass into his doctor's bag by his feet. His behavior seemed curious but she couldn't pinpoint specifics. With a cough he pulled out a suede pouch and held it up to her.

"What's this?"

"Zack's things. They came out of his singed denim pants the night of the train wreck."

"I thought you'd already returned these to him."

"And I thought you had. I found them this morning stuffed into the bedside dresser where he'd been sleeping."

Grabbing hold of the drawstring she tossed the light, soft pouch onto the kitchen counter. The counter was lined with wooden planks that doubled as a chopping block for food preparation. "I'll make sure he gets them when he's finished with his men."

She'd already seen the contents since she'd been the one to slash off his pants and retrieve the small items from his pockets. They were minor, incidental articles that couldn't be too important since Zack hadn't asked for them.

"Where's the cook?" asked Virginia.

"He said he was getting sausages from the smoke-house."

Virginia peered out the sunny window to the plush banks below, catching sight of the heavyset cook walking toward the shack. A blue river meandered through the meadow. In addition to the stables that held fifteen horses, various wagons, sleighs, hoes and ploughs, there was also a chicken coop, a pigsty and two storage sheds for feed. A patch of land had been cleared for an herb and vegetable garden, and she couldn't wait to get out there to discover what had been planted.

"Sure is a pretty view. I don't trust skinny cooks—this one's heavy and he looks like a good one." Uncle Paddy stood alongside her, adjusting the spectacles on his wide nose.

She laughed softly at his assessment.

He walked back to the table and reached into his medical bag, pulling out his wooden stethoscope. "Have a chair. Let's see how you're doin'. It hasn't been twenty-four hours yet since your injury but you're walkin' and talkin' with no problem."

"The laudanum's helping. It takes the ache away."

On his examination he discovered what she knew—all was well.

"Won't you stay for lunch?"

Uncle Paddy lifted his cup of coffee and guzzled it. "Mrs. Dickenson is waiting for me down the road. Her gout's acting up, but I'm sure she's preparin' me a meal to prove how well she's doin'. Don't suppose you could come with me to check on her?"

Zack burst through the door as Virginia rolled down

her sleeve. She buttoned the broad linen cuff from where her uncle had checked her pulse. Zack watched her do it. The air rippled with tension.

Go away, she thought, *and take those big brown eyes with you.*

But Zack stood rooted. "For safety's sake, I think it's best Virginia remain on the property. It would be easier for me not to have to escort her around the countryside."

She was capable of answering on her own. "Could you send some patients my way, Uncle Paddy? To this house? If their medical problems are straightforward, I can handle them. I brought my medical bags and supplies with me. That is—" she glanced at Zack "—if the inspector approves."

"I don't see the harm," said Zack. "As long as you don't send any strangers."

"Too bad you can't assist me with surgery on Mr. Gilbert next week," said Uncle Paddy. "Dental surgery. I can't bring him here for that. He's going to need a couple of days' rest after five teeth extractions."

"I can make the garlic poultice you'll need for packing his jaw afterward, if that would help." She scowled at Zack. Why had he come into the kitchen, anyway? He was crowding her territory with that annoyingly muscled body.

Uncle Paddy rose to leave. He buckled his worn leather bag. "I've got two injured people to care for. One with a fractured arm, the other with a foot sprain. How about my sending them to you to get their splints removed?"

"Sounds perfect."

"And then there's Zack. Don't forget to look after his shoulder."

"Why don't you look after my shoulder, Doc? I think Virginia would probably prefer it."

Virginia prickled at the honesty of the comment, which she couldn't deny.

"Okay," said Uncle Paddy.

"How is Virginia doing this morning? Virginia talks like nothing bothers her, but how is she really?"

Zack's question surprised her. She walked to the water pitcher and poured herself a glass.

"She'll be fine," the older man answered on his way out the door.

Uncle Paddy said his goodbyes and left. Zack was about to follow him outside.

"Zack, wait."

"I've got work to do."

He said it as if *she* didn't. "I won't bother you for long." She led him back into the kitchen and tossed him the suede pouch. "On the night of the train wreck these things were found in your pockets."

"I thought my clothes and things were ripped and burned in the explosion. Totally destroyed."

"They were. But a few things were salvaged."

With nimble fingers, he took the pouch and turned it upside down on the battered kitchen table. The table was huge, enough to seat sixteen men comfortably. But the two of them stood across from each other, totally *uncomfortable*.

Four items fell to the table.

"A ticket stub." He rubbed his dark temple. "I remember there was a train conductor who'd come through. He had his nephew with him—or a cousin—in training he'd said. I'd never seen the younger man before."

"Is that important?"

He studied her for a long moment, as if weighing whether to confide in her. "I'm trying to piece together what happened that evening and who exactly had been in the car with me."

"And who had threatened you about your new bride."

He nodded. He picked up a ten-dollar bill, which was charred along its edges. "This looks passable. I'll exchange it at the bank."

Next came a folded paper. She hadn't read it, allowing Zack his privacy. Now when he unfolded it, she realized it was an old telegram from her. Their gazes locked in mutual discomfort. He'd kept her telegram informing him she'd arrived more than a month ago.

The remaining item, a small red ruby, almost went unnoticed. It was hiding beneath the edge of the suede pouch. "What's this?"

"It looks like a jewel."

"It doesn't belong to me." Then realization blazed in his face. "Aha! This was what I was bending over to reach for when I got shot. If I hadn't been bending over, I might have been shot through the heart. This little ruby saved my life."

She stared at the thing.

"Whoever came up from behind me was someone I knew. Someone I wasn't surprised to see. Either one of my men, or the train conductor and his nephew."

"Where did the ruby come from?"

He leaned back in his boots. "It looks similar to the stones retrieved from the O'Connolleys. A jeweler and his wife who'd been taken hostage the day before. If this little red ruby was in our compartment, then someone had taken it, stolen it, from the O'Connolleys. If I can figure out who stole the jewel, then I'll know who shot me."

"Any suspicions?"

"It could be anyone. All of the Mounties in the compartment were with me and the O'Connolleys. It's also possible that the conductor and his nephew are the thieves. The initial robbery took place on a train and they rode it all day long. It couldn't have been Travis, though.''

''Why not?''

''Because Travis was seated beside me to my right. We were talking about…about the temperature variance in shoeing horses. It would have been physically impossible for Travis to reach over my right side to aim at my left collarbone. There would have been no point. To kill me, he'd only need to pull his gun and shoot me in the ribs. Besides, I know in my gut he's a good man. Brilliant with horses. He's had four promotions in two years—from corporal to sergeant major. Fastest rise I've ever seen.''

''What about his brother, Mitchell?''

''I hope to God he's on our side. He's an expert with ballistics, though. With dynamite and explosives. He could have planned something like this and gotten away with it.''

''Where were the other men sitting?''

''I don't recall. We were getting up and walking around. There was jerky in our packs. We were hungry. The culprit might even have been one of the two killed Mounties. Their fatal injuries were caused when the train derailed and our car rolled on top of the next.''

She knew they'd been crushed to death.

Zack scooped up the items and pushed them back into the pouch. ''You'll keep this to yourself, won't you?''

He trusted her. Was it because she was a doctor and expected to be discreet, or that he'd known her for nearly his entire life? ''You've got my word. I'll discuss it with no one.''

She turned to leave the kitchen, but he pushed the door closed before she could, trapping her. ''You've got to know, when I called off our marriage, I had your best interests at heart.''

She leaned up against the door, facing him. "I know that by distancing yourself from me as your future wife, you attempted to keep me out of harm's way. But now I'd like to keep it at arm's length between us. I'll find a way to repay your parents for my tuition."

He propped his hand on the wall beside her head. "Our reasons for marriage seemed valid—''

"You've got to be kidding. If you think nothing's changed and when all of this is over—''

"I didn't say that," he blazed. "A lot has changed between *us,* but nothing between you and my brother. I saw the look in your eye when you looked at Andrew."

Her hands flew to her hips. "How dare you!"

"You're not over him."

"Andrew means nothing to me."

"Then why did you turn beet-red when he walked through the door? Why did you allow him to kiss you on the cheek? And why did you kiss *me* only when you knew *he* was watching?"

"You have no right—''

"I don't want a wife who's in love with another man. So you see marriage would no longer work for me, either."

He was unbelievable. "*You* don't want *me?*"

He tilted his head and stared.

"I would never marry a man who treats me like I don't matter. I should never have put myself at the mercy of Andrew, believing everything he scraped onto my platter, and I should never have bounced into your arms from his. What I want is peace and quiet from men. A total sabbatical. Maybe after five years, I'll reconsider and receive gentleman callers again, but I'll demand to be courted in a normal way. Nothing prearranged for me, thank you very much!''

His mouth gaped open. ''How long a break from men?''

''Five years.''

''That's impossible.'' His amusement was evident. His mood flipped from solemn to lighthearted. ''You can't stay away from men for that long.''

''I certainly can. I've had my fill.''

He stood so close that, if she raised her hand, she could trace the bristles beginning to erupt on his shaved jaw.

He looked at her lips. ''Then it means you've never been kissed.''

''*What?*''

''Not properly.''

''Kissing would never affect my judgment.'' But the idea sent her senses soaring.

''Our kiss affected you.''

She blushed, maddened by the truth.

''Three kisses. That's all I need to prove your outlandish theory wrong.'' Humor skirted the edge of his words. ''For the fourth kiss, you'll come begging.''

She laughed outright, unsure whether he was teasing or serious. ''The size of your swollen head is only overshadowed by the size of your conceit.''

When she twisted away and rushed out the door, she heard his laughter and felt his burning gaze roving on her backside.

The blasted man was beyond belief.

Chapter Eight

"Are you afraid to be alone with me?" Zack picked his way over the garden furrows, careful not to trample the new shoots of peas with his size-twelve boots. His spurs jangled as he walked. He stopped when one furrow separated him from Virginia. Behind him, the sun burned into his back. It felt remarkably good and etched his bulky shadow onto the dirt, which wove intimately with her shorter one before fading into a batch of berry bushes.

"Don't flatter yourself. Why would I be afraid to be alone with you?"

Virginia leaned into the gentle wind with her hoe, the breeze plucking at the wisps of hair that knotted into a thick strand along her spine. He stood disquieted by the emptiness he had felt since they'd both confessed three days earlier that they no longer wanted nor needed to marry.

Her hands, stained yellow-green from uprooting weeds, fled to her apron. He marveled at the beauty in her stance, caught off guard by the girlish clothes she wore as though she'd bundled up to play outdoors. Yet he knew there was an intelligent, fierce woman beneath the curves.

"I have a note here for you from your cousin, Clarissa."

He extended it and she snatched it.

"Why haven't you spoken to me in three days?" He asked while she concentrated on reading.

"I spoke to you upon rising."

"Only to say good morning." He'd taken the only room across from hers in that end of the house, and was driven around the bend deciphering what she might be doing by the occasional sounds he heard. The thud of a handbag, the scrape of a heel, the hand-winding of her bedside clock at 11:12 p.m. when he couldn't sleep, either.

Her hair, as dark as smoky glass, contrasted with the pale sparks of sky-blue in her eyes. "Well, I spoke to you again at breakfast."

"Only to ask for the honey."

"Between you and Travis, I'm beneath your watch day and night. To tell the truth I—I haven't been giving *you* much thought. I've been busy with patients."

"I don't see any around now."

"Now I'm busy with potatoes."

When he stepped closer, his holster hugging his hips, his arm in a sling across his chest, she backed away. "Do you think your potatoes are going to stop me from getting what I want?"

Her chin riveted upward. "And what is that?"

Three kisses. Goddammit, he'd proved to her that she could no more stay away from men for five years than he could women. He didn't plan on getting involved with her—simply to prove the value of physical satisfaction.

Instead of saying what he felt, he ran a hand through his windblown hair and glanced to the trees. His shoulder ached. It wasn't healing as quickly as he needed it and he still couldn't shoot worth a damn. What good was a marksman who couldn't lift his arm without it trembling?

How could he be called upon to shoot from a distance? To track vigilantes as they raided towns, to go up against the toughest, cruelest gunfighters this side of the Rockies. And how could Zack train the dozens of men beneath him in the handling of a weapon if they were too busy laughing at his shaky grip?

He wondered what she'd found so appealing about his brother. Maybe the serene life Andrew might have given her if she were a rancher's bride.

A crippled marksman or a successful rancher.

"What does your cousin want?" he asked.

"She needs to see me for a medical problem."

"And I have to speak with the commander at the fort. We could go together to town this morning. There's a Mountie patrolling the edge of the property a mile down the road. We'll take him with us."

Her thin gray skirt billowed wide. "Am I...safe?"

"From the Stiller gang?"

"From you."

The steamy insinuation in her tone caused his pulse to kick. His body felt heavy and warm, and his instinct was to pull her tight and give her the first kiss right here. But there were others milling in the background and he wanted unlimited time when he did his kissing. "You'll never be safe from me."

He saw her eyes flicker at the same moment the hollow of her throat tugged. She was so easy to set off-kilter, and Lord help him, he enjoyed every minute. "Well, I suppose I *will* be safe on the ride. After all, it's broad daylight."

Her illogical reasoning caught his sense of humor. "Do you think people don't kiss in the sunshine?"

She blushed. ''But things only get heated at night, in the privacy of the bedroom.''

''Kissing beneath the stars is one thing, but making love beneath the sun's pulsing rays is totally another pleasure.''

On cue, her cheeks turned from pink to red to crimson. She glanced to his holster. ''Then I'll have to pack my own gun.''

His slow swirl of laughter rumbled through the morning breeze. With his strong right arm, he reached out and lifted her chin. His plan was to make her enjoy the kiss, then pull away just when she wanted to yield. He noted with self-satisfied pleasure that, at his touch, her lips quivered slightly. ''You won't need a gun. Get your things together. I'll meet you at the stables in twenty minutes.''

When he dropped his hand abruptly, she shook her head self-consciously, disturbed by his touch. *Good.* He left her.

Twenty-five minutes later they were seated in the open leather buggy. She'd removed her scalp bandages, revealing a healthy two-inch scab, claiming the air would do wonders to heal it. He still felt a stab of guilt whenever he glanced at it, although it was partially obscured by her hair.

''What's that?'' She pointed to a group of men sawing and stacking lumber behind the stables.

''They're preparing for a barn raising.''

''When?''

''Sunday after next.''

She tilted a parasol above her head, shielding her creamy skin from the heat while he flicked the reins of the bay. Its hooves trampled sprouting grass.

He'd never known a woman who could talk so much when she was nervous. Withdrawn to her corner, not an inch of her flesh or clothing touching his, Virginia went on and on about her peas and corn and new dumpling recipe the cook had given her. All the while Zack focused on the soft swell of her upturned breasts, imagining their rosy peaks beneath his mouth, the nape of her beautiful neck and how soft it would feel beneath his hand, the proportion of her full bottom lip to her top one, and how they'd feel surrendering beneath his.

But hell, he had things to accomplish today besides the game he was playing with Virginia. How was it that she engulfed his thoughts whenever she was near?

He stretched his long legs and adjusted his Stetson. "You can sit closer. I won't bite you."

"You might."

Only if he got lucky.

"Relax, Virginia. I'm not sitting here thinking of the perfect time to…to pounce on you."

"I don't give you my permission to do so anyway. You're to stay away from me."

Like hell.

She peered at him. Her pulse beat softly at the base of her unbuttoned collar. Longing coursed through his veins.

"When can I remove this sling?"

"It's barely been two weeks. I suggest you keep it on for at least two more."

He muttered.

She thrust forward. "You want your shoulder to heal properly, don't you?"

"With this hot June sun beating down on me, I feel like taking the sling and stringing it from the nearest—"

Unexpectedly with a rattling heave, the wagon rocked and sank to the ground to Virginia's side. Zack slid down the seat on top of her, still holding the reins. The horse neighed and pawed the air.

"Be still!" he ordered Virginia, reaching for his revolver, bracing his shoulder protectively against hers. With a quick scan, he saw no one else. They hadn't been sabotaged; the buggy had simply popped its wheel.

The horse simmered beneath his soothing hand.

He nudged Virginia by her trembling shoulder, inhaling the scent of her hair as she raised herself from his lap. "Are you all right? We've just broken a wheel."

The force of gravity pinned his body against her own and kept him there.

"Yes, yes I'm fine. I thought—I thought someone was shooting at us again." She tried to pry and squirm herself out of position but couldn't budge.

He was so close to her face he noticed a tiny scar in her eyebrow. "How did you get that little circular scar?"

Her lips nearly grazed his own. "Chicken pox."

He tore away. Safety came before pleasure. "Let me get out first, then I'll help you down." He stretched one long leg over her lap, straddling her. It took work for him to keep his thigh muscles rigidly in control. "Sorry. Excuse me."

"Of course," she mumbled, as if he positioned himself like this above her every day. He swallowed hard as he conjured the mental image.

When his foot touched ground he dived into the soft grass, favoring his injured shoulder. Limber and in control, he crouched on his feet, barrel raised as he pivoted the area.

The wheat fields, a glorious rolling green, shimmered with a hazy heat. Clusters of trees lined old creek beds. A prairie falcon circled the air a hundred yards to their north, scouring the ground for rodents. In the distance the faint blast of a locomotive steam engine indicated the nine-o'clock to Regina had left on time. They were still far from the property line, so he didn't see the Mountie on patrol.

They were safe. But hell, the buggy's wheel had completely rolled off its axle. Leaning beneath it, he noticed the pin was missing. He kicked the dirt.

Virginia crawled out of the conveyance to stand beside him, toting her medical bag and drawstring purse. In the process her skirt accidentally caught on the handbrake, ripping the fabric down its buttoned front.

"I was going to help you get out. You should have waited for me."

"It was taking you forever."

"Can't you, for one moment, sit in one spot and wait—"

"For you to rescue me? Never again."

"You know, giving in to me isn't a sign of weakness."

"It's not a sign of intelligence."

"One of these days some man is going to take you over his knee and—"

Her defiant glare silenced his argument. Her ruby mouth puckered into a straight obstinate line and he realized once again that Virginia Waters was unlike any woman he'd encountered. This one talked back.

Examining the damage on the buggy, he removed his hat and slapped it against his thigh. "How the hell am I supposed to fix this wheel with only one good arm?"

"Don't you dare remove that sling. The mending bones will pull apart. *I'll* help you fix the wheel."

"You?" He snorted. "You don't have the strength."

With a fevered muttering, Virginia tossed her bags onto the grassy slope, then rolled up her sleeves. She was serious.

And he was desperate.

"All right. It would be faster than walking back for

help. Maybe we can work together. I'll push and yank if you could hold things in position when I align them. Let's look for the pin first. Maybe it's fallen out in one piece and we won't have to wire up a replacement.''

First he unhitched the mare from the buggy so it wouldn't spook, tying it to a nearby log instead. After ten aggravating minutes of searching through the cracked ground, Zack found the pin. He could see why it'd come apart. The iron had rusted through on the head, busting it in two, but the half that he'd found—in addition to some added rope he'd wind around the joint—should be strong enough to get them into town.

''I'll hoist the buggy to my good shoulder, if you crawl beneath it and plant the pin between the holes. Ready?''

She yelled from beneath the buggy. ''Yes.''

The weight dug into his back. ''Hurry. It's getting heavy.''

''I'm hurrying.''

He panted. ''I can't hold it much longer.''

''Almost there.''

The pressure of blood was building in his face. ''It's beginning to slip.''

''Be strong.''

Be strong? It felt like every bone and muscle he owned was pulling out of its socket.

''Okay, drop it.''

He let the buggy drop slowly, heaving beneath the torture of a slow withdrawal. Finally he dropped to the ground himself and rolled on the soft grass to join Virginia. Her laced black boots dangled out from beneath the back, while his pointed cowboy boots dangled out the other side. With their bodies at a ninety-degree angle, the tops of their heads touched.

''My, you're strong.''

He knew from the slant of her lashes and the upward tilt of her cheeks that she was teasing him. Still, he couldn't help but feel a bit elated at what he'd accomplished. He'd lifted at least two hundred pounds. Maybe three. "Now I know what an ox feels like. Pass me the rope."

She did as he asked. "Your face is red and sweaty."

"That's what you get when you lift *four* hundred pounds."

"Four hundred? My oh my."

His smile was slow and easy. "Your face is sweaty, too."

"Is it?" She moved a curved shoulder up to rub against her nose. The sheen of perspiration clung to her forehead and glistened like early-morning beads of dew. "It's hot under here. It's not every day a girl gets to see the underpinning of a carriage."

"You can thank me for the experience later. Right now, you have to be my good arm. Tuck that end of the rope under mine."

They had two feet of clearance height beneath the buggy, which meant she had to strain to match the lift of his long arm. Her fingers were coated with axle grease. Grasping upward to clench the rope, she turned herself over onto her stomach, pressing her shoulder close to his temple, but couldn't quite reach the loop.

"Push yourself a bit higher," he urged.

She strained her body. The loose cloth from her leg-of-mutton sleeve dangled against his face.

"Ah, I can't see."

"Sorry." She strained harder until the sleeve passed by his vision, replaced by the luscious swell of one breast.

"Right about there," he mumbled, mesmerized by the sensual twisting of her body. His eyes lowered to the cloth covering where he imagined her nipple to be. His muscles tightened with arousal. The air grew stuffy and hot. Where had the breeze gone?

Hastily he glanced away, but not before he noticed that she'd also become terribly conscious of their positioning.

"Interesting," he whispered. "You're doing a fine job. Keep it up."

She quieted with embarrassment as she twisted and pulled at the rope. "We're almost done," she groaned. "I hope."

And so the pounding of his heart began. Separated from her by an inch, he remained steadfast on his task, tying the rope, bracing his boot against the axle and securing the knot. Every stir of the blades of grass beyond the wheels stirred the hairs on his arms. He noticed how she moved—swayed, rocked, glided along the fragrant grass. Her blouse untucked from her skirt and dangled onto *his* thigh, in a most alluring mingling of cloth, exposing an intoxicating curve of feminine flesh.

A drizzle of sweat beaded along his brow. She was too much temptation for him to bear. He dropped his hand from the knots and lifted gentle fingers to explore her bare stomach.

She gasped, her lips parted. A rapid hue of pink stained her cheeks just before he pulled her down and rolled himself toward her. Taking the dominant position angled to her body, he took her lips in a ruthless kiss.

If she were to beg for her own release, he'd never surrender her. He pressed deeper and fuller until her mouth responded beneath his.

She hesitated for a moment, a heartbeat, then with a silky moan of submission, she gave herself to the kiss. To him.

The sound drove him on. His fingers trailed the smooth

expanse of her soft belly, and her muscles flinched in response. He ached for more, to press themselves together in a locked embrace but due to the cramped quarters, this would have to do.

He wasn't gentle. His lips promised fire and passion and the height of fulfillment, if she would only follow his lead. She would be his conquest.

Her lips were soft and eager, plush beneath his. She was womanly and submissive, it would be easy to—

She pulled away.

He knocked his head on the undercarriage. "What are you doing?"

"Kiss number one won't work on me." With a grunt, she slid out beneath the buggy until all he saw of her were laced high-spiked boots.

With a frustrated sexual groan, he collapsed into the dirt.

What he should have done differently—Zack thought in glum self-examination as they wheeled into the fort with the Mountie guard behind them, dropped off the buggy for repair and borrowed another one to take into town—was go slower with his kiss.

Slower and smoother. That's what women liked. He'd practically attacked her. She was obviously a refined woman, educated and no longer the little kid who stared up at him with flattering eyes while he did as he pleased.

No wonder she'd pulled away. If it hadn't been for the tight space, he would have been reaching for her body as well as her lips.

Women didn't like that. Well, some did.

But not Virginia.

Then what *did* she like?

"I'd like you to stop right here," she said in the buggy,

almost reading his mind and giving him a stroke. "In front of Ashford Jewelers. Hopefully Clarissa is working behind the counter today." She folded her parasol.

Zack tugged back on the reins, easing the horse into a spot by the front door. He jumped off the buggy and circled around to help Virginia. She took his hand and slid to her feet with hardly a glance. You'd have thought from looking at the two of them that they were stilted strangers.

Dammit, he wanted to shout, *why the hell didn't you kiss me longer? How could you resist what I couldn't?*

Her lashes fluttered to meet his eyes and for a moment he wondered if she *had* been affected.

"I'll be right back." She strode to the glass door, adjusting her drawstring purse and medical bag.

Mindful of her safety, Zack stopped her with a brisk hand. He peered in at the three customers. Together with the other Mountie, they deemed it was safe and allowed her to enter.

For what seemed liked ages, Virginia remained inside. Zack followed her movements through the windowpanes as she talked with Clarissa, both women visible between the velvet curtains of the back room. The guard paced the boardwalk.

When Virginia returned outside, Travis asked, "Is Clarissa well?"

"I wrote her a prescription for the apothecary. Female troubles—"

"Say no more."

"I wasn't going to."

"Dr. Waters!" the reporter called from across the street.

"Should I gun the horse?" Zack asked her, half joking, half serious. "Pretend we don't see him?"

Virginia laughed, sweet and clear, much to his surprising pleasure. Maybe the woman preferred a lighter hand in physical satisfaction. An anecdote or two, a humorous tale from his journeys, then short snappy kisses to make her laugh. And *then* she'd submit.

He'd find her soft spot yet.

"You'd better not gun the horse or we might make the front page news," Virginia whispered, leaning against his taut arm in a confounding gesture of friendliness.

Smothering a groan, Zack tipped his hat. "Morning, David."

"Yes, sir, it is. Dr. Waters, I wondered if you might have a look at my wrist. Your uncle saw it last evening, but in my opinion, it's not doing well."

He lifted his arm and pushed back one sleeve before she could refuse—not that she would refuse to help anyone in need from what Zack knew of her. Unwrapping a tightly woven gauze pad, David revealed a blistering burn on his wrist.

Suddenly queasy, Zack preferred to look away, centering his attention on Virginia's face.

Her cheeks dimpled. "It looks like a steam burn."

"It happened yesterday as I was boiling coffee. Your uncle told me to smear it with salve and bandage it, which I did, but this morning the skin looks…soggy."

"Oh, David. Take the gauze right off. Don't put any more salve on it. With the skin sliding off like this, it's best to dry it in natural sunshine and let the air get at it."

"I thought so." David peered up at her, his stick of blond hair poking out beyond his ears and from beneath the brim of his sombrero. "Is your uncle managing on his own since you left for the Mounties' ranch?"

"Yes, why?"

"He…he didn't seem himself last night."

"What do you mean?"

"He was drunk, ma'am."

Her color heightened. Embarrassed, she fidgeted in her seat. "Thank you for telling me. I'll speak with him. Please don't…mention it in any of your columns."

David squinted in the sunshine. "No, ma'am. My father was a drinker."

"Uncle Paddy is *not* a drinker." She rubbed her hands along her skirt. "Please, if there's any more problem with your wrist, come and see me on the ranch."

"More folks would come to you for their problems if…"

"If what?"

"They say you're a bit fickle-minded. Misplacing instruments like you did the night Hank Johnson broke his leg, and sometimes giving wrong instructions to folks about their care."

"What?"

"That's absurd," said Zack. "I was there the night Hank Johnson was taken in and I was there for days after. Virginia's care is nothing but the best."

"I'm only telling you what I hear. It doesn't quite piece together for me, either."

If it wasn't Virginia who had problems delivering a doctor's care, thought Zack, then it was her uncle.

Glancing at her pained expression, he knew she was thinking the same thing.

"Thanks, David," said Zack, clicking his tongue to the mare, hoping to quickly remove Virginia from this troubling and potentially damaging discussion. "We'll be on our way."

The guard followed at a distance.

Although Virginia was subdued and didn't speak, Zack knew exactly where they needed to head next. He wanted to take complete control of the situation himself, to do what he did best and take care of trouble before it happened.

But he tamed his anger that Paddy Waters, the only private doctor not counting the fort's surgeon that the town had had for years before Virginia arrived, was drinking again. Zack would allow her to handle the sticky situation, but he'd jump in the first minute he detected she needed him.

There were many reasons why a man took to drink and Zack had witnessed all of them. Some drinkers didn't know what the effects of alcohol could bring, others did it for the sheer pleasure, some hid their cowardice behind the bottle, and others yet found comfort and hope in the liquid. Zack wondered which of those reasons controlled Paddy.

Paddy was already three sheets to the wind when they arrived at his house. He was stretched out on his parlor sofa, glasses removed, and dozing in a rumpled vest.

"Why are you drinking again?" Virginia's despondency was mirrored in her eyes.

"It creeps up on me. I start with one shot." Paddy tried, but he looked as if he could barely focus.

"You can't take care of sick people when you're affected by alcohol. You'll do them more harm than good."

Millicent entered the room. Dejected, she listened and watched, apparently aware of the drinking.

Virginia stood firm. "Please make a decision between the bottle and your practice."

"I'm not sure I can."

"Then I'm going to the judge. I'll tell him exactly what's going on and then *he'll* tell you to make the same choice."

"I'll stop drinking," Paddy replied.

Millicent put her face in her hands, ran for the kitchen door and burst into sobs.

Zack peered from Paddy's shamed expression to Virginia's stoic one. He realized that, for the first time since knowing her as an adult, he was seeing Virginia in her best light.

And playing hot and cold with her, thinking he could seek pleasure from her body but not touch her soul, was like playing with a keg of ice and explosives.

Chapter Nine

"You should speak up and defend yourself. Tell David it wasn't you making those medical mistakes." Zack turned and hitched the mare to the post outside the train depot. The guard tagged behind.

Virginia sensed Zack's smoldering anger.

"I could never betray Uncle Paddy." Hoisting her skirts off the muddy steps of the boardwalk, Virginia exhaled long and hard. The sound of buzzing insects nesting above her in the rafters made her swerve. She'd never seen her uncle in such disarray and it distressed her.

"Then *I'll* tell David the truth."

"Please don't. I think the matter has been dealt with."

Zack rubbed his dark jaw, making his way through the morning crowd toward her. His cloaked temper gave him an aura of dark appeal.

"Your well-meaning intentions could explode and ruin Uncle Paddy just when he might turn himself around."

Zack flinched at her direct words. She felt guilty for them but it was in Zack's character to take matters into his own hands, and she needed to be clear about this.

The blaring sun cast shadows onto the covered roof and then onto Zack. His body was cut in half by the contrasting shadows, pronouncing the details she found so masculine. Speed and elegance. A black shadow line etched one rugged cheek, down his tapered shirtsleeve, his opened vest and down his lean, long leg. The other half of him blazed in glorious sunshine. His hips swayed beneath his guns and her pulse picked up speed like a thundering locomotive. When he touched the brim of his Stetson and smiled at two young women passing by, Virginia felt a twinge of envy. Women were always noticing him and saying hello.

She could see the attraction. She'd be blind not to notice herself. But she'd opened her heart to him once and she'd learned her humiliating lesson. And no amount of kissing could erase that hurt.

When it came right down to it, she couldn't depend on Zack.

For her life, her well-being, her protection, maybe. But sadly not in other vital things that mattered to her heart.

Zack took her elbow and led her through the depot doors. Conscious of his touch, God, conscious of everything about him, she tugged out of his hold.

Her drawstring purse dangled from her fingers. "Why do you think Uncle Paddy drinks?"

"A lot of men do. The rancher before his meal, the preacher before his sermon, even the judge before his trial."

"But it doesn't drive all men the way it does my uncle."

Zack led her around the ticket counter and through the lineup. "He's quit once before, maybe he'll do it again."

"You were around those years he was drinking. Why did he start?"

"John Calloway told me your uncle had lost two patients after surgery through no fault of his own. It'd gotten to him. He started drinking then.''

"But he hasn't lost any patients recently."

"Maybe it crept back up on him, like he said."

"I hope you're right." She stretched on tiptoe to peer in the direction he so easily scanned above the hats and bonnets. "What are we doing here?"

"Looking for someone." Zack led them around the platform to an office at the far end and poked his head around the door. "Chauncey McGuire, where's your nephew this morning?"

Virginia peered inside, noticing the walls covered with train schedules and yellowed geographical maps.

A big-bellied man looked up from counting rolls of tickets. "He came in on the ten-fifty from Banff." He nodded through the glass window. "There he is." Chauncey puffed on his cigar butt as the other man, skinnier than a shovel's pole but better dressed than his uncle, joined them. "I thought we answered your questions last week."

"I thought of a few more." Zack dug into his pocket and pulled out a ripped ticket stub. "Was it you, Chauncey, or Dirk McGuire who asked for my ticket the night of the crash? I can't remember which one of you ripped the stub."

Chauncey's eyes flickered at his nephew. "I think it was Dirk."

"Might have been," said Dirk, opening his waist pouch, removing a wad of money and shoving it into the corner safe.

"Did you rip my ticket only, or the others in the compartment?"

"I ripped 'em all."

"Even the tickets belonging to Timothy Littlefield and Cameron Peters?"

"The two Mounties who got crushed to death? I took theirs, too."

Zack nodded. "Can you show me how everyone was standing when you took them?"

"That's a peculiar question. But all right."

Chauncey and Dirk indicated that Timothy Littlefield and Cameron Peters had been seated on the far wooden bench but had risen to stretch their legs when Dirk requested to see their tickets. Zack and Travis had been seated in the corner, with Hank Johnson and Mitchell Reid standing by and smoking out the window.

"Do you remember who was in that compartment on the swing train *to* the mountains?"

"I think it rode empty. There were a bunch of farmers, one with a crate of ducks, but they got off halfway to Canmore."

"Any jewelers?"

Chauncey didn't blink. "Nope."

"Someone lost a ruby. I was hoping to find its owner."

Dirk blinked. "Don't recall anyone claimin' a lost ring. Want me to put the word out?"

Virginia frowned but she noticed Zack hadn't twitched at the twisting of the words. Dirk had said ring, not ruby as Zack had explained it.

"No," said Zack. "They'll speak up if they've lost it. It'll be at the fort waiting for them if they do."

Dirk opened the cover of the pocket watch dangling from a chain hooked to his vest. "I gotta go. The eleven-o'clock just rolled in."

When she and Zack said goodbye and left for their buggy, she asked, "What was that all about?"

"Most of what I asked them, I already recall. I wanted to see if they'd lie to me."

"And?"

"They told the truth."

When Zack stopped suddenly in the teeming crowd to let an older gentleman pass by with his saddle trunk, Virginia's lips accidentally brushed Zack's shoulder. The warmth of his skin radiating from under his shirt burned on her mouth, reminding her of the hot kiss they'd shared beneath the buggy that morning. The kiss had been unexpected. Beneath a buggy had been the strangest place she'd ever shared one. It played with her imagination.

Judging by the intensity that had passed between them, there was no doubt in her mind that to Zack, sun or moon made no difference in lovemaking. Passion didn't wax and wane according to the earth's orbit.

"It's getting hot in here, isn't it?" Zack asked, staring down at her hot face.

She fanned herself with her hand. "Yeah."

They continued walking.

"Why'd you let them believe it was a ring you found and not a lone ruby?"

"Instinct to keep my mouth shut. Doesn't mean much. They may have been trying to outwit me or mislead me by misquoting what I said."

"Then you didn't glean any new information."

Zack's cheek tugged upward in a disarming grin. "Who says? Did you see the pocket watch Dirk opened?"

"A sparkling gold pocket watch. Train conductors and engineers all seem to invest a lot of money in timepieces. I imagine it's how they keep the trains running on time."

"Yeah, but not a timepiece encrusted with two emeralds, an opal and one shiny ruby."

She inhaled a short breath. "You suspect Dirk?"

"Maybe."

"But you said you don't recall Chauncey and Dirk be-ing *in* the compartment when you got shot."

"Doesn't mean they weren't."

"Was there a missing stone in Dirk's timepiece that you think your ruby may have slipped out from?"

"No missing stones. Just a gut feeling that he's not telling us something."

Sunshine hit her square in the eye when they exited the depot. The guard was with them. "Where to from here?"

"Our last call of the morning." Zack spoke to Virginia and the other Mountie. "The fort."

When they got there, Zack led Virginia into Super-intendent Ridgeway's office, but when talk turned to po-lice matters, the commander insisted she wait outside. "Would you mind, miss, giving us ten minutes?"

"She's fine here with us, sir—"

The superintendent's stare silenced Zack.

Although she understood the need for privacy, she felt slighted. "It's fine. I'll wait outside."

She waited in the front foyer next to the company clerk who sat at his neat desk, busy entering numbers into the columns of his ledger. Through the closed door, she heard the odd phrase relating to the investigation but couldn't piece things together.

Finally it was time to leave for the ranch again. Their buggy had been repaired, Zack's horse watered, and she was building an appetite for lunch.

They were crossing the grassy courtyard of the fort to-ward the buggy as Lucy Peters and her children came hustling toward the commander's office.

"Lucy, how good to see you again." Zack stepped for-ward to greet her as Virginia smiled and spoke to the children.

Lucy nodded, her face swollen with deep circles beneath her eyes. Seeing the young widow always seemed to trigger an outpouring of emotion from Zack's normally unaffected demeanor. He caught Virginia by surprise each time. Her heart, too, went out to this young family and the loss of a good, strong man.

In the distance, Kyle and his two sisters were patting Zack's horse. The guard who'd accompanied Virginia and Zack held the animal in position.

Standing a good foot taller than Lucy, Zack peered at her with concern. "Have you been getting enough rest and sunshine?"

"As much as I can."

"Did you make it to the picnic on Sunday? You've always enjoyed the quilting contest the Mounties' wives—"

"I wasn't invited." Untying her bonnet, Lucy tried to act casual. But her fingers slid on the knot and her lip trembled.

"Wasn't..."

Lucy pressed her jaw together and attempted a brave front. "I think people confuse mourning with isolation."

Virginia's chest squeezed with Lucy's obvious sorrow. And yet, wistfully, she understood how difficult it was for some women—the other wives—to pass Lucy over for company. How painful it must be to have a constant reminder that the terrifying loss Lucy had could happen to them.

"I'd love to have you to the ranch sometime for tea," said Virginia.

Lucy smiled. "I'll keep that in mind, but I hear you're busy with your appointments and I don't want to be a bother. Come along, children, the commander's asked us to join him and his wife for lunch."

"Lucy, I'm sorry," said Zack. "I'll speak to the other men about their wives—"

"No, please, I don't want to push myself on anyone."

"Well then…you'll come to the barn raising at the ranch Sunday after next, won't you? The men get awfully hungry working from dawn to dusk. We'll need a lot of food, if—"

"I know what you're doing." Lucy's mask of discomfort faded. She broke into a wide grin. Her long ruffled skirt swirled around her boots with her excitement. "I'll bring buckets of my potato salad. And corned beef and pickled beets."

Zack squatted into the courtyard grass to Kyle's level. "And I was wondering if this young fellow would like to visit the ranch tomorrow. I need to do some target practice with my sore arm, and I think he's about the right size to help me out."

Kyle flicked his hand on his overalls and ran his tongue into the pocket of his smiling cheek, trying to hide his pleasure. "Pa used to call you Bull's-Eye."

Lucy put an arm around her two daughters, dressed in matching pinafores. "He's a lot younger than my girls, so he's only got half days of school. Is one o'clock fine, after his studies?"

"I'll send one of my men and keep watch for him."

When the Peters family bounced away to their lunch meeting, Virginia turned to Zack. Beneath the rough skin and block of muscled flesh, he had a pliable spot which he hid, evident in the tenderness he'd just displayed to Lucy.

His face was shadowed by the brim of his hat. It took several seconds for her eyes to adjust to the set expression and angled brows. She was getting used to that cocked half smile of his, but never to the whirling effect it had on her, the tug at her sensibilities and resulting sparks of curiosity.

With his brown hand resting casually on his hip, a flare of desire springing to his eyes, she sensed the potential thrill of arousal in coupling with this man.

She'd never allow it, she warned herself. Men might treasure physical union without a union of the spirit, but she would never surrender her defenses to him again.

Even the commander knew they weren't good for each other and had revoked his permission to marry.

If and when Zack tried, she would never succumb to kisses number two or three.

Oh, yes she would, her heart pounded back.

Virginia had never seen Zack stripped to the waist. At least not while he was standing and conscious.

She opened the kitchen window to welcome the afternoon breeze and watch with anticipation as Zack and Kyle practiced targeting in the garden below. A smile snagged her lips as the young boy unexpectedly unbuttoned his own shirt, removing it to imitate his hero.

At Zack's request, Uncle Paddy had tended to Zack's injury all this time. She'd tried not to feel slighted, but those feelings surfaced.

Despite her argument with him this morning, Zack had removed his sling. The stitches were gone from his shoulder, but the scar tissue and deep dent in his flesh would always remain. The rest of him—acres of golden skin, his broad chest tapering into a V waist down to his tight black breeches, riveted her. His suspenders, having slid off his shoulders to hang at his thighs, dipped with his graceful movements, as graceful as a dancer in a ballroom.

She rinsed the lemon she was carrying in the kitchen's water basin, plopped it on the cutting board in front of the window and sliced. A ribbon of lace from the square-cut neckline of her blouse fluttered, twirling against her skin, making her senses come alive.

She shouldn't watch him.

But holding out became impossible and she glanced up. Although invisible from the window and to the men inside, her laundry hung on the line behind Zack and Kyle. If she'd known Zack would be arranging his tin cans on the cedar fence behind the garden, she never would have rinsed her blouses, nightgown and underclothes to hang them six feet from his nose. She'd considered the vegetable garden her sanctuary.

She'd made arrangements with the cook that she'd tend the plants today, and had strung a short rope between two aspens by herself. Now she'd have to find a way to remove her intimate garments without drawing more attention to them.

Cool tea with sugar and lemon slices, she figured. It was on its way to Zack and Kyle, where she'd then slyly collect her laundry and return inside.

Placing two full glasses into a clean but scratched metal basin that she'd use to gather her laundry, she lifted it and headed outdoors.

The letter she'd received this morning crackled in her apron pocket as she tottered on the path's sturdy steps. The inviting smell of the rich earth, the wild shrubs and huckleberry bushes offset the turmoil catching in her breath. There was nothing she could do about her parents' disappointment over *"yet another broken engagement."*

She'd make her own decisions in her life, and she'd never devote herself to a man again unless she deemed him worthy of her devotion. Spending time with a man was the only way to discern it, not by silly prearrangement.

Instilling herself with patience as she drew nearer to Zack and his nakedness, she told herself that physical attributes meant nothing.

He hadn't hesitated to tell her in a roomful of her friends and bridesmaids, *"I don't want this marriage. I don't feel anything for you. Not now, not ever."* How easily the words had slid off his tongue, while she'd stumbled to collect fallen bread rolls from the floor. He could have included *her* in his plan or been much gentler by saying it in private.

Five years of abstinence would do her good.

"You're too young to shoot a gun by yourself," Zack was telling Kyle as she drew closer. "First you've got to learn how to take care of one. Clean it and load it and practice your aim."

"Can I clean this one?" asked Kyle.

"Sure. Take this little brush between your fingers, roll the barrel up and out."

Kyle struggled to put his small hands where Zack's large one had been but couldn't quite balance all fingers. Zack grinned, squatting beside the boy and showing him exactly how to do it. The boy was quiet and serious.

"Here you are," said Virginia, sliding the drinks from her tin basin onto the top of a sawed log, hoping to disappear without being noticed.

Zack looked up in her direction as she swung around to duck from sight.

"They're not dry yet," Zack called behind her.

She swung back, frowning at the drinks. What did he mean?

"The laundry," he said smugly.

Why did he always have to grate beneath her skin? It maddened her that he could size her up this easily, that she was so transparent. She wouldn't let him know the wet clothes bothered her. "I'm *not* after the laundry."

He took large steps and covered the ground between them. "Then why the big basin?"

Kyle ran out of earshot, twenty feet away to resurrect the fallen tin cans to the fencetop. Morning-glory vines curled their way up the cedar slats. Lily of the valley poked through the loam flower beds in addition to prairie crocus and wild rose. Scents of summer life filtered through the air.

"I was—I was afraid I'd spill the drinks. That's why I brought the basin."

Taking another step closer, Zack lifted the ribbon of lace from her bodice and slid it smoothly between his fingers, his eyes lingering on her flesh.

"I like this." He said it as if he had every right.

He'd barely grazed her skin and her impulses shot to warn her. Stepping backward, she stumbled to find her footing.

His words rang out in the wind as she fled. "I'm glad you didn't come for your laundry, because your petticoats are still damp along the ruffles."

She spun around. "You swine," she whispered.

He raised his head, seemingly amused. "And the cups of your corset haven't quite dried. The rosy one looks like it has, but the pale blue one doesn't."

"Where's your decency?"

The black eyebrows quirked; sunlight hit one side of his newly grown sideburns, making him appear almost like a black-eyed stranger. "Interesting nightgown. I knew it would be made of heavy flannel with a matching ruffle cap, but it's a little worn-out in the behind."

"Shame on you!"

"I thought you hung them there for me."

"For you?"

"On purpose, for my lonesome viewing pleasure."

"I'd like to hang *you* there on purpose," she hollered in the wind, stomping back to the house empty-handed. She slammed the kitchen door closed behind her.

"Don't worry, honey," he called through the open window. "I'll take them down before I come in!"

"Don't you dare touch them!"

Out of view, she placed a palm over her racing heart. She'd never had a man examine her intimate apparel and wondered how much the other men had heard. It would take her a while before she could look Zack in the eye again. She stood there a long time, listening, but never heard him return indoors.

Chapter Ten

The lady was a puzzle. One minute Virginia was cooing softly to Kyle—a warmhearted doctor tending to a child's stomachache resulting from too many gulped berries—the next she was a ferocious tiger daring Zack to cross her. Zack watched with unabashed humor as she collected her laundry just before suppertime when all the men were called in by the cook. She shot *him* heated frowns of disapproval while he lingered on purpose to scrape mud from his boots on the back-porch stoop while daring to glance in the tiger's direction.

Despite their close proximity, she shied away from him for another three days. He *hated* when she ignored him. Hated when he shared a story around the crowded table and she sniffed with disinterest, hated when he suggested a horse ride to the end of the wheat field but she preferred to go with Travis, and hated when he began a conversation only to be answered with monosyllables.

On Saturday evening, a neighbor brought his pregnant wife to be checked due to a rising fever. Virginia assured them it was a mild summer cold, suggested a day of bed rest, then went outdoors for a stroll.

Zack found her in the garden, her lithe figure lit by a

sliver of moon. Dammit, she was wearing his favorite blouse—the pretty linen one that clung to her breasts with the square neckline pulled together by drawstring laces, whose ends fluttered about the hollow curves of her throat. Every time she wore it, he wondered with fascination what would happen if he tugged to release the drawstring.

Wearing a freshly pressed shirt tucked inside his breeches, he followed her around the garden path.

When a twig snapped beneath his knee-high Mountie's boot, she turned up at him. "Please leave me alone. I need a breath of fresh air and then I'll come inside and go to my room like a good girl."

He took in the rope of black hair, the tension in her shoulders, the expanse of milky skin above her breasts. A tiny gold chain with a simple pendant caught the moonlight and glistened on her chest. "You know I can't do that. You need safekeeping."

She motioned to the bunkhouse, smoke rising from its chimney, a holler of voices cascading through its log walls. "I recognize the faces of all of the men who work here. And...and if someone approaches me, I don't know, I've got that little derringer you gave me tucked inside my pocket."

He looked down at the lump in her skirt. "Yeah, but could you use it? You didn't aim it on me just now. You'd wait till the last minute. Till you knew for sure you were in danger before you pulled the trigger, and then it'd be too late. You're too softhearted."

Moonlight flashed in her eyes. "And you're too cold."

He stiffened at the slight, imagining she was referring to how cold he'd been with her in breaking their engagement.

"I can't stay jailed up for another night. I need to

stretch my legs. And you've got guards posted at the gate and the four corners of the ranch.''

''Between the Mounties, farm laborers and stablemen, forty-seven men a day come and go around us. If someone really tried, they could sneak by unnoticed for five minutes. *I* could do it.''

He was right. He was *always* right when it came to his work.

And apparently, she thought she was always right when it came to hers. She began walking, with him looming at her side. ''Why aren't you wearing your sling? You took it off too early.''

''It felt like a noose. I hate the bloody thing.''

''That's not a reason.''

''It's mine.''

''You'll ruin your bones.'' Briskly she rubbed her arms up and down in the slight chill. ''The sling was supporting the weight of your arm. I'll bet your neck and shoulder ache more since you removed it.''

It ticked him that she was right. ''You're a tiger when you want to be. Do you ever soften your blows?''

''Some people need to be told straight out. The ones who are a little *slower* to grasp understanding.''

''You're calling me slow?''

''If the cap fits…''

''A dunce?'' He twirled her around so fast he trapped the breath in her chest. With his large palms gripping the side of her arms, she was his prisoner for one glorious second.

Then he burst out laughing.

She swung free. ''It's not funny. Your health is a serious matter.''

''I have to admit, I did have to wear that stupid cap once or twice in grade school. You, on the other hand, probably sat up straight and never spoke back to the head-mistress.''

''I got good grades and I'm not ashamed of it.''

Since she'd mentioned his achy shoulder, he became aware of its throbbing. He slid out of his suspenders to release the pressure and was immediately rewarded with some relief. ''What was your favorite subject?''

She opened her mouth to respond, then thought better of it. ''You don't want to hear it. You're making fun of me.''

''I'm not. Let me guess…scientific studies. Biology.''

''How on earth did you know that? On your first guess, too.''

He laughed at how obvious it was. Cripes, she *was* a doctor. And he was an inspector, able to piece clues together.

''What was yours?'' she asked.

''Guess.''

''Hmm,'' she said slowly, studying him. ''Sports games.''

''Nope.''

''Geography. Your interest in travel is why you moved across the country.''

''Nope.'' He stared at her. ''Give up?''

She nodded.

''Then say uncle.''

''I will not.''

''Then my favorite subject will go with me to the grave.''

''Why must you be so competitive? For heaven's sake, *uncle*.''

''Singing.''

''*No,*'' she argued, breaking into a smile.

''Yup. I could make a fortune if someone recorded me

for the gramophone doing 'Camptown Ladies' on my harmonica.''

Her laughter filled the air and he realized how much he loved it. Something about the way she tilted her head and genuine affection radiated from her body.

Sometimes Virginia was easy to be with. Sometimes her step fell in line with his.

Moonlight shrouded their silhouettes and nestled them among the golden buildings—the three stables filled with horses and cattle, the chicken coop penned in with cedar logs to thwart weasels and skunks, and finally the row of stacked, quartersawn timber for the new barn.

"Must you always do that?"

"What?"

"Pull your suspenders off your shoulders." She glanced down at the way one suspender slapped against his thigh. Light grazed her cheeks and the movement of her throat. "It's distracting."

"I'm trying to find a comfortable position."

They passed the buildings and were weaving on a rutted path, one side filled with reeds reaching to her slim waist, the other side harboring an arching alley of willows and long-needle pines. Crickets and night birds called to one another. He heard an animal stop ahead at their approach, two shiny eyes glittering among the prairie grasses of an overgrown ditch. They were safe. It was the striped tomcat that lived on the next ranch, similar to one Kyle Peters owned.

Thinking of the young boy, Kyle, brought a steady smile to Zack. Every afternoon running, Zack had spent two and three hours teaching the boy what his late father had started. How to position the butt of the small rifle against Kyle's narrow shoulders and take pretend aim. He took care to explain in detail terms the eight-year-old was eager to learn—caliber, pistol, Colt Navys versus Enfields. The wider spray of a shotgun versus the tight shot of a rifle. Kyle's quiet sisters were harder to understand, being girls and older. Zack was grateful they had each other and their ma to comfort them.

He heard Virginia breathing deeply beside him. "Is there anything new on James Stiller?"

"A few things. We strung together the crimes committed over the past year, then kept going further and realized his gang's been active for longer than we thought. Possibly for three years."

"How do you know that?"

"He likes gold and jewelry. That's what his hits have in common."

"Did you discover…if any Mounties were involved?"

"Not for sure. Cameron Peters seems to have been on the straight and narrow—everything he's done and every place he'd been for the last three years checks out. That leaves Mitch Reid, Hank Johnson and Timothy Littlefield."

"Why can't you clear them?"

"I'm hoping like hell I will. Hank normally deposits part of his payroll into his bank account, but he hadn't been doing that for six months. We don't want to alert him that he's being watched, but we can't explain where his money's going. He doesn't own property and it's not at the bank. And in Timothy's personal things, which we were going to mail to his folks in England, we found a stash of pocket watches adorned with precious stones."

She stopped beneath a cluster of trees and stared up at the quarter moon. The sky was free of clouds and stars were visible. Dancing northern lights—a cluster of pinkish stars somewhere off in the galaxy—twinkled for what seemed like Virginia and Zack's private showing.

He loved Alberta.

"I've never seen that before," she said. "Is that aurora borealis?"

"Otherwise known as northern lights."

"It looks like a puffy strand of cotton candy trapped with a box of diamonds. It's magnificent."

And so was she. With her face turned upward, mouth slightly parted and wonder in her eyes, suddenly he no longer felt like talking about impersonal things, when the sky, the air, the scents breathed personal.

After a moment, she pulled away from the skyward view. She was standing near the back of one of the pine toolsheds. "And then what happened with Mitchell Reid?"

"He's been on a leave of absence for two months. Says he went trapping up north. *Alone.*"

"That's not so unusual, is it?"

"He's definitely a loner. But he went trapping north of Edmonton where the last bank heist occurred."

She raised her face to his. "Why are you telling me this? Why don't you keep your mouth closed like your commander does around me?"

He tried to keep his voice steady, but it came out hoarse and sentimental. "I'm not sure why. Except that when I look into your eyes, I see nothing but honesty."

His answer captured a sigh at the back of her throat. Her delicate gold chain shimmered on a sea of velvety skin. "You don't know how infrequent that is, in my line of work. Maybe telling you is my gut instinct."

Her pink lips pulled together softly. "You seem to do everything by instinct."

"Not everything," he said, slowly, deliberately. "My instinct now is to turn around, march you through the door and lock you in your room before I get into trouble."

She swallowed hard. "What kind of trouble?"

The breeze lifted her scent and carried it the six inches between them. He inhaled all that made her Virginia—her soap, her hair, her fresh skin. "You know what kind. The kind that robs you of your senses and makes you do things you don't understand. That you can't control."

"I told you before...." She blinked and a thud reciprocated in his heart. "Your kisses prove nothing." She whirled around, skirts puffing around her.

He *hated* when she ignored him.

And she'd taunted him enough.

He reached out with a solid arm and yanked her backward.

"What are you doing? Stay away from me."

"I won't. That was a dare if I ever heard one." He growled and spanned her body with his, crushing her against the boards of the toolshed. "What happens when I do this?" He murmured in her ear, then lowered his lips to her throat and with his mouth traced the fine gold chain and her flesh beneath it. She tasted salty and womanly.

"No," she breathed, pulled back, barely audible, trembling beneath his fingers. "Don't."

He tightened his grip on her waist. "I'll tell you a secret," he confessed, breathing, panting, his face pressed close to hers. "I've wanted to do this for days." His smooth fingers came up around her bodice, rolling the lacy ribbon of her drawstring neckline, winding it around his sure grasp, threatening to pull. "And you've wanted me to."

Their eyes met, hers frightened, his dangerous. If she had struggled, he would have let her go, but she seemed caught in a revolution of passion versus sensibility.

With a predatory instinct he tugged the ribbon. The neckline came apart and her rosy corset was exposed in near-darkness. With a smooth, capable hand, he finished what his fantasies urged him to do. He yanked on her stays.

Her breasts spilled into the night air. With a gasp of surprise at the quick speed of his hands, she slid back against the boards. Swollen, pointed breasts, her nipples the same color of her lips, greeted him. He hardened instantly, feeling the want take hold of his body.

Clenching her arms behind her back, he swooped down to kiss the point of her nipple. It was as sweet and soft as a peach. "Kiss number two."

She staggered beneath his hold, out of breath. "That's not fair. It was supposed to be on the lips, not—"

"We never agreed on lips."

"No one's ever—"

"Then it's about time I did." He swirled his tongue in a tantalizing circle around her nipple, then kissed the outer swell, trailing a finger from her pendant, swirling down between her breasts. He *saw* the response in her, the goose bumps, the little downy hairs rising on her skin, *felt* the shudder of urgency beneath his touch. "Tell me now I don't affect you."

She tried to free herself of his grasp but only succeeded in jiggling her breasts. "You...don't affect me."

He kissed the other nipple, sucking and rolling his tongue around the smooth disk, raising it to a swollen point, a hardened nipple. "Tell me now with my lips sealed against your naked breast that you feel nothing."

"I...feel nothing."

He kissed lower, tantalizing the soft round of her belly with his wispy kisses. She responded to him harder and with more fervor than he'd hoped for. "Tell me now."

"What are you doing? Where are you headed?"

"Lower..."

"You can't kiss me there."

"A man and woman can kiss anywhere they want."

"Not there. I've never heard of…no!" She broke free, a tumble of curves and skin, and flushed with a heated mix of dismay and anger.

When she ran, he had no choice but to let her. She did up her corset as she fled. He silently trod ten steps behind, watchful and guarding.

When she fled through the kitchen door, he stayed behind, hidden by darkness. With an unsure hand, he ran his fingers through his hair, fighting for stability.

He'd pressed her to admit how much he affected her but, in truth, it was the other way around.

She affected *him* more than any other woman he'd ever been with. Falling for her was too intense, too involved, too frightening to imagine. He could never live beneath a woman's thumb, to be in love and beholden, strapped and confined. Marrying her for convenience was one thing, but in love with her totally another.

He wasn't in love. He hardly knew her.

The game was over and Virginia had won. He'd make certain they would never share a third kiss.

Never.

A man and woman can kiss anywhere they want.

Standing with her back pressed against her bedroom door, Virginia felt her heart pounding beneath her blouse, breasts still aching from Zack's heated touch. She placed her face in her hands and groaned. She'd made a fool of herself.

She knew nothing about intimacy, primal acts, nor the natural, basest secret of the human race.

But now she knew everything about a woman's longing and curiosity, the thrill of being touched by a willing hand, the delicious coaxing of a man's graze. When Zack had pressed his moist lips against her nipple, the feel of his exploring mouth caused her senses to explode with erotic hunger, a need for him to keep exploring, keep kissing and licking and trailing his fingers where his fingers should never be.

Was she a prude for escaping? Or an easy target, a wayward woman he thought he could control with his deadly looks and easy charm?

Casting a glance to the window to ensure the curtains were drawn, she unbuttoned her blouse and tossed it onto her bed. Next came her corset, the stays of which she hadn't been able to fully close while she'd run. As she slid out of the contraption, the flutter of her hot fingertips against cool skin felt good.

She ran her fingers over her skirt, unbuttoning the side and letting it drop to the floor, revealing a heavy layer of cotton petticoats. Those came off, too, followed by her bloomers. Finally, when she bent over to remove one thigh-high stocking, she caught the reflection of her body in the full-length mirror tucked inside the corner.

She straightened and looked at her reflection, bare except for white stockings that clung over her knees to halfway up her firm thighs, held in place by a ribbon tucked around the edges.

This is what Zack had wanted, she thought, staring at the curve of her breasts, the planes and angles of her abdomen, up the length of her legs and resting on the triangular mound of curls. She pressed a hand beneath each breast and tugged upward, enjoying the slippery feel of the weight, running a thumb over the points, staring at her body the way Zack might. Rosy nipples hardened even as she watched, heavy breasts swollen and ripe, thinking of where his mouth had roamed.

And he'd wanted this. She trailed one hand over the expanse of her stomach, knowing that had she let him, his fingers would have trailed lower.

She could never let him. And yet when she heard his boots thud in the hallway, her heartbeat blasted to the sky and the slow heat of arousal began to throb.

The sound of his door latch closing echoed in the stillness.

If she slipped into his room this minute, naked and willing, she knew she'd soon discover all the carnal secrets he wanted to teach her, but how could she walk away then? He could take her and then simply discard her, as he had before. That would surely be more horrible than a broken engagement.

Glancing back in the mirror, she knew she had more dignity than that. Shame rose to greet her. She was unmarried and they were uncommitted.

But heaven help her, she longed for Zack to kiss her anywhere he wanted.

Chapter Eleven

"**V**irginia! Virginia!"

Millicent Gray's shouting scattered the preening black-birds from the fifty-foot cottonwood in the front yard and jarred Zack from his morning cup of coffee. He threw open the ranch-house door, then leaped off the porch when he saw Paddy's housekeeper bouncing in on Paddy's new leather buggy, careening up the path and yelling at the top of her voice. Several other men broke with their outdoor chores to join them.

Zack dived to her horse's bridle, calming the sweaty beast. "What is it, Millicent? Where's Paddy?"

"He's—he's not here. I need Virginia. Young Diana Peters has taken ill. Lucy's worried sick."

"What's wrong with her?"

"Burning throat and fever. Maybe...maybe diphtheria."

Zack's compassion surged. The poor family. After all they'd been through with the passing of Cameron Peters, they didn't need another death in the family. But he fought his sentiments as he always did when he was dealt a problem.

"Lord, no," said Virginia, coming up from behind,

clutching a basket of gardening tools. Her white cowboy hat sat tilted over her brow, shielding her from the sunshine, the top of it reaching to his eye level. "Uncle Paddy told me someone passing through town on the stage had come down with it, but we were both praying it wouldn't root itself here." She tugged off her gardening gloves, yelling to one of the Mounties. "Please get my medical bag. It's in my room on the dresser."

As one Mountie raced for it, Zack sprang into action and called to another man. "Saddle my horse!"

Virginia scooted to the other side of the polished conveyance. "Travis could accompany me."

Her distancing tactic was obvious. "Travis is off today. He and his brother have some family thing to attend at Quigley's Pub. But *I* can handle you."

His stare was bold, but she gave in first and looked away. She looked as if she'd slept well despite what'd happened last night between them, whereas he felt groggy from focusing on the ceiling for hours. But he pushed those thoughts out of his head to concentrate on how to help the Peterses.

The mare settled. Zack released its bridle.

Virginia threw herself into the buggy alongside Millicent. Shiny springs creaked. "Has Uncle Paddy seen Diana?"

"No, he's…"

"Tending to someone else?" Virginia finished.

"Yes," said Millicent. Then, "No, he's unable…"

Virginia shook her head with disappointment, glancing to Zack with a glum expression. "He's been drinking."

Millicent cast her glance downward. Her tightly woven bun was coming loose, strands of light hair framing her wrinkled face.

"What's his medical bag doing in the bottom of your buggy?"

"I thought I could see Diana and then inform Paddy of…of her condition. He told me what to look for in her throat."

That was odd, thought Zack. Since when was Millicent Paddy's medical assistant? She'd probably seen a hundred different treatments in her years with him, but it was more likely she was trying to cover for his bad behavior.

Virginia gave a brisk frown of disapproval. "Have you seen Diana then?"

"No, I…I realized I don't know much about medicine. I took the chance you'd be here and able to leave the ranch."

A door slammed. The man with Virginia's bag raced from the house. When he planted the bag on Virginia's lap, she clicked her tongue for the horse. "Let's go."

"Wait a minute," said Zack, planting his hands on his hips, fingertips brushing his holster. "Wait for me."

"You'll have to catch up. *Let's go.*"

Zack's mouth dropped open in the cloud of dust they left behind. How had this happened? Of course, she had to help, but he was supposed to guard her.

He dashed toward the stables as a stableman brought around his stallion. Throwing himself into the saddle, Zack took two minutes to fly across the narrow path nestled in the wheat fields, taking a shortcut to meet the buggy along the road. The stallion's muscles strained beneath his thighs, the well-oiled saddle squeaking with the rhythm.

The Peters' home was on the other side of town, eight miles away. It took them close to an hour.

When they finally pulled up, Kyle and his other sister, Beatrice, the twelve-year-old, were playing with sticks beside their apple tree. On the five-acre property behind them, a dozen sheep grazed the grass—a source of income and occupation for Lucy when Cameron had gone off to work.

Kyle hollered, "Ma's in the house."

Virginia climbed out of the buggy and shouted back. "How are you two feeling?"

"Okay," said Kyle with a fearful shiver in his voice. "It's Diana who took sick this mornin'."

Virginia raced to the cabin door, then twirled around so fast her skirts whipped around Zack's boots. "Stay outside with Millicent."

He gave her a warning glare.

"Don't argue. Diphtheria is contagious."

Dammit, why did he never win with Virginia? "I'll be right here on the stoop if you need me."

"That's still too close. That apple tree over there is fine."

"Right. Right. The apple tree."

She nodded and disappeared through the door. Seeing that Millicent was occupying the two children as they watched the flock of sheep, Zack took a hike around the log cabin. It was highly unlikely anyone had trailed them, but he was taking no chances.

A dilapidated lean-to occupied part of the backyard, as well as a pile of old wagon rims, rotting baskets, a pile of branches and half-cut logs. Had Kyle been practicing his hand at sawing firewood?

Good grief, thought Zack. The last time he'd been here, a year ago last summer with Cameron as he'd said good-bye to Lucy before a seven-day trip to the southern border, the place had been immaculate.

She was a widow and no one at the fort had thought to ensure someone was looking after her and her children's day-to-day needs. Zack had just assumed she was being looked after by someone else at the fort. A sense of shame rifled through him. Rolling up his sleeves, still with one eye on the children and another on the cabin, he stacked wood.

Twenty minutes passed. He was swinging the ax and chopping more wood when the commotion started. He heard the front door creak open, the children hollered "Ma," and he left everything to jump in that direction.

When he turned the corner, Lucy was weeping. Zack's heart tugged with sorrow. He was unaccustomed to dealing with such emotions, but Virginia threaded a comforting arm around Lucy's shoulders, leading her to a set of splintered benches. "Sit, Lucy."

The children sobbed. "Diana's gonna die just like Pa," said Kyle.

"No, no," said Virginia. "Your mother's crying from relief. It's not diphtheria. It's that summer influenza that's going around."

"How do you know it's not that awful disease?" asked Beatrice.

"I could tell when I looked down Diana's throat. If she were really sick, her throat would have been gray but it's not. It's pink."

They began to giggle with elation, mixed with more crazy tears. Zack's chest loosened with overwhelming relief.

While the children threw themselves into their mother's arms, Virginia explained further to Zack and Millicent. "Diphtheria presents as a thick gray membrane formed inside the throat, making it difficult for the child to breathe. Usually the youngster will die of a weakened heart, but that's not what Diana has."

"It's pink, it's pink," repeated Beatrice.

Virginia explained Diana's care to Lucy, and Zack stared with respect at the young doctor sitting in the sunshine, fresh out of medical school.

Virginia kept a cooler head than many men would, given the brutal circumstances of the illnesses and injuries she treated. In Zack's line of work, he never felt sorry for the vicious criminals he dealt with, only for the victims he rarely knew. In Virginia's work, her patients were all victims, victims of circumstance, and each required a loving hand.

He could never be a doctor.

As Virginia wrapped a tender hand around Kyle and Beatrice, it reminded Zack of a memory he hadn't thought of for a dozen years. In Niagara Falls, there had been a fuzzy black pup that'd followed her around one summer. She was about six, he recalled, and every time she left the hotel to play in the back alleyway, that wild pup would surface and nip at her heels. No one else's, just Virginia's, and he remembered wondering what her secret had been. Most likely a pocket full of table scraps. Or maybe it'd been the difference in the way she'd treated the animal. All the other children had acted like the playful, energetic children they were, frolicking loudly around the puppy, but Virginia had been quiet and serene as she set the pup on her chubby little legs and patted its fur for minutes at a time.

There was a serenity about her now, sitting in the center of a storm of distraught people, not knowing why or how she soothed them, only that she did. And this time, just like the black pup in Niagara Falls, it filled Zack with tranquility.

He brushed his denims with his hands and peered down the grassy road. Why did he always get sentimental around Virginia? It was a sign of his weakness.

"Lucy, with the things you have to deal with," he said, "you shouldn't be staying alone. Is there someone in town you could stay with?"

"I don't want to leave the ranch. The children love it here and minding the sheep gives us something to do. The school's a short two-mile walk."

"But you're isolated all day."

"No, my sister comes in for two hours each morning. She's the one who went into town to get Dr. Waters. In the afternoon, the elderly couple over the next rise come by to help corral the sheep and keep us company."

Zack teetered on the edge of uncertainty.

Lucy added, "If I shot my rifle, a dozen Mounties would race here to respond."

That made him feel better. The police responded quickly to the sound of all gunfire. It wasn't that Zack felt Lucy was in physical danger, but heartsick trauma from losing her husband and having to deal with emergencies, as she had today, might cause her loneliness.

Millicent removed her hand from her pocket. "I'll stay with her till this afternoon when the neighbors come by."

Virginia smiled and agreed and packed her things to leave. "Can I speak with you a moment, Millicent?"

They stepped to the buggy. Zack followed.

"Where's my uncle at this moment?" Virginia squared her hat atop her head. The sleeves of her blouse were rolled up around her elbows, exposing a flash of smooth skin.

"He's at home, I believe."

"How often have you had to cover up for him?"

Millicent winced. Her Scottish brogue got thicker. "A coupla times in the past two months."

"That has to stop. It's not safe for patients. Thank you for coming to get me on this occasion—it was the right thing to do. Please come and get me in future emergencies. I'll speak to my uncle about trying to shirk his—"

"Please don't be hard on him."

Zack shook his head at the pitiful situation.

Virginia's eyes watered at the request. "Why is he drinking, Millicent? You know him better than anyone."

The elderly woman glanced at Zack, nervously adjusting the broach at the top of her flounced collar. "He's not drinkin' that much, only when…"

"When what?" Virginia grimaced. "Why is he ruining his work and reputation for a few hours of pleasure?"

Millicent's round cheeks sagged. "He's not drinkin' for pleasure."

"Then why?"

"He's drinkin' to forget about *his problem*. And he avoided helping Lucy this morning not because he didn't want to, not because he was drinkin', but because…"

"Because why?"

Millicent heaved a big sob. "Because he can't *see*. I've been beggin' him to tell you." Her shoulders crumpled with her sobs as she delivered the blow that turned Virginia pale. "His vision comes and goes. Sometimes he sees double. He's—he's got some sort of degenerative eye disorder. We've been writin' letters to doctors and professors all over the country seeking answers and solutions, but there's no help. Your uncle is going blind."

When Virginia felt Zack press the cool washcloth against her forehead, she realized she hadn't spoken for a solid ten minutes. She lowered her head, trying to hide her anguish, but the sense of loss she felt for her uncle battered her heart.

"Are you feeling better?" Zack crouched down by her seated figure on the wooden bench, beneath the windblown apple tree. Her spewed skirts spilled between them as Millicent watched. Lucy had taken the children indoors to talk to Diana.

"A little, thank you."

Virginia nodded weakly, took the cloth from his fingers and passed it over her eyes. Cool moisture seeped into her skin, reviving her. Her feelings were too raw to discuss. How could her beloved uncle, the man she admired more than any other, who'd shown her a love of medicine so strong that she'd followed in his footsteps, be going blind?

He was going to lose the very work that he cherished, that he lived for.

"Are you sure you can ride back? We'll need to double up on the horse. Or maybe I should take you into town to see your uncle?"

"No...I...I'd like some time to adjust before I see him. I don't want him to see me weepy."

Virginia heard a sob and glanced up to see Millicent wiping her tears with a scrunched handkerchief. There was more here than the sorrow Virginia felt for her uncle—Millicent's agony was palpable. The woman was deeply in love.

Virginia rose and comforted her, while Zack stood by with his hands tucked inside his pockets, looking as if he wanted to help but not knowing what to do.

"How long have you known?" asked Virginia.

Millicent stared at the handkerchief pinched between her fingers. "About four months. I keep tellin' Paddy that if Ian can do it, so can he, but for some reason that upsets Paddy more."

"Maybe he's not ready to be compared to Ian."

Millicent shook her head. "Paddy will be angry when he finds out I told you."

"I'm glad you did. I'll talk to him soon. Maybe there's something I can say...or do." Virginia tried to appear confident, but inwardly she hadn't a clue what she'd say.

Zack stepped toward the elderly woman. "Are you sure you're able to stay behind with Lucy?"

Millicent nodded. "I told her I'll bake an apple pie while she spends time with the children. It'll do us both good."

They said their goodbyes to everyone, and twenty minutes later, she and Zack were walking alongside the horse, weaving back through the fields. By the angle of the hot sun, Virginia figured it was close to noon.

With the reins hitched loosely between his fingers, Zack looked over the horse's nose at her. "I think you should get into the saddle. Otherwise it's going to take all day. It's another seven miles."

"In a minute. I need to move my legs. They're still shaking."

He reacted to something he saw in her, the honesty in her words, the tremble in her tone, for the crease around his eyes softened, his mouth tugged into a soft, friendly lilt, and those chastening dark eyes glittered with compassion. He crossed the path in front of the horse to walk along with her, looping one masculine arm around her shoulders.

The gesture was the friendliest one he'd ever offered. A link between two friends, one trying to comfort the other over horribly sad news.

And for one brief moment, desperation left her.

She should tell him to pull away, tell him not to overstep his bounds, but the soothing weight of his muscled arm pressed against her shoulder blades, its heat seeping into her blouse and skin was the most relaxing, tempering touch that had passed between them.

She'd always been the one to do the comforting and the soothing, and couldn't recall ever feeling like this.

As if she wasn't alone in the world.

She pressed her head into the crux of Zack's shoulder and inhaled the blissful scent of his black leather vest.

"I should have noticed my uncle was having difficulty with his sight."

"This isn't your fault."

"But I—I've been so caught up with my own problems, I barely looked at him for the past two months. Never looked him directly in the eyes, always in a hurry racing from room to room and patient to patient. I should have noticed something by his gaze."

"There's nothing you could have changed."

"But if I'd seen it sooner, I wouldn't have accused him...gotten angry with him for drinking. I should have noticed that he was wearing thicker and thicker eyeglasses...and last week when he dropped by at the ranch, I should have noticed he was using a magnifying glass to read with, on top of using his spectacles."

"But you were injured yourself. Is there any medical treatment for your uncle? Tonics that can help?"

"I'm afraid not. Many older folks suffer from eye diseases and there's nothing we can do. I've heard tell of surgeons experimenting with new procedures—"

"On an eye?"

"Nothing successful. Ian Killarney is willing to try surgery for his cataracts, but there's nothing anyone can offer him. The lenses of his eyes finally grew thicker and murkier until he could no longer see."

She took a deep breath, still walking in Zack's arm.

"The eye is like a little sphere filled with fluid. Surgeons in this country have tried replacing the lens with one made of glass, but the glass is so heavy it sinks to the bottom of the eye.''

"Good grief. They slice the eye to do that? Isn't that excruciating?"

"They smear cocaine on the area and it numbs it for surgery."

Zack paused, walking alongside the horse. His grip was firm around her waist. "You keep a lot of information bottled up in that head."

"But I won't be able to help my uncle."

"The best way you can help him then is if you learn to deal with it. Accept it so he doesn't have to worry about *you*."

Zack saw her situation with such clarity. It *would* lighten Uncle Paddy's burden if the women around him didn't treat him with pity. Hearing the turmoil in Millicent's voice alone, day after day, had to be difficult.

"You're right. I'll try my best."

Again the feeling of camaraderie looped its way around the two of them as they stood among the wheat shafts, the leather straps of their hats dangling at their throats.

"I'm ready to ride," she said. "How shall we do this? Can you give me a boost?"

"I'll set you in the front, sidesaddle. Then I'll straddle the horse behind you."

She agreed, thinking he'd cup his hands below her knees so she could step into them and hoist herself but he surprised her by wrapping his hands around her waist and lifting her in one fell swoop into the saddle.

"Oh," she gasped.

By the tightening of his jaw and slight moan escaping from his mouth, she realized he must have hurt his already injured shoulder by lifting her weight.

"You shouldn't have done that—you've hurt yourself."

"I'll be fine. Lifting strengthens my muscles." He shoved his boot into the stirrup and swung up, flopping into the saddle. His chest pressed against her side. His legs rubbed against hers.

"Don't move till I slide out your skirt. It's pinned beneath my legs."

With breath poised, she couldn't move if she tried.

He lifted himself in the saddle and tugged her skirt from beneath his thighs, his face so daringly close all she had to do was turn forty-five degrees and she could plant her lips against his.

Heat rose to her face. She wished he'd hurry. She couldn't even don her hat, for its brim would hit him between the eyes.

He swung his arms around her body, one steely arm pressing into her spine, the other trying hard not to press against her breasts. "Sorry, I'll try to rearrange—"

A gunshot rang out, blasting the dirt a foot in front of them into a dusty cloud.

Her pulse exploded. *Danger.* The horse reared at the same time Zack cursed. "Hold on!"

How was she supposed to do that?

A second shot ripped the air, but because the horse had reared, it skimmed beneath them. *Someone was aiming for their heads!*

Zack threw himself over her, leaning into the horse as if he were riding alone, pressing his thighs against her knees and spurring the horse to run.

They galloped at breakneck speed, and she teetered on the edge of falling. She was sitting at an angle to Zack, and her body couldn't bend in the same direction as his. Zack braced her there with unbelievable strength, while all she could do was go limp and pray he had the power to hold her.

He controlled his stallion with the skill and ease of experience. Thirteen hundred pounds of animal flesh pounded beneath them while fear thundered through her veins. Zack glanced backward. She felt his body shift then saw his gun planted in a raised fist. She didn't know who was chasing them, but Zack took careful aim and fired.

"Dammit, I still can't shoot straight!"

He holstered his gun, then screamed into the wind. "Hang on! We're taking a shortcut!"

They made a sharp right and soared through the air. She felt the horse's hooves lift off the ground, saw the tops of a dozen pine trees, then felt the hooves land with precision on the other side of a gully. The impact nearly knocked the breath out of her.

The horse leaped down the embankment, then splashed into a riverbed. Instead of crossing the river, Zack led it back up the same side, fifty feet ahead toward a cluster of trees. "This'll fool them."

When they didn't hear anything, Zack slowed his horse to a trot and slowly angled uphill to view the other side. "It's two men on horseback," he whispered into her ear. "Looks like the same men who shot your bonnet. One horse isn't galloping precisely perfect—it's definitely the same horse and rider from that night. But now *they're* being chased."

His hold loosened and she lifted up off the horse, twisting her body to look between the horse's ears. "By who?"

"Two Mounties probably on patrol. They must have heard the gunshots." He peered toward Lucy's ranch. "I don't know if those men are alone. We can't go back yet.

We'll stay here for a while. Or better yet," he said, looking past her down the river. "We'll go to the dugouts."

"What dugouts?"

"When this land was first settled twenty years ago, the
settlers didn't have time to build log cabins right off. They
dug homes into the side of dirt hills. There are three of
them right up ahead."

They neared the gently rising slopes, which merely
looked like grassy mounds from a distance. But from the
river's edge, the openings that had once held a door, she
imagined, gaped in the sunshine. They were nothing more
than caverns now.

"Let's take the one in the middle. I'll tie my horse to
the tree by the first one. It can graze, unseen, while we
wait."

With capable hands, he grasped her waist and slid her
down to stand beside him. A flush rose to his jaw. He
glanced at the rim of her skirts. "You're wet from splash-
ing through the riverbed. We'll stay out in the sunshine
so you can dry."

She pulled away self-consciously, folded her arms
across her breasts and walked to the cavern opening. She
couldn't see inside for the darkness, but all was still. It
smelled like grass and earthworms. "How long do you
think we have to wait?"

"Long enough to ensure no one else is with them. If
we go out onto the range, we'll be sitting targets. Maybe
we'll wait till nightfall. It'll be safer. I can't shoot worth
a damn yet to protect us."

"Even though it's your left shoulder that was injured,
it affects the stiffness in your body and the speed and aim
of your right arm. Doesn't it?"

He nodded, sank into the grassy slope, unable to shield
his disappointment. He looked like a prize fighter stretched

out in the sunshine, boots peeking out from beneath long denim pants, muscles flexing beneath the fabric of his shirt.

"The one thing I've got that makes me good at what I do is my aim. Do you think it'll come back as good as it was?"

"There's no knowing for sure. Let's see how stiff it is." She wanted to comfort him as he'd done for her with her uncle. Dropping to her knees behind him, she tapped his shoulder. "You'll have to remove your vest."

He slid out of it, leaving him in a blue chambray shirt. When she placed her fingers on the cloth, it was warm and soft.

"Your muscles are stiff."

He moaned softly.

"You've got more than one thing that makes you good at what you do."

"And what's that?"

"Your aim, yes. And your vision, too. It must be acute if your aim is good. But there's also…the way your mind works. The way you piece things together. Then there's your quick response and…and I've seen the natural leadership you command in your men."

"This is the first time you've ever said anything good about me."

"It is?"

"Mmm-hmm."

She yanked on his taut muscles. They slackened beneath her agile fingers while he murmured in sheer pleasure.

His primitive reaction was uncomplicated, unfettered and simple. In turn it roused her.

To have a man react to her touch, her ability to simply ease his discomfort, held wonder.

"You know I won't ask you to stop." He spoke so quietly it barely rustled the air. "When you've had enough, you stop."

Had enough of Zack? *Never.*

Finally he leaned over and pressed his hand on top of hers, resting them both on his good shoulder. Then in one graceful swoop, he was on his knees and lowering her to the grass.

Their eyes locked, their breathing halted.

One unruly lock fell across his forehead, the one she'd noticed never stayed in place. She'd come to recognize many things about Zack—the tiny freckle by his left ear, the scattering of gold dust in his deep brown eyes, the scent of lather on his skin, every scratch on his hands while he drank his morning coffee.

"I never realized how beautiful you are until today when I saw you dealing with Diana, then the news of your uncle."

She swallowed the emotion that formed in her throat.

Zack ran a finger down the bridge of her nose, letting it wind down over her pliable mouth, tugging her lower lip in a strangely sensual way. "Hush...it'll be all right with your uncle...everything will work out..."

The promise was ridiculously simple, yet all she needed and wanted to hear. Zack's reassurance brought her to a warm, secure place.

Gingerly he lowered himself and kissed her throat, letting his lips slide softly over her skin. She shuddered in response.

"Was that kiss number three?" she whispered.

"And four." He kissed the curvy hollow beneath her ear. "And five." He slid an exploratory finger along the top of her collar, then kissed the tingling flesh there.

"And six." He found her mouth.

Chapter Twelve

For a moment neither of them moved except for the driving force of their lips. Virginia could barely believe that this powerful man, a Mountie who everyone held in such high regard, a master of brute strength and domineering will could have such gentle, coaxing lips.

And they were hers.

The sensation of mouth on mouth while no other parts of their bodies touched seemed to her such an intimate coupling.

When his palm came up, he splayed his fingers at her ear, stroking the hair at the base of her temple with his thumb, the faint whisper of contact jolting her like a bolt of lightning. Her heart, her pulse, her breath began to pound.

But he broke the kiss, gasping and pressing his damp forehead against her own, cupping her cheeks with his rugged hand while she reeled from being snatched away. "Do you know what you do to me, Virginia? You set my skin on fire."

Sunshine streamed onto his face, zigzagging around the tousled black hair, the firm brown cheek, the straight, proud nose. Midday heat warmed her clothed body, reminding her they were out in the open, the swirling river crashing over boulders, birds calling to one another in the trees.

She summoned her courage. ''I wish there weren't so many clothes between us.''

He pulled back to gaze at her face. ''You're so innocent,'' he murmured. *And you should stay that way,* were the implicit words he left unspoken.

''I don't want to be.''

There, it was out.

Smooth light swirled in the depth of his dark eyes. ''You tempt me. You really tempt me.''

''Teach me what I should know about men and women.''

His expression dampened. ''You can't talk to me like that.'' Abruptly he turned away and sat up on the grassy knoll.

''Why not?'' She sat on her knees beside him, skirts fanning. Had she been too direct, too obtuse, too clumsy?

''You can't talk to me like that and think I can walk away. I don't have as much control as you. I can't close my door at night and go to sleep as soon as my head hits the pillow. I can't shut my eyes to you across from the breakfast table.'' His voice grew low. ''And I can't breathe in the same room and not be affected by your breathing. So don't do this to me. I'm not some kind of hero.''

He wouldn't look at her, but rose instead toward his horse, leaving her with her mouth agape and senses kindled.

''I think it's almost safe to leave. It's been a good thirty minutes and there's no sign of anyone beyond the rise.''

Now he wanted to leave as soon as possible.

She hadn't thought of the consequences of what she'd

said. All she knew was how she felt. Zack had been her friend for these several hours, guiding her to the Peters' ranch, standing by and supporting her and displaying great compassion about her uncle. She couldn't deny she wanted Zack, but she knew as well as he that it was confusing.

Sunspots dazzled against his blue shirt, the breadth of his shoulders twisting as he walked toward the stallion, which he'd hitched to a faraway tree. He'd removed her medical bag to relieve the weight on the horse, but hadn't removed the saddle, she supposed, in case they needed to fly.

He patted the mount with a gentle hand and turned around toward her.

"I'm sorry," she snapped, clasping her hands together in the cradle of her skirt, watching her sleeves billow back and forth in the sun's rays. "I wasn't thinking. I was only *feeling.*"

Rising to her feet to try to camouflage her humiliation—at not only how direct her words had been, but by Zack's outright rejection—she reached for the back of her hair. The ribbon had loosened from her bun; hair tumbled wildly about her shoulders.

Walking with her back to him, a patch of shrubbery between them, she finished what she had to say. "For the first time since I left for college, I suppose...I didn't feel lonely. I thought our hearts had overlapped this morning, that we'd related in some stupid, silly way over the sorrow we both feel for my uncle. I thought...I felt...forgive me, I thought our sentiments were one."

"Virginia," he said gruffly. "Virginia, please turn around."

She couldn't. The lump in her throat, the sting in her eyes from the tears she was fighting drove her to finish untangling her hair. In a crowd of patients, she had no difficulty tending to the care of men—old, young and everyone in between. She felt no shame in examining their bodies and asking direct questions. But with Zack...

She was good with many, but not with *one*.

She pummeled the soft earth with her booted feet, walking as she combed her fingers through the long black strands, hoping as soon as she'd composed herself, she and Zack would leave this place.

By the time she heard his racing boots, it was too late to run. He tackled her from behind, jostling her to the silken grass. With a soft thud, she squirmed to face him. "What are you doing? Are you crazy?"

He pinned her down. "I told you, you drive me insane."

"You are insane! Let me go!"

"You asked me to teach you something."

"I've changed my mind!" She struggled to escape, horrified at his grip on her wrists, above her head.

"Have you?"

She stilled, looking for an out. "Yes."

Thankfully he released his hold and her hands slid lower to her sides. If he would lift his heavy body off her knees, she'd be free.

"Well, so have I." With a smile so fleeting it simply whispered at the edge of his lips, he raised his hands and ripped open her blouse.

"*Zack!*" Her hands flew across her exposed, pale blue corset.

"Virginia."

"You've ripped my clothing!"

"I haven't. Look down. The buttonholes on this blouse are too big for their buttons. I noticed it a few days ago when you asked the cook to teach you how to make apple dumplings.''

She noted he was right.

''Sometimes the fifth button down, the one around your breasts,'' he said, trailing one fingertip over her corset in circles over the hiding nipple beneath, instantly riveting her attention, ''weaves undone on its own.'' His finger stroked past the corset edge, over her chest bone to the base of her throat, while her body ached for his finger to remain above her nipple. ''Sometimes the one at your throat unclasps and exposes a neck I'd love to bite.''

''Then I must get new buttons! Bigger ones! Get off me!''

''Why?'' But he raised himself slowly. She rose up, sitting face-to-face, a breath away.

''Because...'' He was so obviously skilled with sex, and she so obviously unskilled. It struck her how meaningless this must seem to him, and how much weight and worth she would place on just a kiss, let alone anything more. Zack would hurt her, she knew he would. He'd take her heart in his hand and squeeze hard.

Her blouse slipped off her shoulder; she tugged it up. ''Because you did that with such expertise, ripping off my clothes, I have to wonder how many times—''

''I've never done that before.'' He stopped her hand with his own, allowing the white cotton fabric to brush lower, past her bare shoulder. An artery pulsed at his temple.

Her racing heart couldn't stop. It thundered in her ears, in her throat, in her chest. ''Never?''

Shaking his head, he tilted his massive body toward her, yanking at her blouse. He removed her arm from its sleeve, then the other.

As she met his appraising stare, she listened to the sounds swell around them.

Due to the shrubs, she could no longer see the horse, but she heard the ripping of grass as it grazed. She heard the trickle of water in the sunlight, the swishing of prairie grass, the hum of dragonflies, the groaning of the earth as it turned on its axis.

How could they be doing this, exposing themselves body and heart to each other?

"It's human nature," he said, almost reading her mind, bending her down to the grass to kiss her neck. "When two people care for one another, it's natural and giving, and it erases the sting of loneliness."

Zack was lonely?

She pondered what his life must be like—ten years on his own without a wife, always on the chase, always with dozens of men surrounding him but rarely a woman.

And then she lost herself beneath his expert touch.

His hands slipped from under hers and she felt the ribbon leaving her hair, his fingers winding a path to the back of her neck, nestling and stroking in the hollow. It was another place no one had ever touched her and she tilted her head to one side, luxuriating in his possessiveness. She felt as if her body would soon rebel if she didn't know—feel—more of him.

"No one can hear us, if you want to…be vocal."

What on earth for?

Would it be that painful that she'd need to scream?

His face buried in her neck and hers turned toward the crystalline blue sky. Not a cloud above. Even the sky vibrated with its beauty. He traced his hands over her chest, hands that were wider and longer and firmer than hers.

She closed her lids to enjoy the sensation, picturing him

with his eyes closed while he caressed her, weaving small circles down the middle of her cleavage.

He teased her with patterns of delight above her right breast, under her arm, over the curve of her biceps. Twisting her body, she laced her legs with his, met his lips and they kissed. Gentle at first, he explored her mouth, parting her lips with his tongue, seeking her response. It came naturally for her to respond, sliding her tongue next to his and touching, mingling, swirling in mutual pleasure.

Then almost with a viciousness, he grasped her shoulders and rose on top of her, his body pressed against her, entwined in one direction and then another as he slanted his face across hers to kiss her deeper, with a burning hunger for more intimacy. She felt his body, his center, growing rock hard and gulped in pleasure knowing that he was reacting to her. When his mouth slid lower down her neck, she arched her head so he could reach every part of her throat.

All pretense of self-control left him as he buried his hot lips in her curves.

One hand reached for her breast, first on top of the corset, then with a rapid untying of strings and knots he pried it open and let a breast spill into his hands.

The sensation of her warm smooth skin beneath the firm hold of Zack's masculine hand was a gift beyond compare. While he fondled her beating flesh, she kissed his cheek, his eyelid, his brow, the top of his head as he lowered himself downward. The scent of his hair and skin would stay with her forever.

A moaning escaped from his throat, almost as if he were in physical pain. Then he took her breast in his hungry mouth, suckling the tip in torturously slow motions. She responded with an ache that wove down her legs practically to her toes.

"How do you do that?" she whispered. "How do you kiss me there and make me feel it lower?"

"It's magic," he murmured with a smile.

Wonderful, sheer magic she didn't want to end. It made her tremble for him more, bringing a damp sheen to her skin, moistening the private area between her thighs.

"Let me see all of you." He looked up from her breast into her eyes, and that blissful, sensual yanking tugged through her nipples and her thighs again. He pulled apart her corset, letting the whalebone sides drift beneath her arms.

Her pink nipples pointed toward the sun, heating beneath the rays. Her skin was dented with red lines from the corset's stays. As he looked at her creamy skin, her breasts moving up and down with her breathing, his dark face tensed with wonder. "Virginia, you are something."

She was shy to acknowledge it. "Thank you. So are you."

"More," he whispered, gliding his fingers downward over the waistline of her skirt, unbuttoning the side panel then sliding four fingers into the band of her pantaloons.

A low moan of laughter and excitement caught at the back of her throat as Zack pulled off both items. They were left with her clad only in her parted corset and thigh-high white stockings.

Her heart pounded with life beneath her ribs, her skin flushed to a rosy hue, the grass beneath her naked bottom felt like velvet. She was naked with Zack in the open light for him to see every inch, every flaw, every raw desire that sprang through her body. She'd never felt such freedom.

With a yelp of hunger he ran his hand over her leg, pushing it into the air above them, running his hand down her foot, then ankle, then calf. "Leave these stockings on," he begged.

She would agree to anything. "Can you take off your shirt? I want to see you, too."

With a crooked smile, Zack raised himself off her body. Strong tan hands squeezed her hipbones, turning her slowly to face him as he traced the top of her thighs. She watched in stillness as his Adam's apple glided up and down. With a slowness that drove her wild, he undid the buttons of his blue shirt.

"Let me," she said softly, rising to her knees to undress him. Her white stockings would be stained with grass, but she no longer cared.

Her breasts swayed as she moved and he couldn't seem to get enough. While she slid off his shirt, he cupped a moving breast in his hand. A smile trembled on her mouth and she filled with the thrill of what would happen next.

With his shirt removed, his body glistened in the sunlight. The wide brown shoulders, the broadness of his chest, the texture of his bristly skin contrasted in every detail next to her smooth, slender breasts. On their knees, they kissed. She reached out and unfastened his pants, releasing the pressure on his erection.

He grasped her wrists before she could explore further. "Too much too soon. Lean back, I want to kiss your body."

The hard, hot thrill of his words reverberated through her. Zack caught hold of her arms and gradually lowered her to the ground. A shuddering breath fell from his lips as he flicked his tongue over her breast, not touching her nipple but driving her to a height of desire she had never thought possible.

She wanted him *now,* but he wouldn't let her have it. And that was part of his plan, she realized.

Her eyes drifted shut as she let her herself simply enjoy the ecstasy of Zack's touch. He pressed a palm along her heavy breast as she flattened hers along the angles of his chest. The hairs felt silky beneath her hand, his nipples smooth. His muscles tensed beneath her touch and he groaned with approval.

He moved his tongue lower. The shock of his hot mouth on her abdomen caused her to stiffen.

"If you don't enjoy it, you can tell me to stop."

Enjoy what?

"Oh…" She moaned with dawning recognition as his lips dared to drop farther, in the valley of where her thigh met her hip. *Enjoy his lips there.*

She couldn't fight him if she tried. She wanted this. She wanted him. It would happen.

Gently he parted her legs, and slowly she allowed him.

She was grateful that he couldn't see the multitude of expressions passing on her face—desire, urgency, pleasure, curiosity.

Would she always be so shy?

When he knelt between her thighs, her knees parted around his head. She clung to him and he took her to a world unknown, as pure as Mother Nature. When his tongue swept over her, gliding over the pink folds, she wondered if he'd pull away due to all the moistness.

"Relax," he whispered. "I'm enjoying this as much as you are."

The remaining tension in her muscles left at his assuring words. But tension returned doubly strong as he stroked her with his tongue, kissing, licking, sucking. She hovered on the edge of nature's discovery, the promise of something grand looming in the distance.

His tongue flashed in and out in a rhythm that sent her soaring. Her breathing stopped, she trembled, arching her body to meet his lips, and then her muscles exploded. Her blood raced, climbed a mountainous wave of contraction after contraction, with Zack's tongue steady all the while.

She released and screamed, surprising herself by the sound echoing softly off the whispering trees.

And then finally her body coaxed her down to earth. They stopped moving and she opened her eyes.

"That's what you meant by screaming. I thought you meant from the pain. I've never screamed in pleasure before."

His smile was one of unbelievable pride and accomplishment, which in turn caused her to smile.

He kissed all the way up her body until his mouth rested at her throat. She wondered what it would be like if he kissed her mouth now after what they'd just experienced. She thought she might turn away, but then he did kiss her lips and, to her surprise, it didn't bother her. She enjoyed the feel of Zack.

With a large nudge she pushed him over her side and he fell to the green grass on his back. With her hair draping across him, she splayed her legs and rested on his abdomen, her breasts swaying, her nipples brushing against his hot chest. "And now it's your turn."

He gulped at the promise as she moved her hand behind her, cupping him with an exploratory hand, then stroking his erection.

He sighed and closed his eyes, giving her a thrill that she was pleasing him.

"Show me," she murmured. "Show me how you like it."

He smiled in the lazy, seductive way that flipped her heart.

"Shall I ride you?" she asked.

"I like the sound of that, but it'll hurt you less if you're on the bottom." With that, he tugged her down again.

"You're so wet for me," he moaned. "Hot and slippery. Ready and willing."

"So ready."

He knelt between her thighs, parted her damp flesh, then gently pressed his shaft to her opening. He thrust forward, partially filling her. He felt so big and she so small.

Her body stretched and she tensed. Instead of thrusting deeper, he stopped there, stroked the side of her breast, leading his damp fingers over her rounded stomach, making her think of the tingling pleasure instead of the pain to come. When her body relaxed around his, he thrust fractionally deeper, enough to break through her virginity. Pain sheered up her body and radiated through her belly.

He held her there; she didn't want to move.

"Is the pain so bad?"

"Yes."

His hands wrapped beneath her bottom, grasping the muscled cheeks, then moved slowly around her hipbones to hold her.

"It's getting a little duller," she groaned. And it was. It had been a flash of blinding pain, but no longer.

Zack started a rhythm again, moving so slowly she couldn't be certain he was moving at all, but then she felt his rocking. He took his fingers and slowly slid them against her private spot, the tiny circle of pink flesh. She didn't think she could find pleasure with this coupling, but when she allowed herself to unwind and relax into the soft grass, she went along with Zack's guiding hand.

The steady circling of his fingers provided a delightful shiver up her body. She pulled her legs into her chest and he obliged her by sinking in deeper.

She couldn't have climaxed again without his fingers being there, for all she would have felt was pressure. But the thought, the mental image of what they were doing drove her.

They wove together, heated and lost in each other's bodies. She *needed* what Zack had to offer.

"I love being inside you," he said.

He reached out and cupped her breast, tweaking a nipple. She rode the crashing waves again. Her muscles cascaded, flooding her with light and power.

When she felt Zack tense, she wanted to witness his peak. He closed his eyes and let himself go, one large hand on each of her knees, sinewy brown body flexing out of control, and changing her forever.

Chapter Thirteen

Zack felt the tickle of a butterfly's wing on his nose. He opened his eyes to warm sunshine beating down on his pant legs, with shadows of the dugouts playing on his bare chest. They'd been here for hours. The slanted shadows indicated it was three or four in the afternoon.

Virginia was pressed in close beside him, dozing lightly. He turned on his elbow and rested his head on his hand, gazing at her splendid form.

Her long dark lashes swept down over high cheek-bones. Moist red lips and strong triangular jaw lay loose and relaxed in sleep. Sighing, he looked lower.

Her beauty was astounding. She wore his black leather vest, white stockings and nothing more. Unbuttoned at the front and forming two deep Vs at her thighs, the leather parted, revealing the spheres of her breasts, hiding the tender nipples beneath. His eyes moved lower to her flat-tened white belly and thatch of curls. He fought the desire building in his body. Her curves still teased him, despite his weariness from making love to her another time before they'd both fallen asleep in the gentle wind.

He was insatiable when it came to Virginia.

He'd gone from vowing he'd never kiss her again to kissing her on every conceivable part of her body.

Kiss number one had been on the lips. Number two on the breast. And number three on her private spot, somewhere between here and paradise.

He hardened with the thought. He'd known other women, but the pleasure he'd found with Virginia was incomparable. No one had gotten him talking and laughing like Virginia had. It had always been an act of physical desire, silent mostly, but with Virginia...

What was it he was feeling? Whatever one called it, it had possessed him, and now he analyzed what he'd done.

So far, all he'd done was hurt her. He didn't blame her for being outraged at the way he *and* Andrew had treated her.

But Zack's heart raced with the terror of her expectations of him, fear of not being able to deliver what it was she needed. This afternoon he'd seen the caring look in Virginia's eyes, the doubts at first that gave way to a sharing and openness he'd finally pried from her.

But at what cost had he pried it? What could he promise her that he'd never been able to promise any other woman he'd been with?

And he couldn't forget Stiller.

By growing closer to Virginia, Zack was giving his enemies *more* power.

He was making Virginia more vulnerable. *Hell.* But surely there was a way they could handle Stiller.

She was counting on Zack. He'd seen it in her every gesture, every sound. Besides, he knew it deep in his soul. Counting on him for taking her and her heart to a place it'd never been before.

Well, his heart had never been there, either.

Love was what she wanted.

That's what Lucy Peters had gotten from her husband and that was all she was left with now.

Zack's heart squeezed with disappointment and a feeling of bone-deep inadequacy. He could *make* love to Virginia, but love from the heart was the one thing he couldn't promise.

They prepared to leave but Zack was still bothered.

"You've grown quiet, Zack. What is it?" Virginia tied the waistband of her pantaloons, then slid into her long navy skirt.

Zack enjoyed watching her, her dark oval face with the pretty freckle by her eye, her wealth of black hair, the animation in her movements. It was an odd feeling, tidying up after a session of lovemaking as if nothing had ever happened. And yet everything had.

Already fully dressed, he peered over the thrashing river. "I'm thinking."

"About what?" From her tender expression, he knew she wanted him to say *about us,* to discuss what had taken place between them, its significance and the changes that would occur because of it, but he couldn't. He just couldn't. If he opened his mouth, he was certain he'd regret every word. Until he sorted out what he intended to do, until he got a grip on Stiller's location, it was pointless to make promises to Virginia.

"I'm thinking that something about the third dugout smells different than the other two, but I've searched all three and can't find what."

She studied his face slowly. Her eyes flicked with disappointment. "Oh."

He was right. He was goddamn right. She had wanted to talk about *them.*

Pausing, he rubbed the back of his neck. "The floors

are covered in grass and mud. They've been used over the years by travelers, judging from the coal lumps and charred fire logs.''

She finished tucking in her blouse. Avoiding him, she tossed his leather vest on top of her medicine bag by the tied stallion.

He'd never be able to wear that vest again without thinking about her in it.

She was either too proud or stubborn to ask him directly how she felt about her. He wasn't sure how he'd answer if she did.

When it came to women, words didn't come to him easily.

So by instinct, he fell back to what he knew best. Work. ''The grass has partially grown over the fire. I'd estimate the last one took place about a year ago.''

She crossed her arms, weighing her words. ''Congratulations, Zack.'' Her tone was cutting. ''You're a master at fires. You're a master at inspection. You're a master at being a Mountie.''

But such a bloody disappointment as a lover.

He looped his fingers in his holster. ''Virginia, what went on between us meant the world to me.''

''But it's forgotten now and back to business.''

''I can't ignore what I do for a living. You need protection—''

She clamped a hand over his wrist. ''I need more than that.''

More than he could give.

When he didn't respond, she stalked to the horse and unhitched its reins from the tree. He shook his head with disillusion. It seemed no matter what he said or did with Virginia, it was always the wrong thing.

But it was getting late in the afternoon and the others

would be wondering where they were. He surveyed the dugout one last time. When he spotted a flat brown object flapping from beneath a pile of dirt, he walked toward it and yanked it out.

"How could you see that at your distance?" called Virginia. "Your arm might not be working up to speed, but you've still got your eyesight. What have you found?"

"A piece of burlap, most likely used to start a fire." Four charred letters stamped in blue ink were barely visible—*"toes."* Toes? There was also a jar lid and an oddly shaped piece of wood that had been whittled flat on one end, as if it'd been used as a lever to pry a lid.

He rubbed the dirt off the three items and stashed them in his saddlebag. They headed out.

Virginia swung into the saddle alone, legs astride, seeming perfectly content to let him walk.

"Move over," he called up to her. "There's no reason either one of us has to walk for miles."

She sniffed and slid forward in the saddle as far as she could. When he swung up beside her, he marveled at the tight fit, the scent of her loose hair blowing in the breeze, and finally the rigid stance of her spine, indicating that her anger might never abate.

Only two hours ago, they'd been wrapped in each other's legs!

The horse was well rested and watered so they galloped at a fair clip.

When they hauled themselves into the center of the ranch, men called out, "Where have you been? We've been looking everywhere for you!"

Zack dismounted first, intending to help Virginia but another man got to her and she preferred to accept *his* help.

"We had to hide. We were being shot at—"

"We know. We caught one of 'em."

"Who?"

"A young one, he is. Shame he's up to no good already. The good news is, he's one of Stiller's. The bad news is he won't give us his name. Says he goes by Coyote."

"My brother caught him," said Travis, coming up from behind. "Mitchell chased them for an hour and didn't give up till he brought the youth back, kicking and cussing. He's been put in the jailhouse, awaiting your questioning."

"Mitchell," Zack repeated softly. He turned in Virginia's direction and she stared back at him, also recognizing the significance. If Mitchell Reid had caught a member of the Stiller gang and had him jailed, chances were Mitch wasn't a part of that gang. Mitch hadn't shot Zack on the train that night. A huge relief engulfed Zack. He hadn't wanted to believe that Travis's brother was guilty.

That left two Mounties as suspects. The late Timothy Littlefield and Hank Johnson.

"Good work," said Zack. "There'll be no relief in this camp until Stiller is hanged high for the men he's killed."

With a look of repulsion, Virginia untied her medical bag from the saddle. Her forehead creased with tense lines. Zack hadn't meant to be crude, but the truth was the truth.

He caught up to her as she stomped to the front porch. With a grip on her arm, he reeled her around. "What do you expect, Virginia? When we catch Stiller, we're not going to throw him a celebration."

She wrung free of his hold. "I'm sick of being here. I'm sick of being told who I can see and what patients you'll allow me to tend today. Most of all I'm sick of this violence.''

"He'll get a fair trial.''

"I'm sure he will. But I'm still sick of it. And the thing that scares me is that you enjoy this. This chase.''

A cold knot formed in his gut.

"What happened to you, Zack? You were rough and wild as a child, but when you grew into a young man, you used to be such a gentleman, dressed in your fine suits, accompanying your parents on tours of the falls. You used to be a part of high society. Now what I see is almost…barbaric. Relentless and domineering. You take *what* you want, *when* you want.''

The insult cut him deep. He knew she meant not only his barbaric chasing of Stiller, but also Zack taking from *her* what he wanted, when he wanted. As he had this afternoon.

But they both knew she'd been equally willing.

"Life here is different than back East.''

"*You're* different.'' Her lips curled with distaste. "Now let me pass.''

He suddenly felt ill equipped to deal with Virginia. "I can't do that, not when you're this upset.''

She pushed past him.

"If you think…if you're bothered by…just know this. I claim no hold on you, so don't worry, you're still a free man.''

Virginia craved what she couldn't have.

Peering out from the kitchen window on the ranch toward the stables, donning her hat in preparation to visit her uncle, she settled her hesitant attention on the confident man striding into the stable's broad red doors. Zack.

She craved a return to normalcy, to feelings of security

that she was in control of her own destiny. She shouldn't have allowed him to kiss her, she shouldn't have allowed him to make love to her, and mostly she shouldn't have allowed the sorrow she felt for her uncle to soften what she'd felt toward Zack.

He'd given her the bit of comfort she'd sought, but now he was pulling away from her at a time when she needed him most. She had been harsh on him yesterday, but why couldn't he continue to talk to her, support her, ask her opinion on what needed to be done with her uncle and with their situation here on the ranch? How could he make love to her, *kiss her there,* and then ignore her?

Maybe he was used to treating women this way—ten years to chase any woman who'd caught his fancy—but never in her adult life had she so regretted what she'd said and done with a man.

She'd thought yesterday had made a difference to him.

She hadn't realized how much difference it would make to her. Much more than physical, it had been an emotional outpouring of feelings she hadn't been able to suppress. How could she be longing for a man who treated her as an…equal in bed but a subordinate in every other aspect of their lives?

She wailed inwardly. What was it that separated them? Maybe she'd been *too* harsh on him. Maybe it was *she* who needed adjustment, *she* who needed to develop more patience when it came to Zack's silence.

Maybe she should attempt the first step with Zack.

The screen door banged behind her as she flew down the sunny stairs, adjusting her straw hat with its dried plume of blue wildflowers, smoothing her crisp plaid dress. They were her best visiting clothes. The handle of her reed basket dug into her arm, overflowing with fresh herbs from the garden and six scones she'd baked upon rising with the guidance of the cook. The scones were overly cooked, but if Uncle Paddy ate them this morning, they wouldn't have time to get too rock hard.

Determined to bridge her animosity with Zack, Virginia raced toward the stables. How many times had he told her that giving in to him wasn't a sign of weakness? Maybe she herself was being just as stubborn and pigheaded as Zack.

Men drilled and cut timber along her path. Preparations for the barn raising were well under way, and the thought made her queasy. It was as if she were the mistress of the ranch, responsible for the social aspects of greeting the neighbors, coordinating the meals for the one-day event and planning the barn dance afterward. She had been surprised to know there'd be a dance.

Andrew and Grace had wired that they were coming. Virginia hadn't seen them since the horrible night of her broken engagement. Uncle Paddy was expected, bringing Millicent—and Ian, who was bringing his fiddle—and the secret problems they faced. Lucy Peters would be here in her fragile state, eager to make friends at a time when Virginia wanted to shy away from everyone. Then there were bridesmaids and groomsmen from the failed engagement, the thought of which still brought embarrassment to Virginia.

She squeezed past the stacked timber, the wooden pegs, the precut twelve-by-twelve cedars with the grooved slots. Everything was being carefully measured and cut beforehand so it could be pieced together in a day.

High atop his stallion, Zack rode out of the stables.

"Zack, wait for me!" The weight of the basket rocked against her. Cupping a hand above her eyes, she peered up at his staggering height.

He reined in his horse. "What is it?"

"I heard you were going into town and I'm ready—I'm ready to see my uncle if we could prepare the buggy. We could go together and talk about things—"

"I'm afraid not, Virginia." Every muscle in his unsmiling face flattened into a grimmer line.

Not another argument. Steadying her composure, she would explain herself, then the tender, gentler Zack she'd known yesterday would surface. He wouldn't turn her down after she explained her intentions. "Aren't you headed to the fort to see your prisoner again?"

"I am, but you're not coming with me. Travis is here and he'll watch over you." Zack motioned to the front porch from where Travis tipped his hat. "You got shot at the last time you set foot off the ranch, and I'm not prepared to take that chance again."

Calm down, she told herself, attempting another smile. "Then we'll get six other men to accompany us."

"We don't have that volume of men to spare. *Be reasonable.*"

"Reasonable?" Her eyes dampened and her chest tightened with the hurt of being reprimanded. "My uncle is going *blind,*" she whispered. "There's nothing reasonable about an illness that takes away the vision of a man who's devoted his life to helping others. He's the reason I went into medicine. Don't you see? This is one time *I* can possibly help *him.*" Her lips quivered. "I wish to speak to my uncle and I would appreciate an escort."

Zack shook his head as she stared in total disbelief. "Sorry."

It took all of her strength to suppress the urge to beg.

"Your uncle will drop by in the next few days like he usually does. You can talk to him then."

"Then I'll go without you," she threatened, not thinking of the consequences. Not caring. "I'll take a horse and go wherever I please."

He assessed her. "Yes, I reckon you could. But you'd be putting every man here in jeopardy, not to mention yourself."

She fought her rising temper. "The search for James Stiller could take months. You can't seriously be suggesting I stay put for that long?"

He didn't answer, which made her silently scream.

"What if an emergency arises? What if a patient needs me, like Diana Peters did yesterday? Especially now when you know my uncle isn't capable."

He turned toward the hazy horizon, miles of green and gold pastures. "We'll deal with that if it happens. But not today when your purpose is simply to socialize with your uncle."

Simply to socialize...? Her blood hammered in her throat. Zack had a way of trivializing her dearest wishes.

He galloped off alone, shoulders angled in renewed determination, dust kicking at his heels while she fought her indignation.

How had this happened? Since when in blazes was Zack Bullock running *her* life?

Chapter Fourteen

Fending off his wounded pride, Zack galloped into the center square of the fort thirty minutes later. He dodged two other riders and one wagon carrying barrels of fresh drinking water.

Why did Virginia distrust everything he offered?

The stallion's muscles strained as he hoisted himself to the dirt in front of the busy barracks. Headed to the jailhouse, he had pressing details to think about, not the unforgiving flare he'd seen in Virginia's eyes. Yet he kept returning to the troublesome image.

It only proved what a mismatch they were—Virginia pleading to see her uncle at a time when it was crucially important to her safety and his work that she stay fixed at the ranch.

He hadn't done the honorable thing by Virginia. He regretted ever setting a possessive hand on her satiny skin.

But every time he'd cast a runaway glance in her direction, he wanted to pull her to the grass and do it all again.

He should be horsewhipped for taking advantage of an innocent woman. Horsewhipped for aching to repeat it. And whipped for savoring the memory of her pliant body beneath his own. She might not have known how tangled her feelings could get, but he did.

And why the hell were *his* feelings so tangled? One minute he was dead sure of his goals—nabbing Stiller and his gang—the next he only wanted to pack her up and run away somewhere safe, just the two of them where he could protect her and save her and make love to her twenty-four hours of every day.

He'd never felt this way about any woman and it terrified him that he could be so controlled by a feeling that was uncontrollable. Maybe if he immersed himself completely into his work, he might escape his thoughts of Virginia.

"Hey there!" Zack waved across the courtyard of the grassy barracks. Hank was sitting in a wooden wheelchair, broken leg propped on a stool, playing checkers with the company clerk. Guilt washed through Zack. As well as being responsible for two men dead, Zack hadn't been able to prevent Hank's injury, either, and Doc Waters had mentioned that the leg may never heal up as good as it was.

"Hey!" Hank shouted back. "I've gotta ask you somethin'."

Zack strode toward the men seated in the shade of a quaking aspen. Round leaves clacked together in the wind, rustling the air like a background symphony Zack had heard on Doc Waters's gramophone the night of the broken engagement. Another weight of responsibility loaded on top of the first.

The clerk glanced up and nodded as Zack approached, then went back to the game. A canteen of water hung around the back of Hank's slatted chair, indicating he spent long bouts of time out here. A deck of cards sat on the grass, the town's newspaper folded to the society page written by David Fitzgibbon, a half-whittled wooden pipe with a folding pocketknife beside that, and just so no one would assume Hank was too tough, a clay dish full of oatmeal cookies.

"Help yourself," said Hank.

Zack bit into one. He could never resist a good cookie. "How're you feeling?"

"So good I want to ask you if I could help at the barn raisin' on Sunday."

"You've got a broken leg," Zack replied in surprise.

"I could work around the cuttin' tables. My arms are still strong. I could sort pegs, I could hammer at waist level."

Zack surveyed him. Was this a man capable of betrayal?

Hank squinted up at Zack. "Any particular reason why you don't want me there?"

Zack blinked. *You might try and shoot me in the back again. You might aim for Virginia this time. You might be a rotten bastard.* But maybe inviting Hank would loosen something in the stalemate between Zack and Stiller. Or maybe Hank was just another Mountie trying to feel useful. On Sunday, Zack would double his guard around Virginia and insure Travis never left Hank's side. "No reason. You're more than welcome."

But ten minutes later, as Zack entered the jailhouse, his gut tightened with warning. Something about Hank... something about his manner...

"Coyote, I brought you a cookie."

Slumped on the bed in the corner cell, the nineteen-year-old cussed. He was blond, small and thin. His face was marked with pimples. "Grown men don't eat cookies."

"Is that what your ma says?"

"You're not gonna trick me into tellin' you anything about my ma. You're crazy."

"I'm so crazy that if you don't cooperate today, I'm going to get the judge to keep you in this cage until you grow into a very old man. One with a long white beard, like Smithy here."

The jailkeeper laughed. He was an old retired Mountie nicknamed *Moses,* but useful as the jailer because there always seemed to be a shortage of men. "Yup, I reckon Coyote's got plenty of time to spare, him bein' so young and all."

"What's your real name?" asked Zack.

"I told you. I go by Coyote."

"Where do you live?"

"With Alice in Wonderland."

"Does Alice like rubies?"

The young man stiffened but didn't respond, and Zack knew he was on to something. "Does Alice like gold shipments?"

Standing up, Coyote cursed through the bars. Zack closed in, inches away from the youthful face and simply stared him down. Coyote couldn't hold Zack's cold, unwavering gaze.

Bull's-eye! Zack had figured it out this morning with Travis and Mitch after hours of sifting through maps and land documents and newspapers. There was a gold shipment coming across the Prairies in a week's time, headed to Vancouver to build the biggest opera house in the West—a target Stiller couldn't resist. It meant Stiller maybe had a tie to the railroads, an inner spy who fed him information, for the gold shipment was known only to top-level railway officials. And commanding Mounties, who for security reasons would usually only dispatch men to guard the car at the last possible minute as it wove across the land.

Dirk McGuire from the railroad station had to be involved, but Zack still had no evidence linking him. *Not yet.*

Zack thought about it while he quickly ran his other errands, stopping by Doc Waters's place then racing back to the ranch. Although he was anxious to talk with Travis, he needed to speak with Virginia first.

He found her in the private garden, winding green shoots of newly sprung beanstalks around sticks she was inserting beside the tender plants. If she noticed he was there she didn't let on, not bothering to look up or acknowledge him.

His pointed boots scuffed the dirt. "Your uncle says he'll be dropping by within the next two days on his visit to check on Mrs. Dickenson's gout."

"You spoke with my uncle?" Crouched into a ball, Virginia pushed back the brim of her white cowboy hat, revealing a clear, sun-washed face and ruby-red lips.

"Briefly. Only to ask when he'd be by next."

Virginia swung up to full size, long skirt swishing. Her sleeves were rolled to her elbows and the heat of the day must have gotten to her, for the hem of her skirt was tucked into her tight waistline. When Zack glanced down at her stocking feet, she must have realized the terribly personal positioning of the fabric. With a fluster, she yanked the hem out of her waist. The gathers fell to the ground.

He watched the swell of her breasts rise and fall, her collar tucked inside out at her neckline, exposing her peachy throat. She seemed to have forgotten that she'd tucked her collar that way, and he opened his mouth to tell her…then pressed it closed and swallowed hard as he watched a dribble of perspiration trickle from the side of her neck, where tendrils of black hair lay plastered in heat. The dribble wove down slowly, dipping down the V of her chest and losing itself behind a tight button on her blouse.

It was *that* blouse. The one that'd had small pearl buttons, which he'd ripped open to suckle her flesh, but those buttons had each been replaced with large blue ones that caught the sun and glimmered in his eyes.

Realizing she'd replaced every button brought a sadness to him. Its message was loud and distinct: *Stay out, you're not welcome here.*

Virginia tugged nervously at the loose fingers of her cotton gloves. "You didn't mention to my uncle that I know about his condition, did you?"

"I'll leave that up to you." A slender thread of longing wove between them. Unable to handle it, he nodded goodbye and pivoted.

"Zack?" She called after him.

"Yeah?" He turned around, grateful for the ten feet between them. Her nearness made his head spin.

"Thank you."

He felt his cheeks pull. "You're welcome."

"I guess I'll get back to my plants."

Nodding, unsure of what to say, he rocked back and forth on his big boots, digging into the soft soil and watching as she placed her hoe beside the potatoes. She raked the dirt in mounds around the stalks, providing enough cover for the underground vegetables when they'd need it.

He gasped in dawning recognition.

"What is it?"

He rubbed his sleeve against his mouth. "The burlap sack." He fell to his knees and palmed a mound of earth beneath her hoe. *"Toes.* I was trying to find the significance of 'toes,' but that's not it. The burlap sack was marked 'potatoes.' *Potatoes."*

"And?"

He shifted with unease. Most likely seed potatoes from the biggest potato farm in southern Alberta, about fifteen miles due west. That was the same direction the two assailants who'd shot her bonnet off her head had galloped to that night. If Zack told Virginia, would she let it slip to anyone else?

"Tell me, please."

The image of Hank Johnson rippled through his mind. Stacked in Hank's pile in the grass by the barracks had been a half-whittled pipe. Zack had seen Hank whittle on more than one occasion. With a pocketknife grasped between his fingers, he often did it to pass the time.

But son of a bitch. The clues were crystal clear in Zack's mind. Hank Johnson was guilty as sin.

"Zack, you're going to tell me, aren't you? What's going on? You've pieced something together. *Tell me."*

Hell. How could he confide in her? Hank Johnson would be here on Sunday, and would she be able to treat him naturally if Zack told her? He'd told her plenty enough before and she hadn't spilled it, but this was something monumental he couldn't divulge. Years of tracking Stiller and it might all explode in their faces. She had a will of her own and, so help him Lord, he was about to leave her out of the loop.

"I think I might know where the burlap came from." He said nothing more, willing her to accept his explanation. Part of the reason he was so skilled as an inspector was because he was an expert at masking his emotions. But when it came to Virginia sometimes he couldn't mask anything. It was as if with one glance, she could neutralize his powers.

She returned to her plants as he walked away. By the cool upturn of her lips and the gruff way she kicked up her heels, snapping her body over the hoe, he knew he hadn't fooled her.

So effective with everyone else, so ineffective with her.

Dammit, the two things he prided himself on, which had taken years to hone to perfection—his marksmanship and his ability to hide his emotions—were slipping further from his grasp. He wondered where the hell that left him.

Over the next seven days, Zack wouldn't leave her side. Virginia grew exasperated and ached for a breath alone. Her only reprise was bedtime when she could close her door and unwind without his prying eyes. Even then Zack had begun to leave *his* bedroom door open. His extreme caution made her nervous, and she wondered when and how her captivity would end.

Instead of stepping forward, they were stepping backward in their relations. Mistakenly, she'd opened her heart as well as her body to Zack but he had discarded her feelings, growing more close-lipped and unfeeling as time wore on. Awakening her physically as he had, bringing her to the heights of secret pleasure and sharing the privileged intimacy between a man and woman meant nothing if the act was devoid of love.

He'd discovered something about the clues leading to Stiller, and two weeks ago, he would have shared them with her.

It was also obvious Uncle Paddy was avoiding her. Whenever she heard the clatter of horses' hooves coming up the front path, she raced to the porch to see if it might be him but always wound up burying her disappointment, wiping her hands on her apron and telling herself it didn't matter because he'd come tomorrow.

But Uncle Paddy didn't come tomorrow. Nor the next day. Her tinge of frustration grew to anger for being ignored, then subsided to the deepest empathy for a man going blind and unwilling—or unable—to face it.

The two men she'd cared for most—her uncle, closer to her than any other member of her family, and Zack—had both firmly shut her out of their lives.

Zack was here in form, though, which was worse because she couldn't altogether ignore him.

At six o'clock Sunday morning, Virginia peered out over the breaking dawn sky and walked toward the set of long pine tables the men had nailed together for the banquet of food. She set her pan of apple crisps on the blue checkered cloth.

"Looks like we've got a beautiful day for the barn raising." Lucy Peters, dressed in mourning black, arranged her five pots of potato salad. Her two girls were off playing with the dogs while Kyle was somewhere behind them, following Zack around like a pup himself.

"It's gorgeous weather. Dry and clear." Virginia smiled and tipped her shoulder against Lucy's, determined to enjoy the day. "So glad you made it, Lucy."

Neighbors had begun to arrive at five, before the sun had risen. Two dozen men sorted through lumber. Many of them were Mounties, recognizable by their work clothes—black breeches, white shirts and dark suspenders. Some, like Zack, wore denims.

They dragged twelve-by-twelve posts around flattened soil that would form the perimeter base of the barn called the sill. The ranch foreman called out for beam drills and two-man saws. Young boys stacked barn pegs and cedar shakes behind their fathers and uncles, while young girls helped prepare food trays alongside their mothers and aunts.

Virginia had never been a part of anything like this. These hardworking folks reminded her of a humming army of ants, willing to resurrect a mountain in a day. Everyone had come to help the Mounties. They were the police force who laid their lives on the line to protect the town, and the town acknowledged respect by coming to help today.

When Lucy's daughter brushed by, Virginia pulled her in with a hug. "Diana, you're looking tenfold better."

"Yes, ma'am. I'm feeling mighty better, too. Sore throat's gone." Diana set down a basket laden with preserves and disappeared into the crowd again, heading to the arriving buggies to help unload food.

"She's almost ready to be a bride herself." Virginia smiled, pleased for Diana. Then she suddenly felt old, realizing the new generation of girls behind her were already of marriageable age while she was still unwed. But it was silly to think of it in those terms. Years didn't account for anything. Finding an honorable partner was most important. And if she never found that person, it was better to stay unwed.

Lucy glanced after her adolescent daughter. Diana had budding hips and the promise of a strong body like her mother's. "I'm hoping someday soon."

With a whir of arms and legs, Kyle raced to the table, threw a tea towel off a tray and snatched a stick of honey. It dripped from the honeycomb to his mouth.

"Stop that," ordered Lucy. "Wait till the others begin to eat."

"Let him have it." The deep, familiar lull of Zack's voice rolled through Virginia.

Why couldn't she ignore him? Why couldn't he be a man a woman *could* ignore?

"You're spoiling him," said Lucy with a bursting smile.

"No such thing. He's a growing boy and his stomach's as deep as a pit of quicksand. I remember those days, I never could get enough to eat myself."

"And my," Lucy whispered to Virginia, fanning herself with her hand as the boy occupied Zack's attention, "didn't he grow into a big one?"

At the humorous lilt to Lucy's words, Virginia's skin tingled. She slapped her hands together and pretended to concentrate on a row of Mason jars filled with plum jam.

When she stole a glance at Zack, his gaze dropped to the square neckline of her blouse, the one with the pretty lace ribbon that he'd once undone. Her hands nervously closed on her thighs.

"I like your holster," Virginia called to Kyle as he practiced withdrawing his wooden gun. His toy black leather holster matched Zack's real one, and they looked handsome together.

Kyle turned serious. "My pa gave me the holster, but Zack bought me the gun."

With her eyes on Zack, Lucy sighed with deep gratitude, and Virginia realized how close he and the boy had grown in two weeks. As much as Kyle loved to practice target shooting every afternoon, Zack was always ready and waiting for two o'clock to arrive.

At one time she'd thought she would be carrying Zack's son or daughter, but that dream had faded fast.

"All right, Kyle," said Zack, crouching over the lumber nearest to their table, "let's construct a bent."

"What's that?"

"We're building an L-shaped barn. One of the legs will

have four bays for oxen, the other side will be for feed storage. A bent is a partial frame we'll build on the ground, sort of like a rib cage. Here's a hammer and a peg. I'll hold the pieces and you can pound the peg.''

Lucy stacked plates while Virginia scraped butter from the churn she'd just finished using, depositing the spoonfuls in a large covered jar.

With his dark head bent low in concentration, Zack cast a looming figure of a man. Good Lord, even the young girls were eyeing the muscles straining beneath his shirt, the angled waist and the flexing thighs beneath his tight denim pants. He'd slipped out of his suspenders and had replaced them with a black belt that had a shiny silver buckle. His clothes accentuated his build as he jogged into position next to the slender boy.

Lucy twisted into the sunlight. ''Did you know that Zack ordered two men to my ranch every day this week to get caught up on the chores?''

Virginia felt a tug of sympathy. ''That was observant of him.''

''But I've never seen him *this* interested in farm work.''

''Neither have I.'' Yesterday, while Virginia had been tending to a wasp sting on the cook's arm, Zack had practiced stepping behind the ox plough, leather straps across his shoulders, heaving with all his might. It'd slipped and fallen, and he'd cursed but he'd picked it back up again and again and again. The day before that he'd ordered her to sit on the wagon behind the team of horses so he could watch over her while he helped fork hay onto it, his chest matted with tiny slivers of dry grass, his face twisted as he tried to hide his boredom with the task.

Later that evening, knowing his muscles were likely in pain, she'd rubbed liniment into his biceps and massaged them until the intensity of the moment had gotten so charged that she'd vowed not to suggest it again. Instead she'd recommended he stay away from hard work. Now as she watched him tug on the timber, she realized getting Zack to stay away from strenuous work was impossible.

"Are you thinking of becoming a rancher, Zack?" Lucy called out.

A muscle pulled on his dark cheek.

No, thought Virginia, shocked by the thought, Zack would never quit the force. He *loved* the force.

He tipped his head toward Virginia, a smile capturing the smooth tone of his words. "My duty today is to protect the fair maiden."

Virginia turned away abruptly and concentrated on spooning out her butter.

When he knelt over a second piece of timber, Lucy stepped closer to Virginia and watched her with the churn. "Why isn't it working out with you two?"

Virginia didn't like the direction the conversation was heading. "It's working just fine."

Lucy pressed a hand onto Virginia's, stilling the spoon beneath. "Have you ever noticed that the first thing Zack does when he steps into a space is search the crowd for you?"

Virginia's lips strained. "That's because…it's in his line of work to protect me."

"It's in Travis's, too, and Mitchell's, and the other constables, but they don't—"

"You're making more of this than it needs to be."

Lucy held firm. "Perhaps you're making less of it." Lucy nodded as two elderly women carried a side of salted pork to the table and then covered it with a clean cloth.

Virginia peered to the road, busy with travelers arriving. She wondered if her uncle would make an appearance. When she caught sight of a brown leather buggy way off in the distance, she wondered if it might be his.

Lucy whispered. "Maybe I'm overstepping my bounds and I apologize if what I say offends you. I know you're a doctor and you're smart, but people say…you've got no time for men."

Virginia wished people would mind their own business. She snapped her spoon to the table.

"Cameron wasn't here on earth long enough," Lucy began. "Time is all you have…don't waste it." She walked away.

Virginia closed her eyes. This was different than Lucy and Cameron. Lucy didn't understand. Virginia *had* spent time with Zack, every day and every minute. She'd willingly moved to Alberta for him, had said yes to his proposal, and yet he'd been the one to break her heart. And still she'd gone to him, forgiving and trying her best. They'd spent one blissful afternoon together, reckless and passionate, and in the end he'd cast her aside as he had in the very beginning.

Only the second time he'd done it, he'd stolen even more of her.

Chapter Fifteen

"*U*ncle Paddy!" Virginia shouted across the grass, three hours later, delighted to see him. The midmorning sun shimmered through the blue sky as she dashed toward his buggy. She pulled in a breath of evergreen-flavored air. Her braided hair streamed behind her like a long rope, slapping against her moistened back. "I'm glad you're here. I've missed you."

"Good mornin', Virginia." Seated beside Millicent in the buggy with Emilou squeezed between them, Uncle Paddy tucked in the reins with burly hands and nodded. He was pale but looked wonderful and safe, seated in the impeccable buggy Virginia was accustomed to seeing him ride. The sights and smells of familiarity lifted her spirits.

"I'll take those." Zack stepped around her, taking the reins to the hitching rings, which studded the gnarled cottonwood.

Uncle Paddy's attention darted around Virginia to Zack's broad shoulders. "Mornin', Zack."

With a flicker of uncertainty at Zack's dark figure, cut in denims and flowing white shirt, Virginia wondered how he always seemed to arrive at the most inopportune moment. She wanted to console Uncle Paddy, to discuss his troubles, yet instinctively guarded against revealing herself and her emotions in front of Zack.

Uncle Paddy descended, extending a hand to Millicent. Emilou jumped off the buggy's other side, blond braids jostling against her pinafore.

"What's this bone called?" Emilou pointed to her forehead.

Virginia laughed softly. "The frontal." She tapped the girl lightly above her ear. "And this one?"

"The temporal."

Millicent stood behind her granddaughter and smiled. "She's been studying the book you left her."

Uncle Paddy tugged at Emilou's shoulder. "I think we've got another budding doctor here."

Zack inclined his head in Virginia's direction, eyes sparkling as he watched her.

Emilou hugged Virginia's skirts. "When are your doctor's exams?"

Virginia rubbed the cuff of her cotton sleeve, nervous at the thought. "Tomorrow morning."

"You're still planning to go?" Zack drew himself taller, and she was once again reminded of his overwhelming presence. But by the troublesome distance between them, one would never imagine that less than a week ago they'd made love.

Stalling for time to answer, Virginia spotted her uncle's medicine bag at the foot of the buggy and leaned in to retrieve it. It was a habit for him—and her now—to carry their bags pretty much wherever they traveled. Large gatherings like these were a convenient opportunity for folks who lived miles away to approach the doctor with any ailments.

"The exam time has been set up for weeks," Virginia said carefully. "I was given a note yesterday by one of the Mounties from the town judge saying that the three officials had just arrived from Edmonton and were setting up the study area in the courthouse. They're doing it on my behalf because I'm the only one taking the exams."

"But in view of everything that's happened—"

"It's not something I can—*or will*—decline. If I don't write my oral and written exams, the next session isn't for a year. My license is important," she added, glancing in her uncle's direction, urging Zack to understand. "Especially now."

If Uncle Paddy lost his vision and she wasn't licensed to practice, then what? Would she take her chances, practice without a license, gambling she'd avoid fines and suspensions? It was tough enough to get taken seriously as a woman without making special demands.

Zack came close and slipped the heavy bag from her fingers. "What time tomorrow morning?"

She crooked her neck to look straight up at him. "Seven o'clock. It lasts a full day, till 7:00 p.m. But I'll clear it with Travis and ask him to ride with me, so you needn't get involved."

His full lips drew tighter. "We'll see about that."

He always made her question her own judgment. Virginia had it planned. Superintendent Ridgeway was expected at the barn raising today. She'd finagle clearance for extra men to accompany her to the courthouse and back. *He* would understand the importance of gaining her license—to herself and the town—after she explained her uncle's eye condition.

Emilou spotted a group of children playing ring toss near the picnic areas and tore off in that direction, followed by Millicent.

Zack stepped in line next to Virginia, who walked alongside her uncle toward the house, intending to drop off Uncle Paddy's bag and set up an area where he could see patients if necessary.

"How are you, Uncle Paddy?"

"Feelin' good. Why?"

She searched the elder man's face, looking past his thick spectacles into his dark eyes but seeing nothing out of the ordinary to indicate disease. "I know about what's happening to you. I pried it out of Millicent."

He flinched. "Is that a fact?"

"Is there anything we could—"

"No." The color that had infused his face, the happiness and warmth upon seeing her, faded.

She continued with difficulty knowing she was treading on volatile ground. This was the man who had tutored *her* when she hadn't known the difference between Cobbler suturing and Purse-string suturing, let alone how to knot a stitch around a bleeding gash or handle a fighting patient.

Respect emanated from her shaky voice. "But I could write to—"

"It's been written," he snapped. "There's nothin' left. And I'd appreciate if you kept your thoughts to yourself."

With the reprimand, she felt as if she'd been slapped. Then her grief for her uncle rushed to the surface. She lowered her eyes to the grass as they walked, trying to stop her chin from trembling. Without warning, a large hand came up to cup her shoulder. It was Zack's hand, quietly reassuring. The touch gave her strength. She hoped he'd let his hand rest for a moment longer.

She pressed further with her uncle, determined to point out the brighter side of his situation. "But your eyesight might last for years."

"Or it might go tomorrow. It's a goddamn way to live."

He was right.

Zack's comforting hand remained, squeezing even tighter.

Millicent must have witnessed the exchange, for she joined them as they reached the sun-beaten porch. She reached out and tapped Uncle Paddy on the waist. He tried to be discreet, but Virginia saw him bat Millicent's hand away. The aging housekeeper stepped back and lowered her gaze.

Uncle Paddy squared his arms across his hips and glared at them. "I would appreciate if each of you afforded me the dignity of not spreadin' the news."

Virginia ran a hand along the newly whitewashed handrail. "But don't you think folks should know about their doctor?"

"It's no one's concern but mine. When I need to, I'll let everyone know."

Zack, Virginia and Millicent exchanged looks of doubt. "Promise me."

Millicent and Zack nodded slowly in agreement, but how could Virginia make such a promise? She planned on notifying the superintendent this very afternoon.

"Virginia?" her uncle demanded.

Still she couldn't promise. Although no patients had been harmfully affected by the town doctor, shouldn't they be informed *before* anything happened?

Uncle Paddy's voice rumbled. "I thought *you*, Virginia, of all people would support me."

Virginia winced. He'd done so much for her and she so little for him. And this one request, the only one he'd ever made of her was the one she could never give.

He yanked his medicine bag from Zack's hand, turned and trudged up the porch to the painted front door, shoulders hunched with the weight of his sorrow. Millicent, loving and forgiving, followed him.

"He didn't mean it," said Zack, finally dropping his hand from her shoulder to face her. "His pride is getting in the way of his logic."

"I've disappointed him," she whispered. "The opposite of what I wanted to do. I wanted to help him." She leaned against the porch rail.

With not a second to recover, she heard a familiar male voice calling from the yard. "Hello, you two!"

Bolting to hide her shame from her encounter with her uncle, she whirled around and gasped at the scene of Grace and Andrew, suitcase in hands, closing the distance. Both looked ill at ease, searching Zack and Virginia's faces, turning to glance at the barn under construction. Men were hoisting walls into place. The barn looked like the skeleton of a whale.

"Don't let them disturb you," said Zack gently before stepping out to greet his brother and sister-in-law. "How was your trip?"

Zack chatted to them about the dust and the flies. Virginia realized gratefully that he was distracting them to allow her time to gather her composure. Although she had known the couple was coming today, she hadn't quite believed it, hoping they'd change their mind to save them all embarrassment.

"You don't have to stay with us out here on the ranch," Virginia tactfully said to Grace. "My uncle still has a huge empty house, which he's always offering up to visitors. Perhaps you'd like to use this occasion to spend some time in town."

Cool and withdrawn to this point, Grace brightened at the prospect. She was wearing her hair in the same fashion Virginia had last seen it—braided and coiled above her ears, accentuating its glossy thickness. "Why, that would be lovely—"

"Nonsense," interrupted Andrew. "I've got an opportunity here for the next two days to see firsthand how the Mounties plant and farm. Why, Travis is an expert horseman, breeding his own stallions he tells me, and I could ask him all sorts of questions about my draft horses."

Andrew didn't seem to notice his wife's displeasure, or Virginia's. He ribbed his brother. "I heard you've been trying your hand at haying. How's it going?"

Not well, thought Virginia.

"It's hard work, but I like that." Zack slung his powerful hands into his pockets, thumbs splayed over the belt of his pants. Once or twice, he rubbed his sore shoulder.

"And Travis tells me you've been roping steer. When have you ever been interested in ranching, big brother?"

"I thought I might someday retire from the force and take them up on the offer of free homesteading land."

The conversation halted. Zack a farmer?

She'd heard that after three years of service, Mounties were allowed to retire and, as a bonus, received a quarter section of prime homesteading land. Many enlisted into the force for this reason but soon discovered there was a long waiting list for prime land, and it would take at least double those years to earn it. Virginia had heard that records indicated there were already close to fifty retired Mounties across Alberta successfully involved in ranching. Many were still youthful and strong, in their thirties and forties, and their hard work provided the backbone of Canada's beef industry.

While the other couple stared at Zack, Virginia looped an arm through Grace's. She pulled her and the men to the drink table to save Zack from further criticism. "Lemonade or cider?"

Two hours passed with the women doling out food and drinks to hungry men, while Zack and Andrew rolled up their sleeves to help bang boards onto the barn's foundation.

Virginia had never spent more than ten minutes at a time with Andrew and Grace. She'd never witnessed their relationship, had never noticed the close attention Andrew paid to his wife. He brought her a cool drink at noon, then a platter of food for lunch. He shooed flies off her shoulders and used every opportunity to touch his wife, whether it be on the cheek or the waist, or a fleeting touch on her hand. Grace nodded softly, smiling occasionally, but never opening up to her husband as he was to her.

Zack remained occupied with his work. He had amazing drive and focus, but Virginia wished some of Andrew's attentiveness to his wife would spill over so that Zack might say a kind word or two to her.

Finally at three o'clock in the afternoon, when the cedar shakes were being hammered onto the barn's roof, Grace began to talk. The drinking table where the women were standing was shaded by a group of tall pines.

"Were you in love with Andrew?"

Virginia's hand slipped as she poured herself a cup of spring water. "I thought I was."

"Why did you break up?"

Virginia sipped slowly. "Didn't Andrew tell you how it happened?"

Grace peered at her husband, hunched on the rooftop with Zack. "I'd like to hear it from you."

Virginia glanced over at Zack, who had peeled off his shirt. The sun was beating into his bronzed back. No matter what the man did, he brought attention to himself from the surrounding women who smiled and watched him work.

Virginia chose her words carefully. "It's quite simple. Andrew left me for you."

"I've been asking myself over and over. You're a doctor. You're attractive. Why would he leave you?"

It was clearer to Virginia today than it had ever been. "In the years I've known Andrew, I've never seen him this attentive to a woman. His eyes practically plead for forgiveness. He's remorseful that you've been hurt. He loves you, Grace."

"But he loved you once, too."

"I can see.... He was never mine." Whatever Andrew had wanted to say to her in that meeting in Uncle Paddy's hallway when he'd grabbed her and told her he'd hoped he hadn't made a mistake, it had vanished from his eyes. Perhaps Grace's anger had forced him to clarify his feelings.

And then for the first time in the months since Andrew had written to tell her he'd met someone else, Virginia grew curious. "How did you two meet?"

Grace fanned herself with a paper fan, brightly colored with painted daisies. "At the general store in Red Deer. He was standing in line with his arms full of candles and one honeycomb, and I said 'Excuse me, sir, can you pass me a sack of sugar?'" Grace smiled. "He did, but there was a hole in the sack and sugar spilled onto the floor. By the time we finished cleaning honey and sugar off the candles, we were laughing so hard—" She stopped herself and played with the fan. "I'm sorry, that was insensitive to tell you."

"There was never lots of laughter with me and Andrew. He married *you*. Don't punish him any longer for his inability to tell you about our engagement. I stopped mattering the day he passed you the sugar sack."

Grace reached closer and patted Virginia's hand. "I'm so sorry it didn't work out with you and Zack, either."

The truth zinged across Virginia's heart.

"I've got a brother, and maybe—"

"No, thank you. I'd prefer to make my own choices with men."

Grace nodded. She peered over Virginia's shoulder. "Look who's here. He missed most of the hard work," Grace said with good humor, "but he's just in time for supper and the dance."

"Who is it?"

"It's that reporter, David Fitzgibbon."

Virginia moaned. She peered through the pine branches and watched David hitch his horse and trot down the hillside grass. His right wrist was bandaged, though, and she grew concerned. Hadn't she told him to remove the bandage and throw away the ointment he'd been rubbing into his scalded skin?

Virginia stepped out to greet him. "Are you here to see my uncle?" She motioned to his bandaged wrist.

"You, actually. I wanted another opinion. Again," he said with nervous laughter.

The poor man. Had he gone back to Uncle Paddy and received conflicting advice about his wrist?

She pulled David around the pines to the solitude and privacy of the other side. "Could you remove the bandage for me, please, so I could have a look? I thought I'd mentioned it was best to leave it exposed to the air."

"Quite right, you did. But your uncle was adamant that I continue with the cream. He's—he's been a doctor a lot longer than you, I'm afraid, and I thought I'd go with his opinion. Here, take a look."

When David was done untying the knot and turned his wrist around for her to see, she nearly stumbled backward.

Good God.

Gangrene.

She gulped rapidly and tried to think. *Moist gangrene.*
The tight knot and pressure of the bandage for days had
likely stopped proper blood flow to the scalded area. Or-
ganisms had invaded the flesh and were thriving. She
could see the delineating red line that marked the border
of the affected tissues that would eventually wither and
die.

Her uncle's failing vision had finally harmed *someone*.

"Are you in much pain?" She looked into David's
eyes, noting the dilated pupils and realizing he was on
something.

"Your uncle gave me laudanum." It was an opiate
mixed with alcohol, and necessary for the severe agony
David must be in.

"Good. Come with me to the house. My bag is there."

Frantic but trying to conceal it, Virginia scanned the
grounds for Zack. Her first instinct was that she could
count on him to help. When she spotted him climbing the
ladder off the roof, she motioned him over. He quirked
his brows, grew serious at her terrified expression, then
slowly made his way toward her through the crowd.
Thank God, he knew to remain calm in an emergency.
The quality seemed to come to him naturally.

Turning and smiling at David, she tried to suppress the
horror of the situation from reflecting in her eyes. Within
the next few minutes, David might have his arm ampu-
tated. And her uncle should have seen the danger coming.

Flabbergasted by the news, Zack ran his fingers through
the black hair at his temples and listened carefully.

"It could have been avoided," Virginia whispered as
they stood in his bedroom, her back pressed against the

closed door, his legs digging into the iron footboard of his bed. Across the hall in her bedroom, she'd sat David on a corner chair and asked him to await her return. She hadn't approached Paddy yet, and Zack couldn't fathom how she'd be able to break the news to either man. First and foremost, David was her main concern and Zack admired that.

The corners of Virginia's mouth quivered. Her thick braid swung over her shoulder to drape across the open square of her neckline. "The tight bandage didn't help and may have progressed it. It never should have gotten to this point."

She clenched her hands together, weaving her slender fingers in and out. Desperation reached her eyes.

"What can you do now to help David?" he asked.

She rubbed her cheeks and paced the tight floor, dodging the nightstand and weaving her long legs around the stark bed Zack had made this morning.

"He has to be told his condition. I'm hoping he won't be too angry so he'll understand the choices he needs to make."

"Will he really lose his arm?"

She choked on her words. "He might, depending how much skin and muscle I need to debride."

"Then let's go find Paddy."

They found the gent in the great room, saying goodbye to one of the stable hands who'd needed a sprained elbow wrapped with gauze.

"Uncle Paddy? David Fitzgibbon is here."

"He must be here about his wrist. Send him in."

Virginia twisted her fingers. "Actually, he's waiting in my room for us to join him. I've seen his injury and it's awfully red."

"How red?"

"It's obviously been like that for days." She paused. "It's gangrenous."

"*What?*" The old man paled. He adjusted his thick spectacles. "So quickly? I saw him only four days ago. You must be mistaken." Then he studied Virginia's gloomy expression. "You're not tryin' to tell me that I...*missed* something?"

"I don't know how or why his wrist got this way, but it is this way and we have to deal with it."

"That's impossible!" But Uncle Paddy was already flying out of his chair with medical bag in tow, dashing behind Virginia and Zack down the hall.

Virginia tapped lightly on the door and entered. "David, we're here."

David had parted the curtains and was peering out into the yard. "The barn's almost finished. Amazing. I brought my camera and I'll have to take some photographs before the sun sets." He turned around and looked at the three of them. "Good. I've got two doctors to look after me. Whaddya think, Doc Waters?"

David held out his right arm, which Virginia had insisted he leave unwrapped and unknotted.

"Come here into the light," said Uncle Paddy. "Closer, I still can't see it."

Then by a defeated gasp, Zack knew Uncle Paddy agreed with Virginia's diagnosis. So it was true, Zack thought, every muscle tensing.

"I never noticed before how thick your glasses are," said David. Then he glanced to the windowpane and how closely the doctor was holding his arm to the light. A frown flitted across his blond brows. He dropped his arm and smiled. "Should I continue with the ointment? Your niece seems to think I'd be better off leaving it alone. To tell you the truth, the blasted thing scares me. It looks awful, doesn't it?''

The old man heaved onto the bed.

"Doc?" David snapped his head toward Virginia and Zack. "What's going on?"

"Your arm's in bad shape." Virginia stepped toward the reporter and led him gently to the wooden chair, where he sat. "The redness you see there is dying tissue."

David blinked. "The circulation will come back, though, right?"

"I'm afraid it'll never come back. It's gangrene."

David bolted out of his chair.

"Gangrene! Gangrene is where they—"

"The dead tissue needs to be removed."

"Cut away?"

She nodded. "Or it can spread throughout your body."

"Don't tell me. Please don't tell me what's coming."

"The safest way to stop the spread is to..." Virginia gazed slowly at David's stiffened body, his horrified expression and his shaking head. "The safest way is to amputate your arm."

"No!" When he looked at Uncle Paddy's frozen face, he began yelling. "You're nothing but an old man who should never have been practicing medicine this long! You're goddamn blind!"

Uncle Paddy began to weep. "Yes...yes I am. I'm sorry, David. If I could exchange my arm for yours, I would."

Zack found it difficult to watch the scene unfold.

Virginia was near tears but somehow managed to restrain them. "There's a chance of doing it another way, David, but you'd be taking a huge gamble that the gangrene wouldn't spread."

"I'm a reporter. I write with this hand. Give me any other option, *please.*"

"I could try and debride—remove—only the flesh that's been affected. It would leave a big gouge on your arm, but within the next day or two we'd see if it was successful enough to stop the spread."

"And if it wasn't?"

"It would spread farther and then you'd need a higher amputation."

"Christ," he muttered. He peered at Zack. "What do you think I should do?"

"In all the years I've been an officer, I've never had to witness someone making a choice like this. But I can tell you from what I know and have seen of Virginia, I'd trust my life in her hands."

The realization struck Zack with force. He'd never known anyone like Virginia Waters. She was quiet yet stated her opinion unequivocally when it was sought, and fought with all her strength on behalf of her patients.

And yet who did she have to lean on?

He wished she'd lean on him.

David spoke with greater calm than Zack could have. "All right, let's try the simpler form first. If it doesn't work, then I'll…I'll think about…"

Virginia nodded and moved quickly. She got Uncle Paddy from the room but asked that Zack remain. He hauled buckets of clean water for her, poured them into basins, then helped settle David onto the bed. She put him under, then carefully went to work.

Zack couldn't watch, but peered out the window at the children playing tag and husbands and wives chatting beneath the trees. The supper tables were being set up with people about to sit down and eat. It seemed so long ago from the day that Virginia had walked into his room at

Doc Waters's home and found Zack on the floor, trying to get out of bed after his gunshot wound. So much had passed between them. A friendship had formed, deep and real and solid.

"All finished," said Virginia nearly an hour later. She smiled and he surmised that the procedure had gone well. "I'll give David something for his pain to ensure he sleeps well throughout the night."

"You've been on your feet for hours. Can't you take a moment to sit down and eat something?"

"I'll be fine here."

"The band is starting. Come with me. We'll get something to eat together and listen to the music."

"Well, maybe…I'll get Uncle Paddy to sit with David."

It took her another hour to prepare, with Zack helping to straighten the room and tidy her supplies.

Paddy argued that he shouldn't sit with David, that he couldn't be sure of any of his skills anymore, but Virginia assured her uncle that he was very capable of staying at David's sleeping side. She promised that David wouldn't awaken before the morning, that he was stable, and that her uncle was still very vital and dependable.

It made the old man brighten, Zack noticed, and a peace rolled through the house. When Millicent brought a plate of food to the door, Uncle Paddy murmured an apology and brought a chair next to his, indicating she should join him. Millicent lowered her lashes, but not before Zack caught the glimmer of delight.

"My clothes are soiled," said Virginia, peering down at the soap and water staining her skirt.

"You look wonderful."

"I should change." Virginia removed a dress hanging

in her armoire, bundled it up along with a small leather clutch bag and stepped into Zack's bedroom. "May I use your room to change?"

Only if he could stay and watch, thought Zack. Only if he could pull her to the bed and help undress her. But he nodded yes and left the house, waiting for her on the front porch.

He leaned across the handrail, stared out at the crowd, and wondered whether all that he felt for Virginia was friendship.

No, there was much more. Somehow in the past few hours, the lines had blurred between caring and loving.

It unsettled him to think of her in those terms. But...

The music began from inside the newly built barn. The sound of Ian Killarney's fiddle, a slow melodic winding, almost melancholy in its hum, wafted around the blowing pines and curled around Zack. The shape of Virginia's face lingered around the edges of his mind, the sweet swell of her cheek, the uplift of her dark lashes, that freckle beside her lower lid that intensified the depth of her eyes.

What was he going to do about Virginia?

When he heard the door latch click, he looked up to find her standing there, a dream on a cloud.

His hand tightened on the rail. The evening light rippled over her ivory skin. Long golden earrings glistened off her cheeks. She smiled, standing in a dress he'd never seen before. It was white and dotted with minuscule red rosebuds, gathered off her rounded shoulders revealing a feminine sweep of the upper part of her breasts. Breasts that he'd kissed, a throat he'd devoured, hands that had knotted at the back of his neck. Lips that might never touch his again.

A tight ribbon of velvet, a choker, adorned her neck.

Her black wavy hair, parted in the middle and brushed out of her braid, fell across her shoulders down to her waist, making him wonder what she'd look like naked in the moonlight with nothing but her hair to shield her.

Heat infused his face, throbbed beneath the surface of his skin. "You look stunning."

"Thank you, Zack."

He tingled when she said his name. No one said it as she did, raspy and full of emotion, always on the verge of adding more but holding back.

He held out his hand and murmured into the evening breeze. "Will you dance with me?"

Chapter Sixteen

"Would you like something to eat first? It's nearly nine-thirty and you must be starved," said Zack.

Weaving through the packed crowd in the barn, Virginia felt his warm breath at her temple. His splayed hand nudged her bare elbow and caused a delicious heat to flow through her body. Even in a crowd it seemed to be just the two of them, aware of each other and desperately struggling to fight it.

"Just a bite." She needed to extract herself. Dipping from his grasp, she leaned over the table of food and picked up a bun and slice of curded cheese.

While he helped himself to a sandwich built with ham and lettuce, she stole a glance at his trim shoulders. Her stomach tightened with a flutter. She wondered if it was a good idea to have accepted his dance invitation.

But she hadn't danced for ages, not for a year since she'd attended a friend's wedding back East. Mr. Killarney on his fiddle was mesmerizing, the accompanying flute and harmonica and guitars adding to the harmony. And the fact that the surgery had gone so well with David had her spirits soaring.

Some folks had brought a change of clothing for the

celebration, others clapped their hands in their work clothes. Older folks had already left, reminding the younger ones that tomorrow was another workday.

Virginia stared at Mr. Killarney's face, at his closed eyes and the passion in his stance as he weaved his bow across the strings. How hard it must have been for Uncle Paddy to be playing chess with his blind friend these past months, knowing he was going blind himself. When his condition was disclosed, surely Mr. Killarney would help Uncle Paddy adjust. She smiled into the sultry, darkened room. Perhaps things wouldn't be so bad.

A lantern hanging from the wall beside Zack flooded him with golden rays, highlighting his glossy hair and handsome face, lighting one of her short sleeves to a deep rosy hue. "What are you smiling at?"

"I'm amazed at how well Ian Killarney has managed with his blindness."

"Your uncle will manage, too. He'll find his way."

"I was thinking how in the months to come, I might ask Uncle Paddy to accompany me on my medical calls. It's a way for him to maintain his dignity. But he's also a font of information and could help me tremendously in consultation if we worked together."

She shied away from Zack's appreciative gaze. "It sounds as though you've decided to stay on in Calgary."

"I might. When this is all over with Stiller, I mean," she added. "Will it be over soon?"

He moved closer and lowered his voice, seeming very conscious of those around him. "In less than a week, I predict. My men are in place."

"You mean in less than a week, I could move off this ranch?"

His thick black lashes caught the light. "That's what you've been waiting for, isn't it?"

"Absolutely." She gloried in the great news, her smile broadening. Freedom at last.

But as wonderful as she felt, Zack remained curiously silent.

"Dance with me," he said.

Glimpsing his strong, tanned throat at the base of his open collar made her heart beat rapidly. He was *dangerous.*

Dangerous to be near and dangerous to touch.

He let his eyes drift over her, making her catch her breath. When he placed his flattened hand between the naked blades of her shoulders, her senses leaped to fire.

This will only lead to more pain when we separate again.

But he was too smooth and charismatic to resist.

He led her through the heated bodies on the dance floor, an expert with his hands. A marksman who'd targeted her heart and had hit the bull's-eye.

"Right here." He brought her into a two-foot clearing.

Fortunately the tune had a fast tempo and she'd be able to keep her distance. But then the song ended as she turned around to face him.

Another one began, a slow waltz. She was trapped.

She swallowed hard as her eyes met his. His Adam's apple rippled as he clasped her right hand and brought it to his heart.

Heads turned in their direction, women whispering to their partners.

But the music transfixed Virginia, humming through her body and riveting her against Zack. His grip on her hand and the small of her back was firm and possessive, his appeal devastating. As he twirled her in time to the beat, her skirts swished in pendulum. The invitation in his eyes became a challenge.

When had these changes happened in her? Gone was the shy, elusive woman he'd met weeks ago at the train station and in her place stood a woman confident of her allure, one unafraid to peer directly back at the question in his warm brown eyes.

If she let herself drift, she could picture the two of them on the hillside that afternoon sharing the intimacies of lovemaking, entranced by the way their bodies moved together.

If she allowed him to stare at her mouth much longer, she'd succumb to—

"Pardon me, may I have this dance?"

Virginia snapped her head to the man standing beside them. Yule Vanderveer, instrument salesman.

"No," said Zack gruffly, tightening his grip on her back.

But Virginia was already pulling away. Her face was heated. She avoided looking at Zack. "Yes, of course."

Trying to stifle the desire she felt for Zack, she brushed the folds of her skirt and rearranged her hands into Yule's. Whether he was aware of it or not, Yule was saving her.

From the corner of her eye, she saw Zack's tall body fade into the crowd. She could breathe again.

Yule's timing was slightly off her own as he moved her along the floor. Or maybe it was hers that was off from his. She reshuffled her feet, but it didn't help. The strain between their arms became pronounced.

"I came to see your uncle."

"He's in the house."

"I found him, but there wasn't much time to show him my new collection of leech containers. They're in my buggy if you'd like to see them. Your uncle seems to hold your opinion in high—"

"Yule, please, not now."

He nodded. "I certainly won't push you. No one can accuse Yule Vanderveer of being pushy."

Comically, it was the singular word she *would* use to describe him.

She allowed him to go on about his wares, and as they circled the floor, she searched for Zack. Nowhere to be seen. She looked past the musicians at the sliding barn doors, past the ladders leading to the haymows that had already been filled with hay, past the row of pitchforks, shovels and hoes which had been strapped to the wall. Tomorrow morning the ranch hands would bring the teams of oxen into their new home.

She spotted Superintendent Ridgeway and his wife dancing in the front corner and the mercantile owners, the Rossmans, standing on the sidelines. To their right were the baker and several employees from the train depot, including Dirk and Chauncey McGuire.

On the heels of a dozen more twirls, Virginia caught sight of Zack. He looked disturbed and she wondered why. An elbow and shoulder obliterated her view, and it wasn't until after the next dance began that she found him again.

Peering down at Hank Johnson in his wheelchair, Zack scratched his jaw, said something jovial that caused the two to laugh, then lifted the holsters off the back of Hank's chair and passed them to Travis. Hank seemed to argue, but Zack grinned and shrugged, and Travis walked away with the guns.

From what Virginia knew about these men, for one Mountie to disarm another was strange. Zack was close to finishing with Stiller, he'd said. It would be over within a week. Then she realized Zack suspected Hank and that was probably why Zack had stuck so close to her today. In case Hank surfaced and posed a threat.

The dance ended.

"Thank you, ma'am," said Yule. "Your uncle asked me to give you this." He withdrew an envelope from his jacket. "Doc Waters said he forgot about giving you your mail when he arrived. Says he remembered it in the side pouch of his medical bag and thought it looked important."

Yule walked her to the opposite side of the barn and someone pulled him away to ask about buying a glass thermometer.

With mounting tension, Virginia glanced down at the letter. It was addressed to her at Uncle Paddy's home and appeared to be from Zack's folks. Tearing open the edge with shaking fingers, she realized it was likely a response to the express letter she'd sent them the day after Zack had severed their engagement.

"I got a letter from your folks today, Zack."

Zack looked up and spotted Virginia. It was near midnight. A dozen ranch hands and Mounties were sweeping floors and dismantling tables. Virginia found Zack at the back of the barn as he was trying to convince a group of young men it was time to go home.

It'd been a long day with Zack's muscles tensed for trouble the entire time, but now that nearly everyone had left and no trouble had come, his tension unwound.

The curtain of darkness surrounding the barn combined with the call of cattle and chirping insects, produced a hush between them. Kerosene lanterns hung from pegs along the wall, casting golden arches on her face.

"Why didn't you tell me?" she asked softly.

"I didn't think you'd take it in the way I'd intended." Her lips closed gently. His gaze skimmed her bare shoulders, noticing the rise and fall of her chest. But they weren't alone and couldn't discuss it.

The man beside him, the youngest Smithy fellow who'd overdone it with his drinking, moaned. He smelled of rye and cigars. Zack draped an arm across him. "Whoa, steady on your feet. I'll get you into the back of your wagon with your brothers."

"My folks are gonna kill me."

"Then next time you should cut back." Nodding to Travis that he was leaving for a moment and to keep his eye on Virginia, Zack stumbled into the fresh night air.

He deposited the fellow next to the other three, then instructed their neighbor, who was driving the team of horses, that all brothers were accounted for so he could leave. When Zack reentered the barn, he was still smiling at the sight of the Smithys heaped into the buckboard.

"What's so funny?" asked Virginia. She held a broom and was sweeping the floor planks around the base of the haymow's new wooden ladder.

"His folks are going to kill him for more than just drinking."

"Why?" Her loose hair cascaded down a bare arm.

"There's been a practical joker at work this evening. None of the brothers realized that someone had switched their team of horses and hitched it to the wrong buckboard."

"How do you know?"

"Because the back of the wagon has a different name carved into it than Smithy and Sons, which I'd noticed earlier when I helped unpack their tools for the barn raising. The tools are gone, too. Their father will have their heads."

"That's terrible."

Zack laughed. "It's harmless fun."

"His poor folks."

"With seven sons, I imagine they're used to it. Some-one's probably paying them back for a prank the Smithys played on them. They'll have to wait to hear which neigh-bor hollers first with the wrong wagon."

Virginia saw the humor then. The warmth of her laugh-ter filled the barn and echoed in her blue eyes.

When they both stilled, he sensed she wanted to discuss the letter, but she looked to see who else was left in the barn, then grew pensive. Two of the remaining four men left, saying good-night.

Zack watched the leaving men blow out half of the lanterns. He focused on something safe. "I saw you talk-ing to your uncle in here ten minutes ago. How's David doing?"

She clasped the broom handle between her hands and lowered her head to rest on them. "He's fine. He's still sleeping. My uncle's going to stay the night at David's side. He insists I get a good night's rest before my exams, so I'll take my blankets and sleep in the great room."

"There's no need for you to sleep there."

"But David's got my bed, and I—"

"You can take mine."

She brushed her fingers over her throat. "I couldn't kick you out of your own bed."

Then let me stay there with you, he wanted to say, but knew he shouldn't. "I've got my bedroll and I'll sleep in the hall right outside your door. You can leave your door and David's door ajar. That way you'll be able to hear if he wakes up and needs you."

"You've already got it worked out."

"I've been thinking about it all evening."

She blushed gently. The smoldering flicker he saw in

her expression equaled his own. Yes, he'd been thinking about her in his bed for hours.

One of the ranch hands whisked a large corn-husk broom by their feet. They dodged out of his way.

She bent to the floor, filling the dustpan, then carried it to the wooden bucket in the corner. "I spoke to Superintendent Ridgeway about my uncle."

Zack took the broom from her and leaned it against the wall. He looked down at her soft face. "So that's what you two were discussing."

"He says he'll have two men here in the morning at six to accompany me and Travis—"

"I'm going with you to your exams, not Travis."

She looked to her feet. "Oh."

He felt a sadness that their day was ending.

"Are you sure Hank was feeling well tonight?" She leaned against the boards of the empty stall, which was brimming with fresh laid straw. "From a distance he looked pale to me. I wish I'd had a chance to examine him before he left."

Zack's anger at the man resurfaced. Hank sure as hell was guilty, and he didn't deserve the respect Virginia was allotting him. "The circulation in his foot is fine. I made him wiggle his toes like I've seen you do. The fort's surgeon, Dr. Calloway, has returned from the north and will see Hank in the morning. You don't have to worry."

She nodded and he came around to lean against the beam beside her.

The reassuring weight of his guns shifted in his holsters. "You've never met Dr. Calloway, have you?"

"Actually, I have. He was here for the first two weeks when I arrived. Before you arrived on the train from the mountains."

"It must have been difficult to get to know everything and everyone on your own."

She peered into the dark corners of the stall. "I managed."

"And then I came back and blew everything sky-high."

When she turned to face him, her cheeks glowed in the lamplight. Before she could reply, someone called.

"Good night, all!" Extinguishing all the lanterns except the one beside Zack and Virginia, the last man left the barn. He swung the double doors closed behind him at the back of the barn. The soft thud echoed across the room, dissipating in the piles of loose straw. It was dark, save for the solitary glowing lantern beside Virginia's face.

Now they were alone. Zack's pulse stirred at the thought of taking her into his arms.

"What happened with Hank Johnson today?"

Zack frowned. "I was expecting him earlier to join us at the barn raising, but he said he felt sick in the morning and couldn't come till this evening. He was here for less than an hour. It was an awful lot of trouble for two men to bring him for so short a time. But I could tell from the little resistance he put up when I took his guns that he wasn't here to…shoot anyone. Still, he is up to no good."

And Zack would see to it that he paid for his sins.

"What reason did you give him for removing his guns?"

"I told him it was too hard to wheel him around in his chair with the weight he was carrying. He got the guns when we hoisted him back into the wagon, so I don't think he's suspicious that we know anything."

"Why do you think he was here tonight?"

"That's what I keep asking myself."

With a soft sigh, she removed an envelope from her pocket. A five-dollar bill fell out with it. "Your parents returned the money I sent them."

They were finally alone to discuss it. "I see."

"It took me a month to save that much." Her face was silhouetted in darkness.

It was a lot of money, he thought, considering that a good wage for a man was a dollar a day. Of course, as a country doctor, she earned slightly more. Not a quarter as much as a city doctor, though.

"I figure I still owe your folks one thousand and ninety-five dollars for my education, but they say they're going to decline it."

"That's good."

Her expression grew soft. "They told me you'd already sent them a hundred and eighty dollars, and that they weren't to accept anything from me."

He nodded, fascinated by the delicate way she tipped the letter in her hands.

"It must have taken you a while to save that money. Why do you want to pay for my education?"

Sentiment tugged at his insides. "Because Andrew and I owe you that much."

"But it's not from Andrew, they said. It's from you."

"Andrew left you after six years of stringing you along. When I discovered he'd married Grace after knowing her for less than a month, I gave him a talking-to that made his ears ring."

She glanced down at the straw by her booted feet.

"And then shortly after that, I left you, as well."

Her eyes glistened.

"It seems to me you've been the only honest one among us."

She slid away from the stall. She backed into a patch

of darkness. Her face was hidden. "I'd like to contribute to my education as well, so I'll…I'll continue to send them payment and would appreciate if you'd convince them to take it. But I'll accept your help, too, Zack, and I thank you from the bottom of my heart." She moved away from him. "Good night."

In one easy stride, he caught her hand and entwined his probing fingers with her pliant ones.

"We're alone," he murmured. "Stay."

She wiggled out of his grasp and reached the single barn door. She held the latch. "I can't," she whispered. "It hurts too much to be near you."

He came up from behind, slid his fingers along her arms, buried his face into her scented hair and pleaded, "Stay."

He felt her body shudder.

Her words were a tremor. "Tomorrow I don't want to regret anything I may do with you tonight."

"Don't think about tomorrow."

"Zack…"

"Stay."

Chapter Seventeen

"It doesn't feel right." With a burst of vigor, Virginia tried to push open the door.

Dismayed at the shift in her resolve, Zack blocked her hand with the bulk of his hard body. Peering down into her heated face, he felt a slow smile lift his mouth. He was just as determined she stay.

"Let me out," she sputtered. Her drop earrings jarred with her movements. She clamped down on his firm arm, but he didn't budge.

"Not until we've cleared the air and I tell you—*show you*—what I want from *Dr. Virginia Waters*." He tried to rope an arm around her, but she yanked away and nearly fell backward.

She gaped at him, hair spilling around her shoulders. "You...louse!"

"God, I was stupid to let you go. You could have been my wife and I could have been sampling your charms every night."

"Don't talk to me like that!"

"I talk the way I want."

"Someone might hear!"

"Always concerned about the neighbors. Sometimes I

wonder if you're sorry about your broken engagements because of the way you feel about Andrew and me, or because of the embarrassment it's caused you in front of the town."

"How dare you!" Her hand came up to slap him, but he caught it and held firm.

"There's no one around, Virginia. You don't have to put up that front of propriety with me."

"Let me go! I don't act any different in private than I do in public."

He pulled her up against his chest, one stone-hard thigh pressing against hers. "Yes you do. When we're in public you barely look at me. You say polite things, the things you think you should be saying when all I want is to hear you shout the truth."

"That's laughable!"

"Tell me you *want me* to make love to you!"

"I don't!"

"Tell me that you feel the blood rushing beneath your skin like I do. That you feel the pounding of excite ment—"

"You're so bloody conceited—"

"That you long to feel the thrill of my mouth on your body once again."

Her cheeks flamed. Her other hand came up and punched him hard in his weak shoulder. This time he stumbled and groaned.

"You can't hold me here against my will!"

He caught her from behind, cinched a firm arm around her waist and pulled with all his might. They stumbled backward but neither would let go.

"You don't know what you want!" he panted. He kept pulling until they stumbled through a stall and fell onto a heap of straw.

''And *you* do?'' she shouted, trying to roll away, but he rolled with her, his grip unrelenting until she was lying on top of him.

''Uh,'' he grumbled beneath her weight. ''Can't you see? *I want you.*''

''And I want you…out of my life.''

He stumbled for a second. Then with a slow smile, he found the button on her skirt.

''Leave that button alone!''

She struggled to snatch his hand away but only managed to slacken the wedge between them so that he was able to roll again, this time on top of her.

''You wore this dress for me.''

Sticks of straw poked out of her hair. ''I did not!''

''Then who for? The old cook?''

''For—for myself.''

''Because it makes you *feel* as beautiful as you look. Don't tell me you don't notice the way men's heads turn as you pass. You thought you could tease me and display your temptations and think that somehow I'd be able to resist. *Well I can't!*''

He buried his face at the neckline of her blouse, snaking a hand to her midriff, but this time she hit him harder in his weak shoulder.

''Ugh,'' he mumbled, pain shooting down his arm. Unexpectedly he released her and she scrambled to one knee.

Her words spilled in a nervous tumble. ''You shouldn't have—have done that. I'm leaving now.''

He moaned deep in his throat, gripping his arm, staggering back to lean against the stall boards and trying to catch his breath.

She jumped to her feet. Tiny strands of the dried grass that covered her clothes succumbed to gravity, falling to her feet. The particles shimmered like gold dust, trapped in the moonlight, cascading through a nearby screened window. "I'm going."

"Hmm," he said, nodding weakly. She'd won. "Go."

Quivering, she twisted at her slender waist, but her feet didn't move. She watched him with wary apprehension. He tried not to grunt, but the pain...

"*Go,*" he demanded. "You're free from my hold."

She whimpered, almost inaudible. "Please...I'm sorry. Can I see your shoulder?"

"Sometimes I get an unexpected jolt and it...it stings for a bit, but I don't need you here."

She fell to her knees in the straw. "Zack," she groaned. "What have I done?"

Almost with a frenzy, she began unbuttoning his white shirt, starting from the top where the open collar met with his chest. Although his shoulder still throbbed, the hot feel of the teasing tips of her fingers pushed away the physical pain and replaced it with a lonely squeeze of his heart. She didn't want him, but he *craved* her.

Expertly she slid her hands lower and when she reached his belt, she gave the fabric a good hard yank, pulling his shirttail from his pants.

Astonished, he sucked in the air between them, filling his lungs with Virginia's delicious scent. His arteries pounded. He'd never been undressed by a woman before, doctor or not. And this woman had the coaxing touch that could force a man into any crime.

"If I could paint," he said gently, holding back his urge to possess *her,* tracing his fingers along the velvet choker at her throat and marveling at its softness. "If I were an artist, I'd paint you at this moment."

She quaked beneath his graze. Her fingers trembled on the last button. Moonlight dipped its golden rays around her body, the voluptuous swell of her breasts and gently angled hips as she perched toward him in the sweet grass.

His voice grew hushed. "And then I'd keep it for my private viewing pleasure."

Lowering her head and parting his shirt, she said the most honest thing he'd heard her say. "I want more in my life than a moment's worth of pleasure." Her lips softened into a swirl. "I want to feel great passion and great joy. And I don't want it for only one night."

"Isn't it better to be on an even keel in life? Fewer ups means fewer downs, because along with great joy comes great pain. You can't feel one without the other. Look at Lucy Peters," he offered.

"Lucy would be the first to tell you that every second spent with her husband was a second she'll remember to her grave."

Zack's chest tightened with emotion. Virginia asked for so much. At one time before he'd fully known her, he'd been willing to marry her. Now the thought that he'd never be able to live up to her expectations scared the hell out of him. Why couldn't she be a simpler woman?

Because then she wouldn't be Virginia.

"Let's see," she said tenderly, pulling his shirt down over his shoulder, revealing his tanned torso, making him conscious of how much larger and thicker his body was than hers. Why couldn't he get her to look at him like that beyond when she examined his injury?

"It hurts here," he whispered, raising his strong right arm to pinch the muscle over his left collarbone. His movements were constricted by the half-open shirt slung down his arms.

"Here," she repeated, winding her fingers over the spot and kneading gently.

"Mmm. That's nice." He rocked with her. "And here."

Her touch was gentle and relaxing, but on the other hand, made his senses burst with life. He heard the crackle of straw beneath her ankles, smelled the scent of trapped clover in her hair, could almost taste her salty skin.

She kept massaging. "I hope I didn't break the bone again."

"I don't think so. Earlier today, I picked up a pail of nails and the same thing happened."

"Why didn't you tell me the pain can still be sharp?"

"The pain can still be sharp, Doc." He cupped his good hand over her moving one and slid them both over his heart. "Especially here."

Her lips parted. Her head inclined and her face filled with soft shadows. He dipped his head and slowly slid his lips along hers.

The touch was soft, like cotton against feathers. Softer than he'd ever felt in a woman's lips. Cautiously he coaxed her mouth open with his own, basking in the sweet moistness and her hesitant yet arousing response.

With eyes closed, heavy and drunk with need, he trailed a hand up her throat, large enough to easily encompass it, then splayed his fingers over her soft cheek and ear.

She moaned then, and he knew with damn certainty that she was his tonight.

She was his.

His body hardened. When he slid his tongue along her upper lip, she pulled back slightly, then he felt the exhilarating swirl of her own tongue beckoning his.

She was sin itself, and heaven, rolled into one.

Go slow, he told himself.

With his shirt unbuttoned and torso exposed, he roped her hair with his hand, then entwined it around the nape of her neck, fingering her smooth velvet choker. She responded by hoisting to her knees and lifting her arms up and over his bare shoulders, pressing her body flat against his. Her breasts crushing against his solid chest drove him into a wild frenzy. The kiss deepened and ripened and demanded more.

He always wanted more when it came to Virginia.

Zack pulled her to his lap and, through the fabric of her skirts and his denim pants, he centered her bottom on top of his full erection. She murmured softly, the lamplight exposing her sensual smile.

He'd have her in every position imaginable.

"Why can't I stay away from you?" She slid her arms into the sides of his open shirt, along his bare skin.

He shuddered with the touch. "Because I've hypnotized you."

Her mouth parted into laughter, but he wouldn't surrender her lips and he kept kissing.

She placed her heated hand at the back of his neck and stroked. "What about tomorrow?"

The hairs at the back of his neck where she touched bristled in sexual response. "We can do this again tomorrow."

"That's not what I meant." Her soft smile tugged at his heart.

"I know what you meant," he said, whispering into her temple. He had some thoughts on that, awakening feelings that had come to him as he'd watched her tonight with David, but he was afraid to voice them. "Let's take tonight first."

She didn't disagree. She pressed her hold further to the small of his back, running her fingers up his spine and making him tremble to his boots.

"Virginia," he groaned. Then with one easy glide of

his fingers, he took hold of her gathered off-the-shoulder neckline and pulled it down over her corset. He pulled that down, too, until her breasts popped out, an inch from his face.

"You take my breath away." Taking one succulent nipple into his mouth, he tongued around its perimeter, taunting her, goading her to beg him to suck. Cupping that breast with his hand, his lips traveled across her moon-clad body to the other breast she offered.

The breast swung into his mouth, its flat areola already tensing and pulling to attention. To his delighted shock, he felt her hand sliding along his thigh, aiming for the center of his pants.

With a feather touch, she stroked along his shaft.

Arching slightly to meet her eager hand, he ached to burst out of his confinement.

"I'm curious," she whispered. "Can a woman do it to a man?"

He leaned his head back in disbelief, unsure of what she was asking but hoping like mad it was what he imagined. She was disheveled, her hair in knots around her shoulders, her skin flushed with the fever of lovemaking, her eyes dampened with arousal. And those pretty golden earrings dangled at her throat. "Do what?"

"Can I kiss you there?"

He groaned in ecstasy. "Anywhere you want."

She smiled that elusive smile, kissing his neck and clawing at his sleeves to remove his shirt. She removed her hands from his thighs, and he wondered if perhaps her question was simply hypothetical.

Pulsing with heightened anticipation when he was out of his shirt, he grabbed the hem of her dress and slid it over her head, revealing her underclothes.

"You wore the blue one," he said gruffly. "The blue corset. It's beautiful."

With his help, she unbuttoned it, then slid out of her bloomers. She wore nothing but stockings and glimmering golden earrings.

Taking great pains to restrain himself, to take it slow and make it memorable for her, he lifted her foot and planted it on his chest. Reaching up around her thigh, he groped for the top of her white stocking and, when he found it, began rolling it down her shapely leg.

Her hands fell still. He felt a slow trickle of sweat, a culmination of body heat drizzle down his chest.

When one leg was unclad, he grabbed her by the ankle, turned up her leg and reveled in her beauty. His gaze trailed from her watchful eyes down the soft turn of her nose, the swell of her upper lip, then down her silken throat. It traveled farther over her swollen golden breasts, down the valley of her belly button and the darkness between her thighs.

She was everything any man could ever want.

He desperately needed release, yet he strove to pace himself.

He slowly removed her other stocking, noticing that a trickle of sweat had wound its path down between her breasts.

"Take off your pants." Her voice rippled through the heated air.

"Take them off for me."

She rose to sit on her naked bottom, straw rustling, scents mingling. When she reached for the buttons of his crotch he could barely believe the good doctor was doing what she was doing.

As bashful as she was, whatever doubts she'd had about this evening seemed to have disappeared, replaced by an overwhelming determination to unite with him—the same persistence he felt for her.

His fly came undone and his erection strained forward. With her burning eyes upon him, he raised to his knees, slid off his pants and drawers, then fell to one muscled side to remove the rest of it.

She spoke with caution. "I like seeing you move."

He growled, caught her at the waist and tumbled on top of her. He snatched kisses along her arms, teasing her in places she'd probably never been kissed before: the point of her collarbone, the skin at the fold of her underarm, the tip of her forefinger, the side of her hip, the inside of her knee, and finally the arch of her pretty foot.

Proudly, when he finished his course, he peered up at her only to find her more flushed and desirable than before. She raised her face toward him. The skin of her ankles smelled of night warmth.

"Would you kiss me like you did before, Zack?"

He growled, then parted her knees and began to kiss and coax and slide his tongue along the inside of her thighs.

She turned to jelly and fell back into the straw, muscles unwinding, savoring his touch. He explored the gentle folds of her private area, but this time he wouldn't satiate her with his tongue. He wanted to delve inside her, to hold her in his arms while making love to her and feeling her explode around his erection.

Yet he slowly teased her throbbing center with his fingers, sliding into the wetness and enjoying her scent, licking the firm circle of pink until the rumbling at the back of her throat told him she was near. Taking a moment to catch his breath, he pressed his temple to her knee and buckled his grip around her thighs. He began kissing his way back up her rounded belly, making his way toward her face.

She murmured, "It's my turn."

Gentle hands came to rest upon his thighs, her fingers pressing with urgency.

He didn't want to hurt her spirit, to string her along and insinuate by this union...

But he couldn't stop her and couldn't halt his hands from reaching out to span her narrow waist as she lowered herself to kiss him.

When he felt a flash of fluttering lips at the base of his shaft, he fell like clay in her hands. "Ahh...Virginia..."

Her tongue explored the velvet skin of his erection, causing his sensations to drift to glory. He'd been alone for years and had sought the company of several women to quell his loneliness, but none of them had kissed him where Virginia was placing her lips.

Adrift in pleasure, he lifted his arm and captured her soft, dangling breast. She made a satisfied sound at the back of her throat, and he knew his last thread of restraint had just left.

His fingers slid to her waist. As unbearable as it was to part with her, he peeled her off his body and pressed her to the mound of straw.

"Did you like that?"

He grumbled with the agony of pleasure. "You're irresistible."

Rising on an elbow, he peered into her sparkling blue eyes and kissed her deeply. She wrapped her arms around his shoulders while he eased himself on top of her.

"Spread your legs," he begged.

She parted, bringing her knees up to wrap against his waist. With a moan of intensifying bliss, he eased one hand onto her stomach, parted her moist folds, then entered.

It was a grand rush of heat and pressure, the ultimate joy of man and woman entangled as one. Beneath lazy lids, he watched her mouth part open in a gasp. She arched back, panting while he gazed at the beauty of her rib cage, breasts rolling back and forth beneath his firm, tanned hands. He thrust into her as deeply as he could and she met him with a fervor. Goose bumps arose on her flesh.

He swooped down to her neck and kissed. ''Would you like to try another position?''

''Mmm.'' She smiled in that way that tightened his stomach.

''Then turn over.''

Her nipples jiggled, and she pulled away and rolled over to her knees.

Her hair spilled over one shoulder, revealing the golden arch of her spine and buttocks. Kneading his hands along her creamy shoulders, he then traced her body along her tender waist, pausing at her angled hips. He planted his possessive hands on her bottom cheeks. Balancing on his knees, he plunged forward and encased himself in Virginia.

A gurgle of pleasure escaped from her throat. Dipping over her back so that his chest pressed against her, he cupped her breasts from the bottom.

''That's nice...it feels good,'' she said. ''You feel good.''

But it was too much pleasure for him to last long enough to please her. He pulled out, flipped her over and took her from the front. ''I want to see and kiss your face.''

Nose to nose, she gripped his upper arms as they coupled again. Her eyelids fluttered closed as he twirled the tip of his index finger around her navel, up beneath her ribs, around each nipple, then up her slender throat. Gently but with insistence, his fingers moved down lower to her swollen center, gliding along wet silk. She was ripe and ready for him, and he was so eager to please.

Her body tensed beneath his fingers. He bent lower to kiss her throat as she let the tide take her. He found her mouth and kissed her. When he pulled away, her eyelids trembled, her mouth puckered and her breath grew hot and urgent.

"Zack…" Her words choked out of her throat. "Zack…"

Joy centered in his heart as he watched her wail his name. His hold grew stronger, more rhythmic, primal in its need.

He raised her buttocks with both hands, calloused from the day's work, and held her in midair as he lost control. His muscles exploded in the timeless beat of lovemaking.

His heart leaped inside his chest with a thousand new sensations. Nothing in life had prepared him for Virginia.

Virginia was unaware how much time had passed, but nestled in Zack's arms, she watched the moonlight filtering through the window and yearned for the night never to end. She reprimanded herself for wanting more. She *knew* there'd been no promises about the future. He'd *told* her outright.

For a moment she could barely breathe, barely think about the things they'd done.

It's been heaven.

She struggled to push away regrets. "What time do you think it is?"

Zack wove a strand of straw from her hair, brushing

his fingertips across her bare shoulders. "It must be past two. Maybe three."

"Mercy." She bolted upright, still naked but clutching her dress to her bosom. "I'd almost forgotten about my exams this morning. I need to get some rest. And Uncle Paddy will wonder what we've been doing as soon as he sees me stumble in looking like—" She stopped herself from finishing and wondered if Zack were right. Was she overly concerned about what others thought of her?

"Your uncle's probably asleep." Zack shot up beside her and reached for his pants. "Your exams, though, I apologize. You need to be able to think clearly, and here I've kept you up for hours."

"I've managed on less sleep." She struggled into the straps of her corset, sliding buttons into place.

"But these are crucial exams." He whisked her up, stopping briefly to plant a full kiss on her mouth.

His nearness calmed her, yet she wondered in a panic how many more kisses there'd be. Or if the bliss she felt would suddenly end.

"Here," he said, holding her petticoat for her to step into. He was only wearing his shirt, his hips still bare and thighs exposed, and the vision enthralled her. She'd never tire of looking at Zack.

But time was essential. They dressed briskly, ran fingers through their hair as best they could, and when Zack stole into the ranch house slowly leading Virginia, they were still picking bits of dried grass off each other.

Travis peered unexpectedly around the corner, nodded when he saw it was them, then disappeared before Virginia's flush of cherry-red cheeks could greet him. He was on night watch, awaiting their return. She felt guilty for keeping Travis awake, for when the officer was extremely tired, he limped from an old bullet wound to his thigh.

Between Zack and Travis, Virginia knew she owed them her life.

On tiptoe she peered into the open door of her bedroom. Uncle Paddy and David were both sleeping. Her uncle was propped in a worn leather chair which someone had carried in from the great room. Lying in her bed, David exhaled peacefully. She stepped beside him to place a finger on his wrist, liked the slow steady beat of his pulse, then took her nightgown and slid into Zack's bedroom to join him.

He was gathering his bedroll when she entered.

The square room smelled of masculinity, of shaving supplies and leather boots and laundered shirts from the Mountie fort. The plain wool blanket symbolized all that was Zack—sleek and to the point, not a flounce of decorative stitching on it, but bulky and clean and promising of warmth.

The moment exemplified the very things that were right and wrong between them. She'd sleep in his bed tonight. She'd be cozy and tight and surrounded by the things she loved about him. Yet she'd be waking up alone.

It crushed her to think of parting. Zack kissed her temple and slid his fingers beneath her chin. Although his face was cast in shadows, she noticed the furrow between his brows and the unspoken words that clung to his lips.

Good night. Goodbye.

He took his duffel cloth bag and she heard rather than saw him unwind his bedroll in the hall.

Unsettled, she picked up his cotton undershirt that he'd earlier tossed onto a chair.

After changing into her nightclothes, tucking her feet into his sheets, his blankets, his bed, she bundled up his undershirt and placed it beneath her head.

Things were gearing up for a showdown with Stiller.

Zack wasn't ready. His aim was still slow and poor, and she sensed that around her he sometimes lost his cool demeanor, his concentration. Her presence seemed to weaken rather than strengthen him. He didn't think clearly around her.

She knew it was wrong to bargain with God, but she bargained anyway. *Please keep Zack safe. If he's safer without me beside him…I promise I'll step aside.*

Turning quietly so that the three men outside her door couldn't hear, she buried her face in the soft cotton. She inhaled the scent of the man she now realized she was in love with and fought the sob in her throat.

Chapter Eighteen

There was much Zack wanted to say to Virginia, yet he hadn't deciphered in his heart what it was he wanted to express. When she was with him, he could think of little else. That wasn't good, he thought, given the danger surrounding them.

Squinting in the clear-morning sunrise, with Virginia seated beside him on the buckboard and two constables on horseback behind them, Zack hurried the horses. It was past six o'clock and she was due for examinations by 7:00 a.m. "Are you reviewing material in that pretty head?"

Virginia nodded. "Going over the names of the muscles of the upper body."

He patted her knee. "I enjoyed last night."

He couldn't read her expression as she glanced at her hands.

"What are you thinking?"

She turned her face into the sunrise and it colored her skin orange. "About the clinical presentations of rheumatism."

He was put off by the distance in her voice, although

knowing she needed to think about her studies. They finished the trip in silence.

It wasn't the time or place to talk about last night, but he'd barely slept for reliving those midnight hours, making love to her again, her body on top of his, her lips warming his throat. The memory rattled him as he clutched the reins tighter.

They rolled into town along Macleod Trail, past the cutoff to the fort and past the storefront windows till they stopped in front of the courthouse. Judge Dodd would be supervising as Virginia wrote her papers and John Calloway would administer the oral questioning. As Zack understood it, the district of Alberta licensed physicians under the North-West Territories Act, and Virginia would know the final results of her testing before the week was finished.

John Calloway was waiting for them at the front doors. Dressed in a light deerskin jacket and wearing his Stetson, he turned to wave hello. With quiet reassurance, he placed one hand on his gun and holster, indicating to Zack that the commander had explained the need for Virginia's safety.

As the fort's chief surgeon, John had returned two days ago from his emergency call in the northern fort. Due to a buildup of patients he needed to see in Calgary, he wasn't able to attend the barn raising yesterday. He'd also told Zack he wanted to spend every extra minute with his wife, Sarah, and young son, who'd just learned to walk. John had once been an untamable bachelor, but his mail-order bride had won his heart. The couple initially had problems in their marriage but had fought hard to solve them. Maybe, thought Zack, his own problems with Virginia were worth fighting for, too.

"Where will you be today?" Virginia asked Zack as

she slid to the ground. "Will you be waiting for me here?"

Zack nodded hello to John and answered with regret. "I've got to see the commander first."

John stepped forward and took Virginia's medical bag. "You won't be needing this inside. I'm afraid nothing's allowed except paper and quill. I'll hold it for you."

"Thank you for coming today, John."

"My wife, Sarah, would have killed me if I hadn't returned from Edmonton in time to let the only female physician in Alberta write her exams."

Virginia's eyes lit with gratitude. "I've met Sarah and little Colton. Please say hello for me. As far as payment for writing the examinations, do I give it to you? I've got the bank draft here in my bag." She unsnapped a buckle and handed John the note.

He held it up. "I'm supposed to take it to the bank manager. He knows in which account to deposit it. But I think I'll wait till this afternoon when my payroll gets in to save me another trip. Anything else I can do for either one of you?"

Virginia shook her head then frowned as she caught Zack rubbing his sore shoulder. "Is your shoulder still sore from last night?"

He wouldn't admit it, because she felt bad enough as it was. "Just a little tight." Hell, it was sorer than it'd been for two weeks. Last night she'd hit him square in the nerve.

"Let's go," said John.

Zack swung his legs off the seat, about to disembark to say goodbye, but she was already walking away.

"Bye, Zack!" she hollered over her shoulder. John held open the courthouse door.

"Good luck, Doc!" Zack hollered, but was afraid his words got lost as she entered the building.

She hadn't glanced back and it bothered him.

He rode into the fort, noticing how empty it was, but normal for this time of day. Most of the able-bodied Mounties were out on patrol over the prairies, or tending to problems in town, or investigating crimes and accumulating evidence. Only the older men, retired or unfit for physical duty, remained to tend to the horses, or the smithy, or stock supplies.

Zack thought about the dismissive glance Virginia had given him, kept thinking about it as he watered the horses, and then as he strode into the commander's office.

He thought about her reluctance to speak about last night as the commander explained how many dozens of men had been dispatched along the railway line to the mountains. They were being centered in areas deemed weakest points of attack by Stiller and his men, who would undoubtedly strike the opera house gold in four days' time.

Zack thought about how hard he'd fallen for her as he explained to Superintendent Ridgeway how curious Hank Johnson had behaved at the barn raising, as Zack listed the names of everyone who'd been there yesterday, while both he and the commander tried to piece together the significance.

Finally, close to ten o'clock, Zack took one of the horses from the stables and rode to the courthouse to check on Virginia. John had left to tend to his patients at the hospital, promising to return in the afternoon to start the orals. The two constables stood outside the courtroom guarding the door.

Zack pushed the door slightly and peered inside. Virginia was hunched over a stack of papers. Large diagrams of the human body were propped on tables around her, and Judge Dodd had his feet propped up on a table while he read from his law books.

"I'll be outside." Zack nodded to his men and walked out into the sunshine.

There was an oddity in…the situation. He was missing a key piece of the puzzle. An overlooked detail. It didn't have to do with Virginia's situation, it was something else.

Then with a mounting urgency, he jumped on his horse and rode back to the fort. "Something's not right," he told the commander. "Are you sure about the timing of the gold shipment? Was it double-checked?"

"Triple-checked. It's leaving Wednesday night from Regina, should be passing through the Rockies Friday morning at five o'clock. Our men are lined up and ready. We've got Dirk McGuire cornered. Hank Johnson's about to unravel. What's missing?"

"I don't know, but I'm taking three more men with me to wait at the courthouse while Virginia finishes."

"I haven't got three men to spare. The fort's empty. You've got two already *plus* John. Plus yourself."

Zack was galloping to the courthouse when the pieces fell together.

"Goddammit!" He reined in his horse tightly, his mind reeling with the puzzle, his blood pounding with the realization. His mount neighed and bucked.

"Stiller's not going for the gold shipment!" He turned his horse around and raced back to the fort to notify the commander and stop it before it happened.

Even though Zack hadn't witnessed it, he was damn sure the reason Hank had appeared last night at the barn raising was to give Dirk a message.

And Calloway had casually mentioned that same message this morning at the courthouse.

The message was that the Mountie payroll was due in this afternoon by stagecoach. The payroll gold was coming in from the south, from Fort Macleod as it did near the middle of every month. Exact dates were a secret for security reasons and changed every time. It wasn't nearly the cache of gold Stiller could steal from the opera house. But by scooping it from under Zack's nose, crippling the town's protection, by sending half the Mounties on a false chase to the Rockies, Stiller would be teaching Zack a lesson he'd never forget. Stiller was smarter, faster and fearless.

The son of a bitch was after their payroll gold!

With a long-legged leap, Zack crashed through the commander's door. It was empty.

"Where'd he go?" Zack demanded of the clerk sitting at his desk outside the commander's office.

"His wife came by in her buggy, and they've gone to lunch like they do every day."

Zack strode to the gun cabinet and removed two rifles. "Send word to him immediately. Tell him I'm pulling the two Mountie guards out of the jailhouse. Tell him I need more men. Stiller's after our payroll gold, and I'm heading out to stop him."

The corporal jumped. "Yes, sir!"

Zack bounced out the door and ran the fifty yards to the jailhouse. "Smithy! Apricot!"

The two guards, one as old as Moses, grandfather to the Smithy boys who'd binged last night at the barn raising, the other a new recruit so young he was barely shaving his peach fuzz—hence the nickname Apricot— jumped to the call.

Their prisoner Coyote thrust himself off his bed behind bars. "What's goin' on?"

"Your time's up." Zack motioned to the gun rack, indicating the guards. "Take yourselves two rifles apiece and lots of bullets for your handguns."

"Where we goin'?"

"To seek justice."

"What about our prisoner?"

"As long as the cell's locked, he'll be fine here."

Coyote rattled the bars. "I *demand* to know what's goin' on."

"Demand? That's a funny choice of words for a man who still won't answer any of *our* questions."

Coyote glared back at Zack. "I never will."

"Even if I ask your mama on the potato farm?"

The young man flashed a look of horror, then rage. "Shit!"

But Zack, Moses and Apricot were already running through the door. Zack had a horse but the other two didn't.

"Grab those!" Zack pointed to the two hitched to the commander's post by the clerk who was about to mount his gelding.

They tore off in a southern direction. When they heard a distant echo of gunshot blasts, Zack felt a sick pounding in his stomach. Gunshots. That wasn't good. He cursed and urged his horse faster. The other two men barely kept pace.

Zack spotted something peculiar half a mile into the blowing grassland. He flagged his men behind a line of trees. "There's the stagecoach, but I don't see the accompanying four Mounties. I see two other horsemen riding behind."

The three men stared glumly at the lonely coach. They knew what it meant. By the gunshots they'd heard, Zack had been right. Stiller had already taken control.

Zack shook with violent rage. He knew that if he had to, he'd fight to the death. As the coach drew closer, he squinted. "Do you see the two men, strangers by the way they're dressed, sitting inside the coach? They've got their arms propped outside the window."

"How can you see that far, sir?" asked Apricot. "I can barely make out the coach and horsemen."

"They don't call him Bull's-Eye for nothin'," said Moses. "He's got the sharpest vision of any marksman I've known."

"They're pulling away," said Zack. "Hell, they're turning around. Let's go!"

While Stiller's gang raced along the road, Zack led the other charge, invisibly racing parallel on the lower slopes behind the trees. They were only a hundred yards from the coach when they were spotted.

Gunshots rang out at them as they trailed and raced. Zack was unsure if there were any Mounties inside per-haps still alive, so he commanded no shots to be returned.

With a team of six horses, the coach sped faster and faster through the trees and wheat fields. When it turned the corner, the right wheels lifted off the ground and ev-erything careened. Catching its balance again, it headed in the general direction of the Peters ranch.

"No," Zack whispered.

But the coach headed straight for it. When it reared to a jostling stop in a cloud of dust beside the cabin, Zack ordered his men to stop.

Moses and Apricot followed Zack's dismount, ducking behind the barn. When Moses climbed off the com-mander's stallion, Zack swore. "Smithy, you've been hit."

"It's nothin'," said the old man, clinging to his rib cage. But blood was spilling onto his pants.

Zack tore a sleeve off his shirt and wound it around the man's waist. "Sit here and don't move."

Then he ordered Apricot up around the other side of the barn. The area seemed absurdly quiet, as if Lucy and her family weren't in. Zack prayed the house was empty. When he heard the faint sound of a horse and buggy coming in from the west behind the barn, Zack peered in that direction. He had difficulty seeing through all the trees, but was grateful Stiller and his men had their view totally obstructed by the barn.

Paddy Waters was approaching in his sparkling buggy, and sitting beside him was a bandaged David Fitzgibbon. Paddy had a good horse who could lead them home even if Paddy couldn't see an inch in front of his face. Zack grumbled at their arrival.

But the good news was three more riders were coming in from the other direction. Two of them were Mounties and...goddammit—someone with a skirt. Virginia.

When they rode in, shielded by the barn, Zack slid out to meet them. He flashed his eyes at Virginia but spoke to her accompanying guards. "Why the hell did you bring *her?*"

"The clerk was in a panic. Said you needed help. We're the only ones he could reach so far. We couldn't very well leave her behind, unguarded. And we thought if anyone got harmed on our side, we'd need a doctor. Judge Dodd offered her his horse. The clerk's still looking for the commander and said he'd get word to John Calloway, too."

Zack watched Virginia's expression grow tense. He told her, "There are four wounded Mounties somewhere out there in the field....but Smithy, here, needs your help."

She took her bag and ran to the fallen Mountie.

Paddy's buggy rolled in and stopped at the side of the road. "Where's the widow Peters?" he called.

Zack motioned a finger to his lips to silence the man. When Paddy and David joined them behind the barn, Paddy explained himself. "I'm taking David home as planned, and thought I'd stop by and explain to Lucy what happened to me last week when Diana took ill."

David, ashen from his surgery of the night before and dazed on pain medicine, glanced at the coach. "This could make a good story."

Zack shot him a cold look of warning. "Keep still, don't open your mouth, and stay behind the barn or I'll shoot you myself."

Turning back to the situation at hand, the cutthroats inside the house, Zack's fear escalated. Where was Lucy? Where were her children?

Zack cocked the hammer of his six-shooter. He held two guns, but the weight of the one in his left hand ratcheted the pain in his left shoulder. Of all the bloody times to have his injury flare up.

He called into the air. "Leave the gold and we'll work out a deal."

Zack waited so long for an answer that he wasn't sure the four men inside had heard.

Then a voice bellowed through the air. "The deal is...you let us ride out of here with the gold and we won't come back to kill Virginia Waters."

"Christ," said Zack. "That's Stiller's voice." He'd heard it once before in the mountain cabin with the O'Connolleys, but it'd been too dark to make out Stiller's face. Zack stumbled back, his spine hitting the wooden planks of the barn. "Who've you got inside?"

There was another long pause. "A couple of youngsters. One boy and an older girl."

Chapter Nineteen

Having controlled the bleeding on the Mountie jailer, Virginia sagged against the barn boards in terror when she heard the exchange. Peering over at Zack, she watched his look of alarm spread. The gang had captured Kyle and one of the girls.

Through the splintered walls pressing along her spine, she felt a vibration—the movement of large animals inside. They were the cows most likely, for the sheep were in the meadow.

Where was Lucy? It wasn't like her to—

Another sound came from inside the barn. Muffled sounds.

Human voices!

Virginia bolted to her hands and knees, and raced to Zack.

"Lay down!" he commanded.

She ducked but kept coming.

"What is it?"

"There's someone in the barn," she whispered, her blood pumping. "I heard noises, like someone telling someone else to be quiet."

His gaze flickered. "It must be Lucy and her other daughter."

"There's more than two of them inside. I'd swear I heard three, maybe four voices. Young voices."

"Are you sure?"

"Yes." Her heart raced with the excitement, the possibility that Lucy and her children were safe.

"Then who the hell does Stiller claim to have?"

Virginia stared wide-eyed toward the cabin.

"Slide down," Zack whispered.

She slid onto her belly.

Zack called out to the cabin. "What are the names of the children you've got inside?"

"You can ask 'em yourself in a minute when you step back and let us pass."

"He's bluffing," Zack said softly to Virginia. "He's got no one."

"Then how does he know children live here?"

Zack took a minute to think. Then he nodded to the far right of the cabin. "The clothesline. Look. Lucy's got their clothes hanging on the line."

Virginia turned in the same direction, then with relief, she spun back to Zack. He was rubbing his left shoulder. She groaned with fright. "I punched you hard last night. You can't put yourself in the line of danger. You can't shoot. Let the others handle—"

"Shh."

In an instant the sound of a barn door creaking open scattered her heart in a thousand directions. "Stay inside," she pleaded to whoever was peeking out.

"No!" Lucy Peters's voice crackled through the air. "Kyle! No!"

A thunderous bellow escaped from Zack at the same time his body flung through the air toward Kyle. "Kyle!"

Both Zack and Kyle were standing out in the open, exposed to the mercy of the men in the cabin. A cry burst from Virginia.

The boy held a gun between his hands and raced away from his sisters and mother at the barn door, and also away from Zack. Virginia could only see their backs. Ten feet behind the boy with his arms in the air, Zack stopped short when four rifle barrels cracked through the window-panes and aimed.

"Which one of you killed my pa?" Kyle sobbed.

Zack's voice was low and steady, but Virginia recognized a frantic plea that equaled her own. "Kyle, this isn't the place for you to practice your shooting."

"You taught me how to aim. I can do it."

"Not against four men. Put your gun down."

One of the men at the window stood up from his knees and aimed straight at the boy. "If you shoot, kid, it'll be the last thing you'll do in your life."

Zack addressed the men. "Which one of you is Stiller?"

When the tall man with the rifle pointed at Kyle grinned, Virginia felt a twinge of vomit rising to her throat. Stiller was dark-haired, bearded and fit.

"Leave the boy," Zack growled. "I'll ride with you as far as you want out of town. No one will shoot while I'm in the coach beside you."

Stiller studied him with a lean, hungry look.

"Right, guys?" hollered Zack behind him.

"That's right," said the youngest-looking Mountie. The others grumbled in agreement.

"Drop your guns!" said Stiller, and one by one the Mounties tossed them aside.

Virginia's fingers were clasped so tightly around her

knees she could feel the imprints. *There had to be another way*.

Could she do anything?

She looked to David, but he was hunched over a shrub, weak and unable to move. Uncle Paddy's face churned with indecision as he stepped closer and closer to the wide-open space where Zack and Kyle stood, looking as if he desperately wanted to do something. But no one knew how to help.

"Drop your gun, kid," said Stiller, "and move away from the door."

Kyle didn't.

Zack took five slow steps forward with his arms firmly planted in the air. He had such muscled control over his body that he swiftly kicked the gun out of Kyle's fingers from behind, shocking the boy and likely bruising his hand. But Virginia knew it was necessary to disarm Kyle before he was killed.

Stiller and his men came slowly out of the cabin. "Hop into the coach, Bullock. You're going for a ride."

Virginia rose from her bottom to her heels, about to make a move.

But Uncle Paddy jumped out from behind the barn instead, with a gun drawn in the direction of Stiller's voice. He shoved Kyle to the dirt and the boy rolled to safety behind the clothesline.

Uncle Paddy would get himself and Zack killed!

As the sun was streaming down upon them, Virginia knew Uncle Paddy couldn't see five feet in front of him.

Could Stiller tell?

Could the others?

The gunmen stared at the old man who aimed his revolver at Stiller.

The distraction was enough to give Zack the split second he was seeking. In a flash Zack hit the dirt, taking Uncle Paddy with him, pulling out a small gun from his boot and blasting Stiller through the gut.

Virginia clamped her eyes shut in horror as the other Mounties came out with guns blaring.

Within two hours, the Peters ranch was swarming with Mounties, some from the ranch Virginia had been staying at, some who'd been on patrol. Fortunately, Lucy's children hadn't witnessed the bloody battle, Kyle's hand wasn't broken but only bruised, and Luke had two men whisk away the children along with Lucy, Uncle Paddy and David to Uncle Paddy's home in town until the Peters ranch was cleaned and settled. To Virginia, they looked as if they were nearly finished.

She heaved a frayed sigh of relief at what had occurred. Stiller and his men were dead.

"Miraculously," said Dr. John Calloway walking up behind her and Zack, "three of the Mounties who'd been guarding the payroll coach are still alive. They were shot and left for dead in the grass. They're on their way now by covered wagon to the fort hospital, along with Smithy. Unfortunately, one man didn't survive."

"Anyone we know?" asked Zack.

John shook his head sadly. "No, they're all from Fort Macleod. New recruits, they told me."

Virginia winced. What an awful introduction they'd received to the force. She slipped in between John and Zack, feeling safe for the first time in a long while.

Cupping a hand over her eyes, she peered up at John. "Can I help you with the wounded?"

"They've been stabilized. I can manage fine, but I'll holler if I need you. Seems to me you need to rest." Then he squinted in Zack's direction. "This has taken its toll on both of you."

"It's over," Zack whispered as John left, circling an arm around her shoulders.

It felt good to be near him. He was alive. He'd lived through an ordeal she hoped he'd never have to witness again, but recognized in the same fearful moment that in his dangerous line of work, he was likely to face it more than once.

She thanked God for men like Zack.

"Your uncle was really something," he murmured.

Still light-headed, Virginia managed a smile. "I've never met two braver men."

"Virginia, I—"

"Zack!" hollered the commander.

Zack and Virginia whirled toward Superintendent Ridgeway, who was dismounting from his horse—not the stallion Smithy had taken, but Virginia knew his horse was around someplace because Smithy kept begging her to see that the stallion was returned safely to the commander.

She spotted it hitched beside the barn. "Sir, your horse is over there."

He looked where she indicated. "Glad to see you're safe, ma'am. It's interrupted your examinations, though."

"Judge Dodd told me he'd certify that my papers were under his lock and key until I'm ready to finish them. John told me he's available for the orals tomorrow afternoon."

"Tomorrow?" repeated Zack with amusement. "You don't upset easy. You still have a steady hand and clear mind to think about exams?"

Her emotions whirled at the compliment, but she remembered her promise. If Zack was kept safe, then she'd step aside and no longer interfere in his work or his life.

The commander cleared his voice. ''I thought you'd like to know, Zack, that Hank Johnson is in custody along with Dirk McGuire. McGuire's doing an awful lot of talking, but Johnson denies any wrongdoing.''

''We've got evidence, though.'' Zack adjusted his Stetson. ''Travis witnessed them talking at the barn raising, and we've found a trail of money. Johnson was being paid by Stiller. He deposited five-thousand dollars into a Vancouver account. That's where he's been sending some of his payroll money, too, keeping it all out of our sight. He thought he could avoid our suspicions by hiding it, but his behavior alerted us even more. I know where he's been meeting Stiller's men for the past two years. In the dugouts. He's been whittling pieces of wood—a pipe I saw him with—the same cut of white oak I found whittled in one of the dugouts. A useless lever of some sort used to pry open jars.''

''What about Timothy Littlefield?'' asked Virginia. ''Remember those expensive watches you'd found in his possession?''

''It turns out,'' said Zack, ''that the watches are heirlooms passed down from his father, who's a watch collector. Sarah Calloway is a watchmaker, and she verified the dates of origin and value.''

''So who was it who shot you on the train?''

Zack swallowed hard, his bitterness evident. ''McGuire. It was his ruby that had dropped out of his pouch. He'd been paid that day in the precious stones they'd stolen from the O'Connolleys. And it was his voice that had uttered the threat about my bride.''

''They're all facing murder charges. Including Coyote for attempted murder of Virginia,'' said the commander.

She took a minute to compose herself while it sank in. "What does Coyote have to do with potato farming?"

Zack answered. "He grew up on the largest potato farm in the township. His real name is Frank Orynkowski. Unbeknownst to his folks, he uses the farm as a hideout for Stiller's men. He pretends to hire them as transient workers, but in their spare time they scout the banks and businesses for potential hits."

The superintendent reached into the inside of his jacket and pulled out what appeared to be a property deed. "Here you go, Zack, you've earned it."

Zack handled the paper with care as he read.

Unease settled on Virginia. Her words were rushed and brisk. "What's that?"

He looked up. The tree above him caught in the wind, casting shadows of leaves and branches across his face. "I've put ten years of my life into the force. I've earned a hundred and sixty acres of ranching property along with retirement."

"Retirement?" she said in disbelief.

"Christ, I wish you'd reconsider." The commander pulled out an unlit cigar and chomped on its end. "But all you have to do is sign it. I'll give you a minute alone." He sauntered toward the house.

"Why do you want to retire?" asked Virginia.

"I thought it might be something you'd be…. A rancher is an honorable way to make a living."

"But not for you."

"Andrew's done right by it."

"Andrew is not you."

"But I thought you might—"

"I don't ever want you to be like Andrew. *Ever*. Ranching *is* an honorable profession, but it's not for you. You hate it. You love police work."

"But I've given it a lot of thought—"

"Zack!" called one of his men. "Zack, we need you to come back to the jailhouse so we can properly report this."

Two men strode to Virginia's side. "Sir, we'll make sure she gets back to the ranch safely. You're needed at the fort."

When Zack confirmed, the man left. This was Virginia's chance to say goodbye.

Zack leaned back and appraised her. When he spotted the commander exiting the house, Zack left her side to whisper something to the older man.

The commander looked to Virginia, rolled his cigar between his teeth and nodded.

What was Zack asking?

The commander handed Zack a quill pen.

Virginia ran a hand nervously over her skirt pocket and raced forward. "Don't do it, don't sign it."

Zack's dark expression was unreadable, but he gave the pen back without using it and tucked the deed into the inside of his shirt.

Called again by his men, Zack placed a decisive hand on his saddle horn and swung a leg over his horse.

Tall in the saddle, he was a man of pride and passion. And he was leaving, trotting out of her life surrounded by a sea of Mounties.

Twenty feet away, he turned and shouted from atop his saddle. "Have you still got your wedding gown?"

Horses stopped and heads turned to stare at her.

Her heart leaped forward. She mumbled, trying to fathom his question. "What do you mean?"

All hands ceased working and focused on Virginia.

His horse was restless. It tried to stray, but Zack controlled it with a firm snap of the reins. "Your wedding gown! The one you were supposed to be wearing when we had to cancel! Do you still have it?''

''Yes.'' Was the question he'd just asked the commander one seeking permission to marry?

Zack's mouth twisted with pleasure. ''Then wear it for me in two days!''

Was he proposing marriage? Why did he want to see her gown? At times, his gall was maddening. And she had plans to leave him. ''Without talking about this? I can't just put on my gown and appear for you like a genie from a bottle! I won't be commanded like one of your men!''

His men snickered.

''You're abnormal!'' she shouted to more laughter.

But he was Zack again—bold and outspoken and confident as hell. ''Atta girl! You no longer seem to care what the neighbors think of you! Wednesday afternoon at five o'clock!'' Zack galloped away, a broad, dangerous figure on a powerful horse. ''Meet me at the church!''

Chapter Twenty

If Zack thought he could whistle for her like a comfortable steed, and that she'd come running...well, he could whistle all night.

Standing in Uncle Paddy's kitchen the next day preparing lunch, Virginia slammed the cutting board to the table and lopped off the fish's head. Propped on the table well away from the splatter was a medical study book opened on the herbs and roots page. She read and memorized.

All she'd wanted was a normal man to court her in a normal way, but what she got instead was Zack Bullock.

Had that been a proposal? And if so, what sort? Or maybe not one at all. Zack did more to confound Virginia's state of mind than any man she knew. Just when she'd thought she had it settled that she was backing away from him, he wanted to pull her closer. Were they good for each other or did they only create havoc in each other's lives?

He'd moved back to the barracks last night and she'd moved back to her uncle's home. But Zack should be here beside her, telling her how he felt about her, *asking* her if she were interested in marriage, not asking off the tail end of a horse whether she still had her blasted gown.

At the market this morning, why even the fishmonger and his wife had heard the silly story and had asked about it. Then later when she'd dropped by David's house to check on his healing arm, even he'd joked with her. She couldn't blame David for his exceptional mood—it appeared that his arm wouldn't need further surgery, and she, too, had walked back to Uncle Paddy's with a spring in her step.

She wouldn't go to meet Zack tomorrow at five o'clock. And that was that.

She chopped with renewed vigor. She had no intention of being made a fool for the third time this year. How would it look if she—

Pondering it, she let her knife drift to the board. She wiped her hands on the towel tucked to the waistband of her apron.

Zack did seem to be right—she was always concerned about how she looked in front of others. It was because if she trusted her soul to Zack, met him at the church and it wasn't a marriage proposal but *something else,* then she'd look foolish.

But what if…she took Zack at his word this time, slid into her gown and ran openly into his arms as he was asking? The feelings she had for him weren't of weakness and vulnerability. And although other folks had mentioned the lack of time she might have for *any* husband while working as both doctor and wife, Zack had never once criticized her choices. She'd wanted to change everything about him since she'd known him—his aloofness, his take-charge attitude, his arrogance—but maybe it'd been she who'd needed to take a long look in the mirror.

Still, he was asking for an awful lot of trust.

She glanced to the clock on the pine shelf. A minute after twelve. On top of her problems with Zack, she was running late for her examinations.

"What time is it?" Standing in the church hallway between the empty kitchen and the fully seated congregation, Zack straightened the collar of his scarlet uniform, inhaled a nervous breath and looked to his best man, Travis Reid.

Also in official uniform, Travis grinned. "Don't worry, she'll be here. She's got two minutes left before the clock strikes five."

"It's just…I want to do things right and I wonder what in thunder I was thinking, ordering her to wear her gown and to show up on the church steps. I should have *asked* her."

"I don't claim to know anything about marriage, but if she's interested—and it appears to me she is—she'll be here."

"Maybe she won't," called Travis's brother, Mitchell. "Maybe she'll stand you up."

Of equal height and dark stature as his brother, Travis scowled at Mitchell. "Why did you go and say that?"

The younger Reid laughed. "I don't often get to see the famous marksman look nervous."

"Maybe," hollered one of the other six groomsmen, "she found another man between Monday and today."

The priest walked in, solemn and dressed in full robes. The men silenced their laughter. They cleared their throats, some looking in the other direction. When the priest glanced to Zack for an explanation of the bride's tardiness, his nerves were uprooted.

Zack scooted out the side door. "I'll wait for Virginia on the steps."

They were gathered in the small church in the middle of Calgary, centered above the town square on a grassy hill. The square was where they held the fruit and vegetable market every morning, where people congregated before a trial in the courthouse, where musicians played in the summer for disembarking passengers off the railway, and where he hoped to someday walk past as he led a son or daughter to school.

Virginia, his heart called. *It all depends on you.*

He strained to peer above the milling crowd, looking beyond the buggies headed down the trail, but there was no sign of them. Paddy had promised to bring her. Her bridesmaids awaited in the church entry, peering curiously at him through the open door, wondering as he was *if* Virginia would arrive.

It'd taken a small miracle to orchestrate the wedding ceremony and the reception slated afterward without alerting Virginia. He'd ordered everyone to secrecy about the size of the wedding—he wanted it to be everything she'd planned for them in the beginning, but didn't want to scare her off in speeding it through in two short days. Even Clarissa had promised to keep it secret, which was nearly as impossible as it seemed.

The community hall had been adorned with flowers and tablecloths yesterday while Virginia had finished her exams. The baker had baked five wedding cakes, the men on the Mountie ranch had been eager to barbecue the steer, goat and venison. All Zack needed was one fair maiden.

Brimming with frustration, he slid a hand along his temple and slicked-back hair. When he glanced around the stone edge of the community hall, he caught glimpse of a shiny iron wheel on a fresh leather buggy. He'd recognize the doctor's impeccable buggy anywhere.

His pulse kicked forward.

Seated in the back seat alongside her flower girl and behind her uncle and Millicent, who was holding the reins, Virginia caught sight of him through the bustling crowd. She gripped the side rail of the covered buggy, and didn't let her gaze fall from his.

His breathing intensified.

She was engulfed in a satin cloud of swirling white fabric. A circle of white roses adorned the top of her head and off it trailed another yard of wispy white netting, mingled with her mane of wavy black hair. Her blue eyes shone with anticipation, her nose tilted straight and proud, her lips parted ever so gently. Her V neckline plunged to her bosom, the fabric gathered tightly in pleats around her narrow waist.

The horse pulled up beside him. He bowed slightly and held out his hand. With a tender smile, Virginia slid her slender fingers, encased in white leather gloves that reached above her elbows, into his.

Their clasp held more meaning than any words that might have been spoken.

"Virginia," he began. "You took me at my word."

"I wasn't sure. I didn't know if you meant this." Peering at the scads of women fighting for a view at the church door, Virginia raised one hand, smiled gently and waved. "There are so many people here. How did you manage when I didn't hear a word about it? I even asked Clarissa yesterday if she'd heard of any plans and she wouldn't admit to anything."

"Good old Clarissa. She's in the church helping David set up his tripod and black tenting for the photographs. He can't do much with his arm, but they're in there together arguing about it."

Zack grasped the sheath of his ceremonial sword to

keep it at bay. "Let me help you to your feet and then I've got a few things that need to be said."

"But there isn't time," said Millicent, adjusting her straw hat.

"Sure there is," said Paddy. "Leave the carriage here. We'll take Emilou and meet Virginia at the top of the stairs just inside the church."

Still with her warm hand tucked inside of Zack's, Virginia pressed her skirts together with the other hand while Emilou grabbed her train of smooth satin. Gracefully Virginia placed her slender foot, encased in a leather skin, high-buckled white boot onto the ground and leaned into Zack. When she was anchored to the ground in front of him, he heard the jubilant clapping of hands in the church behind them. His grin spread as he craned his neck to peer down at his bride.

"You were worth waiting for. You look lovely."

"I've never had a good look at you in uniform." She swallowed hard.

He inhaled deeply then watched Millicent lead Paddy up the stairs, with Emilou holding the man's other hand.

Zack searched for the right words. Clasping both of her hands, he knelt down on one knee.

"Zack," she murmured, the blueness of her eyes deepening.

"Since the moment I met you, I haven't done this right. I pushed you and goaded you and shoved you out of the way when all I had to do was put my arm around you."

"You did what you thought best to protect me. I know…I know how *I* feel trying to protect Uncle Paddy from being hurt by the world, and I imagine that was how you felt trying to protect me from James Stiller."

His throat tugged with the understanding of what she

said. "And I apologize for the things I said to you—accusing you of harboring feelings for Andrew."

"As an adult, I can easily decipher which brother had the higher moral standard to begin with. But as a child, I followed in the footsteps of my friends and believed because Andrew was more popular, he was the better one. I was wrong."

Happiness filtered through Zack. "When I first set eyes on you at the train station that night, God, you were so tough tending to me and my men."

"Before you go on..." She could barely catch her breath. "Zack, I need to ask. Are we right for each other? Before I came along, your life ran smoothly, you were always in command. You never had to choose between your work and those you care about."

"Before you came along...I was nothing. Virginia, I'm in love with you."

Her lips softened into a lush curve. Her eyes shone.

"And now I'm asking...would you share the rest of your life with me?"

She let out a sound that was half sob, half laugh. "Yes."

The folks inside the church must have realized he'd finally popped the question, for they cheered. Grinning widely, Zack got to his feet and outlined her cheek with a finger, amazed at the clarity in her eyes.

"Did you sign the deed?" she whispered.

He shook his head slowly. "I followed your advice. I'm staying with what I love."

A soft smile tugged at her cheek.

"My left arm is never going to heal as good as it was, is it?"

She didn't cower. "No," she said softly.

''Then it's a good thing my right hand is still as fast as it is.''

''You were exceptional against Stiller.''

He knew he'd remain a marksman as long as he could lift a gun.

Her smile beckoned. ''I passed my exams. John told me this afternoon.''

''Congratulations, Doc. This is one damn lucky town.'' Then realizing where they were, he disentangled his hold and whispered. ''I'll meet you inside.''

He walked backward up the slope and headed to the side door but he was unable to pull his entrancement away from the pretty woman standing at the bottom of the stairs.

But moments later, flanked by Uncle Paddy, Virginia walked down the aisle toward Zack.

Ian Killarney raised his fiddle and let out a lone, beautiful wail that seemed to capture the entire emotion of the congregation.

Repeating his vows, Zack felt the comforting warmth of Virginia's presence. Kissing his bride at the end of the ceremony, he felt that same surge of excitement she elicited from him every time he breathed her air. And as they accepted congratulations at the bottom of the church steps, he thanked God that the young girl from his childhood had accepted his invitation to travel west.

At 6:10 p.m., finishing with the handshakes at the church, and when bride and groom were about to join the others inside the hall for dinner and dancing, Zack heard the call of Lucy's voice.

''Virginia! Zack!''

Hand in hand, he and Virginia wheeled around to see Lucy, dressed in widow's black along with Diana, Beatrice and Kyle dressed in their Sunday best, pulling up in their family wagon.

"How are you all?" Virginia asked, breathless with the same excitement and concern as Zack.

"Fine," said Lucy. "We came to thank you for everything and to wish you luck on your wedding day."

Zack watched Virginia's sentiment gush to the surface as each member of the Peters family climbed down to give them a handshake and hug.

Virginia glanced at Lucy's clothing. "Won't you come inside for dinner?"

"It—it wouldn't be proper."

Zack understood they were still in mourning. He bent down on a knee, catching his sword before the tip hit the ground, and shook Kyle's hand. "You're a good shot, Kyle. Just like your pa was."

Kyle's face strained to contain his sorrow. "Yes, sir. I'm going to be a Mountie when I grow up."

"You'll be the best."

"We won't keep you," said Lucy. "Please come by and see us sometime when you're not busy. *Please*." They scooted back into their wagon.

"Lucy!" called Virginia as they headed out.

Lucy turned around.

"We'd love…we'd love to have lunch with you tomorrow, if it's all right to drop by."

Lucy's face broke into a trembling smile. "I'd like that very much."

Zack squeezed his wife's hand with compassion as the Peters family rolled away.

"Is that all right with you, Zack? I haven't even asked where we're staying tonight."

"I've rented a room at the big hotel for three nights. Not a suite, nothing fancy, because I'm saving to pay off your tuition. Then I figure we might rent part of your uncle's home for a little while. It'll be a couple of years before we can afford to buy our own house, but I figure this way you could be close to your uncle and he could help with the practice. I've spoken with him already, but needed to check with you first.''

Her warm gaze settled on his face. ''It sounds wonderful.''

He led her into the fold of friends and family awaiting in the town hall. They rose on their feet and clapped as Virginia and Zack made their way to the front table.

Virginia smiled and found her footing across the rose petals Emilou had strewn as a bridal path. She tucked herself next to Zack's side, and for the next hour of dinner and wine and moving speeches, Zack gloried sitting beside her.

He filled with pride, looking at the men around him he'd grown to think of as more than comrades, as brothers. The veterinarian, Logan Sutcliffe, and his wife, Melodie, and their two-year-old boy and one-year-old daughter, then Sarah and John Calloway struggling to keep their toddler quiet and satisfied with his drink, then Travis and Mitchell Reid and their sister, Shawna, and folks.

Andrew and Grace were here, holding hands in the corner. In the end, Andrew had followed his heart, and perhaps there was something there for Zack to learn.

Ian was sitting with Paddy and Millicent, head bowed in deep conversation and from Paddy's comforting nod, Zack knew the old man would be all right, that Ian would help him through his blindness. Whatever story had occurred between the three of them, Millicent had chosen Paddy.

She belongs with Paddy Waters, Ian had told Zack yesterday when Zack had stopped by his place to ask if Ian could play at the wedding. The conversation had turned to Paddy and then their mutual feelings for Millicent.

Each one of these people factored into Zack and Virginia's lives.

Zack was called upon to give the bride's toast. "To my remarkable wife and best childhood friend." He remembered how she'd fought his threat of three kisses and how intimately they'd come to know each other since then. "To our third kiss."

Their third kiss was the first time they'd made love.

Color infused her face. After the crowd murmured and they drank their wine, he sat down and slipped his shoulder next to hers.

Lowering her head in privacy, she slid her hand beneath the tablecloth. She placed her warm fingers on top of his, which rested on his thigh, and whispered, "I love you."

When the orchestral music began, a rich bridal waltz, he took her hand, caressing the smooth fingers and her simple gold band. "Mrs. Bullock, may I have this dance?"

*   *   *   *   *

Be sure to watch for Travis's story,
THE PROPOSITION,
coming only to Harlequin Historicals
in September.
And now for a sneak preview of
THE PROPOSITION
please turn the page.

Chapter One

Alberta, July 1892

Unaware of it, the man astride the horse dominated her attention. For three days running, Jessica Haven had watched Sergeant Major Travis Reid exercising the stallion on the oval track inside the fort, desperately trying to have a word with him, and for three days running the officer had ignored her. Today she'd force him to listen.

Sitting in the bleachers beside her, awash in early-morning sunlight, a small group had gathered to watch. The men concentrated on the dangerous bucking of the unbroken mustang, but Jessica knew the women focused on Travis.

''It's a pity he's leavin' his horses,'' said the banker.

''Sad shame what happened to his wife,'' whispered the commander's sister.

The officer twisted in the saddle. Leaning forward in concentration, his dark head tilted and body flexed, he melded with the sculpted lines of the horse. Dressed in the work clothes of the North-West Mounted Police— loose white shirt tucked into tight black breeches—he ran a large hand over the stallion's neck and whispered something into its mane.

His hard muscles coaxed the animal into submission.

Jessica fanned her heated face and rearranged her flowing cotton skirts around her ankles, uncomfortable that it was obvious the man stirred her. Her absence of two years hadn't changed his ability to dominate her senses.

Roughrider, his men had nicknamed him, a man skilled at riding untamed horses. The name suited him, she thought. He was rough. Travis was a master horseman, the Mounties' best. Jessica had heard he also excelled at tracking outlaws, that he'd been promoted four times in three years. He'd risen from corporal to sergeant major faster than prairie lightning. But he still had a way of brushing her aside.

"Sergeant Major!" she shouted, jumping out of her seat and racing into the stables behind the intimidating man and beast. Rows and rows of horses filled the stalls. Warm gashes of sunlight filtered through plank walls; the soothing scent of fresh straw and oats drifted around her.

Travis eyed her, then turned sharply on his black leather boot, broad shoulders twisting, ready to leave.

The insult burned deep. "Travis! I'd like a word with you! Please!"

She dashed out and nearly stumbled over a cluster of barn cats. Four small kittens froze in her path, the smallest one, a tawny fur ball, hunched its shoulders and peered up at her.

Laughter bubbled in her throat. She lifted him, tucking his entire body into one palm. Pressing her face into the downy neck, she enjoyed the tickle on her skin and its barnyard scent. "You're so soft. A child would adore you."

Travis turned around. The rippling shadows beneath his

white shirt tightened in wary response. He said nothing, simply stared down at her as she drew closer.

Don't be nervous, she told herself. *Remain cheerful and simply ask the man.*

Stroking the kitten, Jessica swallowed in a stew of emotions. Travis had the same solid jaw and firm cheeks she remembered. She looked lower. And there was something compelling about the physique of an active man, the straining and stretching of ropey muscles knotted from hard work and perseverance.

"Hello, Travis."

His lips tugged into a cool line. "Back from charm school, are you?"

Her face heated, even as she nodded in agreement. *Charm school.* It was what her father had told everyone to cover his shame, but so far from the truth it was laughable. And her own shame made her go along with the story.

Travis's deep blue eyes, almost navy in color, flickered. "The mayor's daughter has returned to Calgary. Let's all bow and bid her good welcome."

He tilted his head in mock acknowledgment, a finger of his black hair falling forward on his brow.

Hiding her humiliation, she lowered the kitten to the ground near a bowl of water where his bigger black-and-white brothers and sisters were drinking. "Make way for the little one," she coaxed. The kittens parted and she smiled softly.

She felt Travis's gaze beating down on her tilted head. She wished she could erase the past.

He'd once called her a spoiled young woman. And shamefully, it'd been true. It had begun five years ago when she'd convinced her father to outbid Travis on a feisty stallion so they could buy it and she could learn to ride. Travis hadn't had the money to compete, but he'd tried to convince her the horse wasn't suitable for an inexperienced girl because of its size and temperament. She remorsefully admitted now that the stallion had attracted her simply for its color—a speckled gray with almost purplish mane and tail. And Travis had been right. She hadn't been able to handle the horse and got such a fright she was still put off by large animals.

She *had* been rude. Self-absorbed. But in her defense, she'd also been young and inexperienced, and she'd learned a lot of things in the last grueling two years.

Remain cheerful. "I heard you're leaving for Devil's Gorge tomorrow. I came to offer you a proposition. To pay you to take me along." Her mouth parted with a silent plea. He had to say yes for her world to regain its balance.

"Absolutely *not.* I'll pass on your proposition. This is a personal leave. And a difficult seven-day journey. Ask at the livery stables if you want to hire a guide."

The fluttering in her stomach tightened. Desperation trembled in her voice. "I already have, but they've got two men out on trail and only one left. He…he leers at me and I just couldn't spend an entire week…. Even though I'd bring a chaperon. You know our family's butler, Mr. Merriweather."

"You've got to be kidding." Travis stalked down the middle of the stalls, ducking buckets and workmen. Horses' heads turned to watch him as he passed. "Ask at the big hotel. They hire out to travelers and tourists."

She raced behind him, barely keeping up with his long stride. She felt like a silly child tagging behind.

"Wait!" She chased after him. "There's no guide at the big hotel as qualified as you. And now that my father has discovered my plans, he won't let me go unless I'm escorted by a Mountie. Devil's Gorge *isn't* a light jaunt into the mountains and no one seems eager to go.''

He spun around. ''Then, why do you?''

She had prepared for the question for days, but it still prickled her skin. ''I'm trying to locate a—a Dr. Finch.''

Travis frowned. ''I know him. He came through here last year. Helped a lot of folks.''

Helped was not the right word.

Dr…*Mr.* Finch had hurt a lot of people. She believed he'd gone by another name in Montreal—by Dr. King. When she found him, she'd expose him and Travis could jail him.

''Listen, I'm prepared to pay you as part of the bargain. *Lots.*''

He walked away.

''One hundred dollars,'' she shouted after him. ''And another hundred on safe delivery.''

He turned around, his eyes misty. ''It's always about money with you people, isn't it?''

Her throat clamped. ''Not always.''

Not anymore. But no one knew about her problem—or at least believed how Dr. Finch had deceived and devastated *her.*

''Let me make myself clear, Jessica. I don't care what you're up to, who your friends are, or what you do with your time. Leave me alone.''

She knew his response stemmed from Caroline, and Jessica was sorry that she'd caused the woman any grief. But it was unfair of Travis to blame Jessica for everything.

''I'm sorry to hear about your wife,'' she murmured.

He didn't respond. His mouth tightened.

''I said, I'm sorry to hear about Caroline's passing.''

''Hmm.'' The pain that settled in his eyes was enough to stop her heart.

"Poor Caroline," she continued. "It was a terrible way to go. I—I know it happened months ago, but I heard it only last week when I arrived on the train."

"Did you now?"

She flushed at his insinuating tone.

His body stiffened. "Let's not coat things with honey. You never liked Caroline and she never liked you."

A flash of tears pricked her eyes, but she blinked them away. It was too difficult to remain cheerful, to keep begging him face-to-face. She whispered as she left, "A person can change."

FALL IN LOVE WITH
FOUR HANDSOME HEROES
FROM HARLEQUIN HISTORICALS.

On sale May 2004

THE ENGAGEMENT
by Kate Bridges

Inspector Zack Bullock
North-West Mounted Police officer

HIGH COUNTRY HERO
by Lynna Banning

Cordell Lawson
Bounty hunter, loner

On sale June 2004

THE UNEXPECTED WIFE
by Mary Burton

Matthias Barrington
Widowed ranch owner

THE COURTING OF WIDOW SHAW
by Charlene Sands

Steven Harding
Nevada rancher

Visit us at www.eHarlequin.com

HARLEQUIN HISTORICALS®

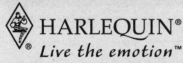

Savor these stirring tales of romance with Harlequin Historicals

On sale May 2004

THE LAST CHAMPION by Deborah Hale

Once betrothed, then torn apart by civil war, will Dominie de Montford put aside her pride and seek out Armand Flambard's help to save her estate from a vicious outlaw baron?

THE DUKE'S MISTRESS by Ann Elizabeth Cree

Years ago Lady Isabelle Milborne had participated in her late husband's wager, which had ruined Justin, the Duke of Westmore. And now the duke will stop at nothing to see justice served.

On sale June 2004

THE COUNTESS BRIDE by Terri Brisbin

A young count must marry a highborn lady in order to inherit his lands. But a poor young woman with a mysterious past is the only one he truly desires....

A POOR RELATION by Joanna Maitland

Desperate to avoid fortune hunters, Miss Isabella Winstanley poses as a penniless chaperone. But will she allow herself to be ensnared by the dashing Baron Amburley?

HARLEQUIN HISTORICALS®

HHMED36

COMING NEXT MONTH FROM

HARLEQUIN HISTORICALS®

- **THE COUNTESS BRIDE**
  by **Terri Brisbin,** author of THE NORMAN'S BRIDE
  Count Geoffrey Dumont must marry to secure control of his lands
  in France. Though she's completely unsuitable for a man of his standing,
  Geoffrey knows that Catherine de Severin is the only
  woman for him…so he kidnaps her! Will he convince Catherine
  to elope with him before they are caught?
  HH #707 ISBN# 29307-0 $5.25 U.S./$6.25 CAN.

- **THE UNEXPECTED WIFE**
  by **Mary Burton,** author of THE LIGHTKEEPER'S WOMAN
  Everyone in Matthias Barrington's tiny Montana town knows that
  he needs a wife. And since the struggling single father refuses to find
  a bride, the townspeople take matters into their own hands and find
  Abby Smyth, mail-order bride. Though Matthias has vowed never to
  remarry, would he deny his sons a mother…and deny himself a second
  chance at love?
  HH #708 ISBN# 29308-9 $5.25 U.S./$6.25 CAN.

- **A POOR RELATION**
  by **Joanna Maitland,** author of RAKE'S REWARD
  To avoid fortune hunters, heiress Lady Isabella Winstanley allows
  the ton to believe she is an almost penniless poor relation. When
  Leigh Stansfield, Baron Amburley, meets Isabella at a ball, he falls for
  her disguise, but thinks she's greedily trying to snag a wealthy husband.
  As Isabella finds herself attracted to Amburley, how can she show him
  she's not a wanton gold digger without giving away her secret?
  HH #709 ISBN# 29309-7 $5.25 U.S./$6.25 CAN.

- **THE COURTING OF WIDOW SHAW**
  by **Charlene Sands,** author of WINNING JENNA'S HEART
  When Steven Harding finds Gloria Mae Shaw lying unconscious next
  to her dead husband with a bloodied knife in her hand, he takes her to
  the one place no one would ever think to look for her—his mother's infa-
  mous brothel. Steven's not sure if she's guilty of murder and Gloria
  has no memory of the night in question, but a secret from Steven's past
  compels him to protect her.…
  HH #710 ISBN# 29310-0 $5.25 U.S./$6.25 CAN.

KEEP AN EYE OUT FOR ALL FOUR
OF THESE TERRIFIC NEW TITLES

HHCNM0504